Mary Torjussen grew up in Stoke-on-Trent. There was no television in her family home so books have always been her escape – she spent hours reading and writing stories as a child. Mary has an MA in Creative Writing from Liverpool John Moores University, and worked as a teacher in Liverpool before becoming a full-time writer. She has two adult children and lives on the Wirral. *The Girl I Used To Be* is her second novel.

Praise for *Gone Without A Trace:*

'Suspenseful and subtle, this novel tions. Not to be missed!'
Shari Lapena, author of *The Couple Next Door*

'I practically inhaled this book. A clever and uncompromising thriller'
Katerina Diamond, author of *The Teacher* and *The Secret*

'A page turner with a cracking ending'
Jenny Blackhurst, author of *How I Lost You* and *Before I Let You In*

'This fast-paced story kept me guessing – great twist at the end'
K.L. Slater, author of *The Mistake* and *Liar*

'A taut, suspenseful debut very much rooted in reality: any one of us could come home to an empty house and want to find out the answers. With a twist that will knock your socks off, Torjussen is one to watch'
Gillian McAllister, author of *Everything But The Truth*

'*Gone Without A Trace* is exactly the kind of book I like to read. It not only pulls you in, but it also makes the reader think. I loved it!'
Amanda Reynolds, author of *Close To Me*

'Has a twist I really didn't see coming'
Cass Green, author of *The Woman Next Door*

Also by Mary Torjussen

Gone Without A Trace

THE GIRL I USED TO BE

MARY TORJUSSEN

HEADLINE

Copyright © 2018 Mary Torjussen

The right of Mary Torjussen to be identified as the Author of
the Work has been asserted by her in accordance with the
Copyright, Designs and Patents Act 1988.

First published in paperback in 2018 by
HEADLINE PUBLISHING GROUP

1

Apart from any use permitted under UK copyright law,
this publication may only be reproduced, stored, or transmitted, in any form,
or by any means, with prior permission in writing of the publishers or,
in the case of reprographic production, in accordance with the terms
of licences issued by the Copyright Licensing Agency.

All characters in this publication are fictitious and any resemblance
to real persons, living or dead, is purely coincidental.

Cataloguing in Publication Data is available from the British Library

ISBN 978 1 4722 4081 1

Typeset in Meridien by Jouve (UK), Milton Keynes

Printed and bound in Great Britain by CPI Group (UK) Ltd, Croydon, CR0 4YY

Headline's policy is to use papers that are natural, renewable and
recyclable products and made from wood grown in sustainable forests.
The logging and manufacturing processes are expected to conform to
the environmental regulations of the country of origin.

HEADLINE PUBLISHING GROUP
An Hachette UK Company
Carmelite House
50 Victoria Embankment
London EC4Y 0DZ

www.headline.co.uk
www.hachette.co.uk

For Rosie and Louis
And for my mother and my late father
And for Ann Perkins in Aberdare
With love

Prologue

Fifteen years ago

Thursday, August 15

When I think of that night now, I remember the heat, clammy and intense on my skin, and the sense of feverish excitement in the air. I think of the taxi ride to the party with my friend Lauren, her body soft and scented against mine as we sat crushed into the back seat with her boyfriend Tom. The radio was on, the windows were open, and 'London Calling' started to play. I remember the surge of happiness I felt then; I'd just been accepted by London University and would be there within a month. Whenever I hear that song now, it takes me straight back to that taxi ride to Alex's house. It's as though I *am* that girl, the girl I used to be.

But I'm not.

I can feel the sandals I was wearing as though I'm wearing them now. I could hardly walk in them; I wore them that night for the first time and within an hour I had blisters. I can remember the feel of my dress, its soft cotton brushing my skin. When I close my eyes I can feel the breeze lifting my hair. I can smell the perfume I wore, taste the lip gloss on my mouth.

But always, always, when I think of that night, I think of Alex.

It was mid-August, the summer we were eighteen, and over two hundred of us from school were going to celebrate our exam results at Alex Clarke's party. Lauren and I had got ready together at her house, and I'd sneaked in the little pink dress that I'd bought with the money I was supposed to be saving for university. We were tanned from the summer sun; each day we worked until mid-afternoon in the café in our local town, and then we'd strip off our sweaty nylon overalls, pull on our shorts, and spend the rest of the day down at the beach. That afternoon we'd spent an hour or so topping up our tans before going back to her house to get ready for the night ahead. This was the start of the rest of our lives, we told each other. We wanted to look different, like we were ready for our new lives away from home.

We had a few drinks before we went to the party. Lauren's mum came into her room with a bottle of champagne to celebrate our results, and insisted on refilling our glasses whenever they were empty. We didn't tell her we'd already had tequila shots. Lauren had more to drink than I did, but she always did back then. As soon as I was seventeen, I passed my driving test and my dad bought me a runaround so that I didn't have to ask him for lifts. I loved driving and was happy to have soft drinks and ferry everyone about. I suppose that's why it hit me so hard that night.

It was a Thursday in the middle of August and we had to go to the school office first thing that morning to get our results. We felt they were life or death; if they were what we needed, doors would be opened to the top universities, the best courses, and a life full of promise. Just a grade down and we'd be screwed. The lives we'd hoped for just wouldn't happen. Or so we thought. And while we knew – we'd been told often enough – that everything would work out no matter what, that other universities were still good, we were young enough to believe that no, actually, things wouldn't be okay. We all knew people who'd failed to get into their first-choice university, who'd talked about it for years later.

But that wasn't our fate that summer. It was a stellar year. Everyone seemed to get the results they needed to do what they wanted to do. It was exhilarating, the way we opened our envelopes and screamed, one after the other.

And I remember Alex and his friends, all of them bound for Oxford or Cambridge, trying to hide their elation behind cool exteriors. They were fooling no one. They'd seen themselves as separate from the rest of us – they *knew* they were different – and now they were proven to be right. Or that was how I saw it then. I didn't even know him; I'd only spoken to him once, but that was the impression he and his friends gave.

Lauren and I were standing behind their group that morning in the queue for the exam results and overheard his friend Theo ask, 'The party's on then?'

Alex nodded. 'Spread the word around. People from here only. No one else.'

I'd nudged Lauren and she'd giggled; we'd been looking forward to it for months and had everything planned, right down to the nail varnish we'd wear on our toes.

The local press was there in full force that morning, pre-arranged by the school, and there were photos taken of us all, grouped into sets, our expressions happy and free. Our teachers stood with us, their faces so tanned and relaxed I could hardly recognize them. The relief among all of us was palpable.

Alex's house was in the middle of the countryside, ten miles out of town. We'd guessed it would be bigger, more expensive, but the scale of it surprised us. It was a detached house set in pristine landscaped gardens on the edge of a village. There were no near neighbours; the garden was surrounded by fields, beyond which we caught glimpses of the river.

He and Theo were standing at the front door when we arrived, making sure that they knew us all. There'd been stories in the news that summer about parties where crowds had gatecrashed and the police had had to be called; it was obvious from the way he checked everyone as they walked up the driveway that he was on guard for that.

'Hi,' he said. 'Come on in!'

Behind Alex was Jack Howard, one of his friends, who was taking photos of everyone as they went into the house. We'd known for a long time that he'd had a crush on Lauren, and when he saw us, he blushed and busied himself with his camera. She slung her arms around Tom and me and we posed there on the doorstep, giddy and excited at the thought of the night ahead. After Tom went through the front door, she turned and blew a kiss at Jack and turned to wink at me.

Whenever I think of Lauren, I think of us giggling. Just about anything could make us laugh. When Alex had greeted us, we giggled and nudged each other and went through the large hallway into the kitchen at the back of the house. It was full of food and alcohol. People had gone overboard and brought spirits and crates of beer and armfuls of wine bottles. I heard Jack say that Alex's parents were away on holiday; they'd agreed that if he got top grades – which meant he'd be accepted by Oxford – and if he paid for a deep clean afterwards, he could have a party to celebrate. They would be back a few days later and didn't want to see any sign there'd even been a party. That was a bit optimistic, I thought.

Everyone in our year was invited to that party and most were there. There were so many I only knew by sight, but we were all on such a high that pretty soon we were kissing everyone and anyone, congratulating people we barely knew, just grateful that we'd done well and were going to have our chance to get away. You'd think we were living in some sort of hellhole, the way we carried on, as though our only chance of a good life was to leave behind the one we had.

Lauren and I had done well; Tom too. We were all off in a month's time to different universities. She and I had been friends since nursery school, and it would be almost the first time Lauren and Tom would have spent more than twenty-four hours apart in the two years she'd known him. I thought our friendship would last the separation, and guessed she'd stay with Tom, too; there was an ease about them that I envied. That night their arms were entwined and I noticed when she kissed a friend that she'd align herself with Tom, as though they were one person, so they embraced the friend together.

I drank so much that night. All of us did. It was the first time we'd all been together like that and we knew it would be the last time, too. Despite that, people didn't seem drunk. Not really. Nobody was staggering or falling, and apart from my friend Lizzie, who was sick into an ornamental bay tree on the patio before it was even dark, nobody was ill. We were all outside and then the music was turned up and everyone was dancing. I lost Lauren and Tom somewhere along the way. When I saw her later, her dress was buttoned up wrongly and she had a fresh love bite on her neck. She was telling someone she hadn't ever spoken to before that she would always miss them.

Then all of a sudden, past midnight, it hit me. I realized I was more drunk than I'd ever been. I'd been drinking more and more as the night went on, and most of it was punch from a huge bowl that one of Alex's friends had been in charge of. God knew what had been in it – there were bottles of every spirit and liqueur you could think of lying around, and I was sure that most had ended up in that bowl. Lauren and Tom were lying in a hammock nearby by then, and when

I turned to them, clinging onto the back of a garden chair for support, she smiled lazily and closed her eyes. I knew she wouldn't want to go home yet. I was staying at her house that night and we were sharing a taxi home. Her mum had promised to leave the money next to the front door and the key under the doormat, so that we didn't have to take our handbags with us.

My heart sank. It could be hours before Lauren wanted to leave. I started to walk back towards the house and staggered, falling into a bush. I didn't mind; I thought it was funny. One of the girls from school yanked me back up again and asked if I was all right. I nodded. I don't think I could have spoken if I'd wanted to.

When I reached the house I was suddenly desperate for the toilet. There were several portable toilets at the bottom of the garden but I didn't think there was a chance I'd reach them in time. I searched for a cloakroom inside the house and found a door under the stairs, which I thought was probably what I wanted. When I tried to open it, I heard a boy laugh and a girl say 'Shh!' and I realized what was going on. I gave a deep sigh, knowing there was no point in waiting, and went further into the house. I could hardly see by then and was smiling at just about everyone. The mood was high, voices were loud, everyone was happy.

At the foot of the stairs there were a couple of chairs, with a note telling people to keep out. I couldn't wait by then, though, so I squeezed past them and found a bathroom just at the top of the stairs. I stumbled in and sat down so fast I nearly dislodged the toilet seat. I found that funny, and wondered just what was in that punch. I wasn't so drunk that I didn't wash my hands, though, and saw that my face was flushed in the bathroom mirror, my eyes bleary and half closed. I knew I'd suffer the next day; I would have even if I'd stopped after the champagne and the tequila shots at Lauren's house. I remember grimacing as I thought of the headache I'd have. The following afternoon I was going on holiday to France for two weeks with my family, and already I was dreading the long car journey with a hangover.

As I turned from the basin, I slipped on a towel someone had left on the bathroom floor. I probably should have picked it up, but I realized pretty quickly that if I bent down, I would fall. I doubted I'd be able to get myself back up if that happened, so I kicked the towel to one side and opened the bathroom door. It was quiet upstairs, though I could hear the sounds of the party continuing downstairs and out in the garden. I tripped at the top of the stairs and grabbed the handrail. I didn't think I'd make it down without falling. My head was spinning by then and I had a sudden vision of myself hurtling head first down the stairs.

I backed away from the staircase and stumbled back into a door. It opened behind me. A lamp was lit next to a double bed. From the hockey stick propped up against the wall, I realized it must be Alex's room. He played for the school team; the only time I'd spoken to him was when he dropped his kit when he was hurrying to get to a match. Posters from the Glastonbury music festival he'd gone to that summer were on his bedroom wall. I'd known he was going to it, just after the exams ended. Lauren had heard him talking to Theo about it when they were all queuing up to leave the hall after their last exam. A local band, The Coral, were playing at Glastonbury that year, and Alex was wearing their T-shirt at the party. A drum kit was in the corner of the room next to a guitar and a huge amp. I remember wondering whether he was any good and thinking he wouldn't play if he wasn't.

I sat down on the bed. Suddenly I was so weary, I just wanted to sleep. My head was spinning and everything was blurred. I couldn't summon up the energy to go back downstairs, and I knew that when I did, Lauren would want to stay longer and wouldn't want to spend time with me. Only that night she'd said that she and Tom had just three weeks left and they were going to spend every single minute together.

So I lay down. The bed was so soft, its covers clean and fragrant. It smelled like my own bed when the linen had just been changed. I loved the scent of clean sheets. And I knew Alex wouldn't know I'd been here – he was a party boy; he'd be outside until dawn.

My head relaxed onto his pillow. I had a fleeting thought that my make-up would be all over the pillowcase, but I couldn't care about that then. The door was half open and I knew that Lauren would come to find me. She'd know I hadn't gone home; how could I? I had no money on me and I wasn't going to go back to my own house as drunk as this. The bedside lamp cast a soft glow over the room and the light from the landing flooded the entrance to the room. *She'll see me here*, I thought. *She'll tell me when it's time to go home.*

I turned to face away from the lamp. I've never liked to sleep with a light shining on my face. As I turned, I felt my dress ride up and I made a half-hearted attempt to pull it down. The scent of the pillow and the alcohol in my bloodstream and the lateness of the hour and the fact that I'd been awake until dawn that morning, worrying about my exam results, meant that when I turned back, my head buried in the pillow, I relaxed completely. I remember sighing as I slipped into sleep.

It had been a great night. A really great night.

Part I

Part I

1

Present day

Friday, June 16

When I saw him for the first time, I didn't think he'd be trouble. He was tall and broad, built like a rugby player, nice enough, but not the kind of man you'd necessarily look twice at in the street. At first glance he seemed harmless enough. That's how men like him operate, I suppose.

I saw him that morning, looking at the advertising boards in the window of the estate agency I own, but didn't take a lot of notice at first. Over the course of a day maybe a hundred or so people will look at the boards, trying to decide which house they'd buy if they had the chance, and I'd quickly learned that an expression of interest did not mean a sale. He lingered for a while, moving from the cheapest houses to the most expensive. I remember idly wondering what he was looking for.

When he did come in, he hung about in the doorway, as though he were waiting for someone. I glanced around and saw that Rachel, our sales negotiator, was at the photocopier and Brian, our lettings manager, was busy with a tenant. Usually we leave clients to look around, but he seemed uncertain, so I caught his eye and smiled.

'Good morning,' I said. 'Can I help you with anything?'

'I'm David Sanderson,' he said, coming to sit at my desk. 'I have an appointment.'

'Oh yes,' I said, flustered. He was an hour earlier than I'd expected and I'd planned to run out to meet my friend Grace for coffee for half an hour. 'Hi. I'm Gemma Brogan.' We shook hands. 'Just a moment, I'll call up your details.'

While I did that, I surreptitiously sent Grace a quick e-mail. Sorry, can't meet. Another day?

'So you're looking for somewhere in the city centre,' I said. 'I can see you've selected a number you like the look of.'

'I'm still not sure whether to go for a flat or a house,' he said. He smiled then, a great smile that made his face light up. It transformed him from someone you wouldn't really notice to someone you'd definitely remember. I couldn't help but smile back. 'I'm not sure if I'm ready for a house. I'd rather be near some bars and a gym.'

'Will you be buying on your own?'

I could see Sophie, our junior administrator, who was always on the lookout for a boyfriend, giving a sidelong look at Rachel. I could tell from the way they both became very still that they were waiting for his answer.

'Yes, I'm single,' he said. 'I'm just looking for somewhere for myself.'

I reckoned he was around my age, in his mid-thirties. Now that he was at ease and smiling, it was hard to believe he wasn't snapped up already, though of course he could be divorced.

'Are you from Chester?' I asked. 'I'm trying to place your accent.'

'I grew up in the north-west but I've been working over in

the States for the last ten years or so. Boston. My company's transferred me to the UK for a while. A few years, I guess. I've sold up over there; no point in keeping the old place going.'

'Who're you working for?'

'Barford's. I'm in sales.'

I nodded. Barford's was a large pharmaceutical company that had its headquarters on an industrial estate just outside Chester. I'd found properties for a couple of people there; it was supposed to be a great place to work.

He clarified the amount he was willing to spend; it was in the upper ballpark of properties in Chester, and I started to get excited. We had plenty of properties on our books. Things were moving more slowly than usual and I knew I could find him something. He'd named a great price and he was willing to try out a lot of different areas. I *had* to sell to him. I didn't want to have to come back to the office and tell my staff that he had decided to go elsewhere.

'I'll get some details,' I said. 'I won't be a moment.' I saw that Sophie was busy with a client, so I called over to Rachel, who was putting brochures in the window. 'Rachel, would you make Mr Sanderson a drink, please?' It wasn't her job to do that, but in such a small office we all had to take on that duty if someone else was busy.

She came over to my desk. 'Would you like tea or coffee?'

'I'll have coffee, thanks,' he said.

'How do you like it?'

I glanced at her and had to stop myself from laughing. Her face was pink and she couldn't bring herself to meet his eyes. She and Sophie were always the same when a good-looking guy came into the office. They were both young and single, though Sophie had nerves of steel when it came to dating, while Rachel seemed more shy and nervous.

He smiled at her. 'White, no sugar, thanks.'

She blushed again and disappeared into our tiny kitchen behind the office. Sophie swiftly followed her and I could hear muffled giggles.

We drank the coffee and went through the details of some of the properties I had. He seemed particularly interested in the flats that overlooked the River Dee and others that were in the centre of the city.

I glanced at the office diaries online. I would normally send Rachel out, but she had another appointment that morning. I had a valuation in several hours' time, at four P.M. 'You said in your e-mail you were free until three P.M. I can take you to view some properties now if you like.'

'That would be great,' he said. 'I'd love to look around this area; I don't know it well at all.'

'Just give me a few minutes,' I said. 'I'll make some calls and get my keys.'

'I can drive us if you like.'

'It's fine, thanks,' I said. 'It'll be easier if I drive. I know the quickest routes.'

I asked Sophie to take some details from him and he went over to sit with her. Sophie was only eighteen and fresh from school. She was still learning the ropes; I'd had to weigh up experience versus cost when I'd employed her, and still wasn't sure I'd made the right decision. As I made my calls I saw her, her face bright with excitement, asking David for his details and laboriously entering them into the computer.

I always drive round to the front of the office to pick up clients, so that they don't have to go through the back and into the car park. As soon as he got into my little car I could see I should have let him drive his own. He was over six feet tall, with long legs and broad shoulders, and he looked really cramped in the passenger seat.

'I'm sorry!' I said as he struggled with the seat belt. 'Shall we go in your car? I can direct you.'

'It's fine.' He turned and grinned at me. 'I used to drive a Mini.'

I laughed.

'My mum bought herself one when I was seventeen,' he said. 'I think she thought it would put me off borrowing it.'

'And did it?'

'No, but I saved up for my own car much quicker than I would have if she'd had a bigger one.'

'Clever woman. I'll have to remember that when my son's old enough to drive.'

'How old is he now?'

'Three.' I smiled. Every time I thought of Rory, I smiled. 'Plenty of time to go.'

The first property I took him to was a block of flats set in a gated courtyard within the city walls. As I drove, he asked questions about the area and I talked to him about the old Roman walls that encircled the city.

'Walking around the walls of the city is a great way to get to know Chester,' I said. 'It's a couple of miles and you follow the wall around – it's virtually complete. You get to see the racecourse, the castle, and the cathedral as well as the River Dee. So you can see, it's a pretty small city, but it's got a lot going for it.'

'Have you lived here long?' he asked.

I nodded and told him I'd grown up on the Wirral, twenty-five miles north of Chester. 'I moved down to London to university and then came here.'

'You were in London? I was there too. Imperial. I studied maths. How about you?'

'Queen Mary. Business. I graduated in 2005.'

'Me too!' He grinned at me. 'That's weird. And then you moved back north?'

'I always wanted to work for myself, but it's virtually impossible in London, so I moved here about seven years ago when I decided to open my own business. I love it here.'

'That's your own agency? You've done pretty well.'

'Thanks. I love having my own place.'

I was really proud of myself for running my own business. It had always been my dream. I trained as an estate agent immediately after graduating, and worked down in London for a few years. Sales were high in those days, so my commission was too, and I saved as much as I could, knowing I wanted my own place in the future. When I met Joe, we decided to head north so I could set up on my own. I have a few properties that I've bought to rent out, too. It seemed crazy not to, when there were cheap houses coming up at auction. We're managing agents for a number of landlords, so it's just as easy to manage mine at the same time.

'It's a big responsibility, though, isn't it?'

I nodded. 'It's a lot of work sometimes, but I prefer working for myself.'

'I'd love to do that,' he said. 'I'm in a great job, but there's something about having your own business . . . I'd really like to try it. Did you buy an existing agency?'

'Yes, I bought one that had been running for a few years.'

'What did you do about staff?'

'Brian, the older guy who was in the office when you came in, was someone I inherited. He was a lifesaver; he's worked in lettings for years and knows all the local landlords and tradespeople. I leave the letting side to him, though he's heading for retirement now and works shorter weeks. It won't be too long before I have to look for a replacement for him, I suppose. I hired the women myself.'

We arrived at the first block and took the lift to the fifth floor. The previous owners had already moved, so a sale could go ahead quickly.

'Hmm, this is pretty nice,' he said. 'How long has it been unoccupied?'

'They've just moved out,' I said. 'Last month. May. It's much better that it's empty; you could move in within weeks. You'll probably find there's room to manoeuvre on the price, too. If the vendor's still paying a mortgage, they'll want a fast sale.'

He went over to the window and opened the doors to the balcony that overlooked the central courtyard. There was space out there for a small table and a couple of chairs. He closed the doors without comment, then went into the bathroom. There was nothing to complain about there and he went into the kitchen, pulling out drawers and opening cupboards. Everything there was high spec; it was just the kind of place I thought he'd like.

'What do you think?' He smiled over at me. 'Could you see me here?'

I laughed. 'It's a great city-centre flat. Well, on the edge of the city, which is better, really. You don't get the noise.'

'Oh, I don't know,' he said. 'It's pretty noisy out there, when the French doors are open.'

'Really? It seems quiet to me. Well, it's the middle of the day, so there'll be a lot of tourists and shoppers. At night it'd be much quieter.'

He nodded. 'Let's go. Where's next?'

Next was a house in a popular area a couple of miles from the middle of town. It had its own busy centre, with bars and restaurants, gyms and shops.

'Houses move quickly here,' I said as I showed him around. 'This one's only been on the market for a few days and I'm expecting it to go by the end of the month.'

'Sounds great,' he said. 'I could be living here within a couple of months.'

I smiled, absolutely certain that pretty soon he'd be making an offer on one of our properties.

* * *

By mid-afternoon, though, I'd shown him six places, and although he'd enthused about them all, when I dropped him off at the office he made no suggestion that he'd be taking any of them further.

'I'll be in touch in the next few days,' he said.

'Great!' I smiled at him. 'I'll look forward to it.'

'Any luck?' asked Sophie as I entered the office.

I frowned. A number of people were looking at houses listed on the boards and glanced up in interest when she called out.

'Can I see you for a moment?' I asked, and went into the kitchen to wait for her. She bounced in, but the smile left her face when I reminded her not to call out in the office. 'Just e-mail me or ask me quietly if it's busy out there.'

She squirmed with embarrassment. 'Sorry.'

Rachel came into the kitchen and filled the kettle for tea.

I said, 'That's okay,' to Sophie. I didn't like to reprimand her while anyone else was around.

She was only down for a moment, though, before she nudged me, saying, 'How did it go with that guy? He was nice, wasn't he?'

I laughed. 'I could tell you liked him.'

'Tall, dark, and handsome,' she mused. 'Fit, too. Gorgeous. Rachel thought he was too.'

'I did not!'

'Yes, you did. Pity he's too old for us.'

I raised my eyebrows. 'He's my age, thanks.'

'That's what I mean.'

Rachel, her face scarlet now, nudged her, and I left them to it.

But later, before we closed the office, I called a meeting so we could thrash out some ideas for properties for David. We got together a list of another six that we thought he'd love, and then I e-mailed him to see whether he wanted to view any of them.

He replied immediately.

> They sound great. I particularly liked the third one we saw today, the one with the view of the racecourse. I need to get my mortgage sorted out first, though – will be in touch soon.

I sighed. He'd told me he had his mortgage sorted. It seemed he was yet another client messing me around. I'd learned from experience that until someone had got a guaranteed mortgage, they weren't seriously looking. I guessed we wouldn't be seeing him again, but I wrote back saying he should let me know if he wanted me to recommend a financial adviser.

Will do, he replied. See you soon.

2

When I arrived home, I walked through the house towards the happy sounds I could hear in the garden. I stood unnoticed at the patio windows, watching Rory run up the lawn and into the paddling pool, splashing water and shrieking. The hosepipe lay on the grass, filling up the pool, as it emptied every time he jumped into it. Joe sat on the patio, a beer in his hand, wearing just his shorts. He had his Kindle on the table in front of him, one eye on the screen, the other on Rory.

'Hey,' I said, and he jumped. I kissed him on his cheek. 'My two boys.'

'Hi.' He put the bottle down on the patio and I stooped to pick it up again and put it on the table. 'Good day?'

'It was okay.' I sat beside him and sipped his beer. 'I spent hours taking some guy round a load of properties that I don't think he'll be buying.'

'Argh, time-waster,' he said. 'That's the way it is, though, I suppose.'

'You weren't the one wasting your time! Mind you,' I said, looking Joe straight in the eye, 'he was very attractive . . .'

He laughed. 'Perk of the job.'

Joe was a stay-at-home dad. We'd been married for a few

years, but still it was unexpected when I got pregnant with Rory. Joe was working in IT, and though he was paid well, he wasn't enjoying his job much and was looking for a change, whereas I was really happy at work and was bringing in quite a bit more than he was each month. I didn't want to hire a manager and lose control of the place, so when Joe suggested he should stay at home with the baby, I jumped at the chance. My hours were awkward, and I knew I'd never find a childminder or nursery that would keep Rory late at short notice. We were typical prospective parents in that we thought our lives wouldn't change much when our baby was born; Joe had sworn he'd be able to take on part-time jobs while Rory slept, and I'd believed him. That first year had been a massive learning curve for both of us.

And now, well, house sales were down nationally and that was showing no sign of change soon. I had to work longer and longer hours to try to keep clients happy and to keep staffing as low as I could. Any ideas I'd had of taking days off to care for Rory were suddenly blown out of the water. Only two days ago Joe had told me his skills were now three years out of date and he'd suddenly found that he could no longer apply for certain jobs even if he wanted to, as technology had moved on so rapidly. The thought of being the only wage-earner was now making me panic. It wasn't that I minded, just that houses didn't seem to be shifting at the moment and I couldn't think of a way to make more sales. I was worried, too, about the rentals I owned; they were mortgaged up to the hilt and it would only take one defaulter to mean we'd lose hundreds of pounds each month. And if houses weren't selling, I wouldn't be able to sell mine either. Or not unless I made a loss. The thought of that would keep me awake at night. And Joe . . . I had a horrible feeling that he'd stopped looking for work. He changed the subject when I brought it up, and I could never bring myself to press the matter.

Then Rory saw me and all thoughts of that left my mind. He yelled with delight and ran towards me, his arms outstretched.

I leaned down to kiss him, my face buried in his hair. 'Hello, my lovely boy. Have you had a good time?'

'I've been in the paddling pool all day,' he said. 'But I'm starving! What's for tea?'

'It's in the oven,' said Joe. 'Lasagne. It'll just be a few more minutes, so let's get you into the bath and it'll be ready by the time you're out.'

'I'll take him,' I said quickly. 'Come on, Rory; let's go.'

Rory stood between us, indecision on his face. 'I want Dad to take me.'

I felt a familiar prickle of hurt. 'Come on, sweetheart; I haven't seen you all day! You can tell me what you've been up to.'

'Go upstairs with Mum, Rory,' said Joe. 'Come on, be nice!'

My eyes smarted. My own child shouldn't have to be persuaded to spend time with me!

'But . . .' said Rory, and then he looked at my face and I knew he'd seen the hurt there. 'Okay, but will you be a lion? Growl just like Dad does.'

'I'll have a go,' I said, but when I did, it clearly wasn't up to scratch.

He gave me a pitying glance. 'Don't worry, Mum,' he said. 'Dad can do it when we get back downstairs.'

I ran a bath for Rory, and sat next to him as he played and sang and splashed. Hopefully he'd forgotten he was with his second choice. I started to think about the work I still had to do that day. I tried to get home as soon as the office shut at five so that I could spend time with Rory before he went to bed, though often I couldn't manage that because of evening viewings, but the cost of that was that I had to work late. As soon as he was in bed, I'd be on to my e-mails, making calls, trying to match clients to properties they'd love, keeping track of the finances, and preparing for the meeting we had first thing every morning. The legal work had to be up to date, too, and often I did that at home, as it was easier to concentrate outside the office. Often I'd look up from my laptop late at night to find Joe asleep on the sofa, with something neither of us had been watching muted on the television.

Now that Rory was three, I knew Joe was anxious for us to have another baby, so that the children could grow up together. He loved being at home with Rory, but I was worried that if he was struggling to find work now, he'd find it impossible in another few years' time. And if the property market was still in a slump, what would we do? I tried to forget these problems in the time I had with Rory each evening, but they were always there at the back of my mind.

I took Rory up to bed after he'd had his supper and lay on his bed to read him some stories.

'Do the voices,' he urged. 'Make them scary!'

I tried to do it, but he sighed. 'No, do them like Dad does. Make me shiver!'

I tried again, more forcefully, and he laughed, but said firmly, 'Tell Dad to come up and do it.'

Shamefaced, I called to Joe and he came into Rory's bedroom on all fours, growling and snarling so that Rory screamed with excitement. I stood and watched, and though I loved it, I was hurt, too, that he'd wanted Joe instead of me.

Later, when Rory was asleep, I sat at my laptop, typing up notes for the property valuation I'd seen after I'd dropped David off. I was just about to start to e-mail clients who'd sent me messages that afternoon when Joe came back from the gym.

'You don't mind if I watch this, do you?' he asked, and flicked the television on. A football match was about to start. Wonderful.

There was no way I could concentrate while there was background noise, so I took my laptop into the kitchen and sat at the dining table. Joe came into the room and took a bottle of wine from the fridge. He raised a glass to offer me some, but I shook my head violently.

'Come on, Gem,' he said. 'It's Friday night. Start of the weekend.'

I was so tempted to say, *What weekend? I'm working!* and I think Joe must have recognized the expression on my face, because he put the wine back into the fridge and sat down beside me.

'Give me a job to do,' he said. 'Any job. Come on, I can handle it.'

I laughed and he nudged me, his leg tanned and hard against mine. I nudged him back, feeling a frisson of desire as our bodies touched. 'I've got all the bank statements here,' I said. 'And here's a list of all the fee payments that have come in from solicitors. I need to marry them up and check for outstanding debts. You wouldn't do that for me, would you?'

He moved an inch closer to me. 'Maybe. What's it worth?'

I leaned over and whispered in his ear.

'Pass me that file and my laptop,' he said, 'and give me half an hour, and then I'm going to hold you to that.'

3

Monday, June 19

'So you'll definitely be able to work on Friday afternoon?' I asked Rachel the following Monday.

She nodded. 'The course is on Saturday, then?'

'Yes, in a hotel in London. Covent Garden. I'll go down late Friday afternoon and come back Saturday night.'

She looked at the rota in front of us. 'And you're at work on Sunday? Are you sure you won't want a day at home?'

'I can't. Brian's off on Sunday. You'll have Wednesday off in exchange for Friday?'

This happened every week. We were short-staffed, but unless the housing situation changed soon, I couldn't afford to take on anyone new. I had to juggle around the rota to keep everyone happy and the place staffed. That was the problem with having a business that had to be open every day of the week. I tended to work most days, taking half-days off where I could, but it was hard and I seemed to be permanently exhausted.

I was happy to work long hours, but I did miss Rory and loved nothing more than to just be on my own with him.

I loved those times we'd spend at the park or having a milkshake in our local café or at the swimming pool. Joe usually came along too, and I liked that, I really did, but sometimes . . . well, when Joe was there Rory would often turn to him if he was upset and I'd stand there feeling useless, whereas on our own he was totally reliant on me. It sounds selfish but it can be hard for a mum to watch her child run to someone else for help, even if that person is his dad.

Often I'd daydream about the time when Rory was older, when he could walk from school at the end of the day and come to the office and do his homework for an hour while he waited for me to finish. Joe would be out at work, then later, in my daydreams, it would be just Rory and me, in the kitchen, making dinner together while he told me about his day.

It was a strange fantasy, I knew that. It wasn't as though things were bad now, it was just that I felt I'd missed out on that lovely one-to-one time that most mums seemed to have. I shook myself. I loved Joe. I loved Rory. I loved my job, most of the time. There was no reason to live in fantasy land.

I looked up to see Rachel staring at me.

'Sorry!' I said. 'I was miles away.'

'Anywhere nice?'

I shook my head. 'I was thinking of Rory and what he'd be like as a teenager. At secondary school.'

Sophie saw the chance for a gossip and came hurrying over. 'He'll be gorgeous. Totally gorgeous.'

I looked at the photo on my desk. Rory was riding his tricycle in the park, his face serious as he concentrated. His hair was blonde and floppy and glossy, and far, far too long. The photo had been taken a month ago, just as summer started, and already his skin was tanned, his body lithe. Joe and Rory had given me the photo when I got home from work, just as Rory was going to bed, and as soon as he was asleep I'd started to cry at what I was missing.

'He's just like Joe, isn't he?' asked Sophie.
I smiled. 'Yes, beautiful!'
They laughed.
'Would you like another baby?' asked Rachel suddenly. She blushed and I guessed she thought she'd been too forward.
They both looked at me, an eager look in their eyes.
'I'm not sure,' I said slowly. 'I think so. I think Rory would love a baby brother or sister.'
'And they'd love him,' said Sophie, a sentimental look on her face.
'I wasn't going to have another,' I said. 'Not with working full time. It's just something my mum said.' I thought back to Christmas, when she and my dad had come to stay. 'She said the best present I could give Rory was a brother or sister. I've got an older brother and we used to get on really well when we were kids. He's working in Edinburgh now, so I don't see him as much as I'd like, but we're still great friends.'
'She's right!' said Sophie. 'He'd have a friend for life.'
I smiled. 'That's a lovely thought.'
Rachel picked up the coffee mugs. 'I'll get these done,' she said, and went into the kitchen.
'So you decided against going down just for the day, then?' asked Sophie.
'I couldn't face getting the six A.M. train. Joe wanted me to so that he could go to the pub on Friday night, but I couldn't face it.' I left a pause, and then admitted, 'So I told him it wouldn't get me there on time.'
She laughed.
Rachel came back in to put away the biscuit tin. 'What time did you tell him it started?'
'Nine A.M. instead of nine thirty. The train gets in at eight fifty, so I'd have had to rush to be there on time.'
She shook her head in mock disapproval. 'Lies to your husband. What next?'

I laughed along with the others, but I was well aware that I was telling Joe more and more lies lately. Some nights I'd sleep in the spare room, telling him my head was aching, when all I wanted was to be on my own for a while. Or I'd creep in with Rory, just to spend time with him, even though he was asleep. And I knew that Joe suspected I wasn't happy. I'd seen him watching me at times, and when I'd smile at him, he'd seem lost in his thoughts and take a while to respond.

Last night, when we were in bed, I felt he was about to ask me about it and suddenly I thought, *I'll tell him everything, tell him exactly what I'm feeling*, but then he turned away from me and went to sleep. I was still sitting up, putting my face cream on, and I wanted to lean over, to kiss his cheek, to try to regain some of that closeness, but I just couldn't. So I turned away from him too, but I couldn't sleep.

I seemed to have gone from someone who was always honest, always open, to someone who said whatever had to be said for an easy life. I didn't know how that had happened.

4

That night I took Joe up on his offer of wine. It was Monday, that was his excuse, and I realized then that virtually every night lately he'd had an excuse to open a bottle. 'It's Thursday!' he'd shout from the kitchen. 'Nearly the weekend! Come on, let's have a glass.' He was pretty good at having just one or two glasses, though, and so was I, now. I hadn't always been like that.

So that Monday night Joe poured us a glass of wine and we did what I loved best, and lay at either end of the sofa, legs entwined, and talked. We put some music on and I lit some candles and for a while nothing existed but us. Our family. We talked about everything and nothing, as we always did, but the conversation always came back to Rory. It was our favourite topic, guaranteed to put me into a great mood. Joe told me about swimming and the park and how Rory had befriended a dog who lived across the street from us, and I soaked up those stories. I could never hear enough of them.

I told him what the women at work had said about having another child. 'Do you think we should have another?' I asked, suddenly overcome with sentimentality. 'Do you think Rory would like a little brother or sister?'

Joe looked startled. 'Of course! He'd love it. *I'd* love it!' He reached out to pull me to him. 'I thought you didn't want to. You shouted at your mum when she mentioned it, remember?'

I winced as I remembered my mum's shocked expression on Christmas Day when she'd given me her advice and I'd given it back to her with both barrels. She'd instantly looked down at the glass in my hand and I knew she thought I was drinking too much. That had made me even angrier. I couldn't think now why I'd reacted like that. I'd felt so much pressure at work, and the idea of getting pregnant on top of that had seemed just too much.

But now, in the candlelight, with Rory asleep in his bed and my work for the evening all done, I couldn't seem to recapture that feeling of anger and frustration.

'What's changed your mind?' Joe asked.

I shook my head. 'The women at work, I think. Sophie . . . she agreed with my mum. She said he'd have a friend for life, and she's right. Look at you and Caitlin. Mind you, look at you and Brendan.'

Joe laughed. He was probably his elder brother Brendan's greatest fan; he was never happier than when the two of them were together. 'Oh, I wouldn't want one like him. That would be a nightmare.'

Despite the haze of wine and sentimentality, I couldn't help but think how hard I'd have to work to bring in the money needed for a bigger family. Perhaps I could expand the business? But how could I do that when houses weren't moving? My heart sank. I was exhausted as it was, without bringing more pressure on myself.

And then I thought back to when I was pregnant with Rory. It was the first time I'd felt relaxed in my body since . . . well, I could hardly remember. The feeling of a baby inside me, those first tentative movements I'd felt so early on, like a butterfly's kisses. I'd loved him from that moment. Before then, even. He'd been part of me then; he'd always be part of me. And the thought of going through that again was exhilarating.

'Do you think we could love another child as much?' I asked.

'Of course we could.' Joe's hands were in my hair and I closed my eyes as he kissed me. 'Especially if we have a redhead.' He ran his fingers through my hair and kissed me again. 'A redhead with green eyes, just like you.'

'Maybe we could think about it later in the year,' I said.

'That would be amazing.'

'And maybe I could look at changing my hours so that I can spend more time at home.'

I got caught up in his embrace then, but later, when we were lying in bed and he was sleeping soundly beside me, I lay awake trying to think of ways I could work fewer hours. Joe had kissed me then and I was distracted; it was only later that I realized he hadn't agreed with me.

5

Friday, June 23

I caught the afternoon train from Chester to London the following Friday and it was packed. As I hurried past the relatively empty first-class compartment, I saw a couple of women relaxing in the large, comfortable seats, glasses of gin and tonic already in their hands, and wished I'd spent the extra money and upgraded my ticket. I couldn't justify it, though; the business wasn't doing well enough for me to throw money away like that.

My heart sank at Euston when I saw hordes of people queuing for the escalator to the underground. There was a notice saying one of the tube lines was out of service, and I knew there'd be bedlam. The station was crammed and stifling with the summer heat, and I felt so hot by the time I reached the escalator that I decided to walk instead.

I stepped outside onto Euston Square. It was early evening by then and I walked down Tottenham Court Road towards my hotel in Covent Garden. Crowds of office workers mingled with tourists, and I thought of the days I'd worked here when I was in my early twenties. I missed those days. I was working for an estate agent's in North London and it was fast and furious then, before the downturn. Flats and houses would sell quickly for more than the asking price, and the agency could afford to be generous with bonuses and drinks after work.

I'd known it wouldn't be like that when I moved to Chester. And by the time I met Joe I was ready to move on. I was twenty-six then, with five years' experience under my belt, and I was up for the challenge.

We had a great time in those early days. I met Joe when I was in Ireland for Brendan's wedding; Caitlin had invited me and we'd gone to her family's local pub the night we arrived. I'd been over to Ireland to stay with her in the long summer holiday a couple of times before then, but Joe had been off backpacking those summers and I hadn't met him. That night she and I walked into the pub and she stopped in the doorway to talk to an old friend. I went to the bar to get us drinks and watched as a band played, badly, on a makeshift stage. Joe was standing watching them too. We hadn't yet been introduced, but I knew instantly he was related to Caitlin; they had the same tousled blonde hair, the same blue eyes, and besides, his mother had shown me enough photos of the family to recognize him. He winced at every bum note and then saw me looking over at him and laughed.

I said, 'That bad, eh?'

'It's my friend's youngest brother,' he said. 'I don't think he's quite ready for stardom yet.'

I looked at the guitarist, who'd dropped his head so nobody could see his face. I could tell he was aware how badly he was playing.

'Poor guy,' said Joe.

When the band came off stage he went over to the guitarist and clapped him on the shoulder. I could see he was being kind to him, shaking his head as the young man protested. 'It's nerves,' I heard him say. 'Next time you'll be fine.'

He came over to me and said, 'So, you're Gemma.' I remember I blushed then, and he said, 'I've heard a lot about you.'

We stood together at the corner of the bar for hours that night, and it was only when the pub was closing that I turned to see Caitlin smiling at us. She bundled me into the ladies' loo before we left, and as soon as we were alone, she said, 'I knew you'd like him!'

I couldn't deny it. I couldn't stop smiling either. 'Why didn't you introduce me before?'

She hesitated, and immediately I knew what she was about to say. 'Now's the right time,' she said eventually, and I knew she meant she couldn't have risked it before. She was right. I'd been a bit of a mess for years, but she'd helped me get through it.

'You planned this?' I asked.

She grinned at me and refused to answer.

Joe was staying with a local friend, as his parents' home, where I was staying, was full of visiting friends and relations. He offered to walk me back there that night, but we were talking so much by the time we got there that he didn't want to let me go. He said he'd take me on a tour of his old haunts, and we walked for miles around the deserted streets of his neighbourhood. I think I knew that night that he'd always be in my life.

Now, as I approached the hotel, I stopped to send him a text.

```
Just walking through Covent Garden. I know it's
not Dublin, but it's making me think of the night we
met xx
```

He replied:

```
Oh that was a great night. One of the best nights
of my life. Last night was pretty good too xx
```

I blushed. It certainly had been.

```
For me too. Missing you both xxx
```

6

It was a hot night and I felt sticky and horrible from the journey and the walk to the hotel. A big corner bath was calling to me, but when I heard the sound of people talking and laughing out on the terrace below, I decided to have a shower instead and go down to see if there was anyone I knew in the bar. If there wasn't, I planned to come back up, order some food and wine, and have a long bath and an early night.

After a quick shower, I changed into a dark green silk dress with spaghetti straps that I'd brought with me in case I went out to dinner. I put some make-up on, slipped on my sandals, and wondered who'd be there. I had to do these training days every now and then, and often I'd bump into the same crowd. It wasn't that we kept in touch with each other outside the events, but over the years we'd gravitate towards each other whenever we met. Those of us with our own agencies understood each other's problems, and it was always good to talk freely, in a way I didn't like to do with people I met in Chester. I didn't want local people knowing anything about my business worries.

I switched both bedside lamps on, ready for when I returned later, and went down to the bar.

'A gin and tonic, please,' I said to the barman.

'Single? Double?' I hesitated, and he said, 'Why not? Kick-start the weekend!'

I laughed. 'Go on then.'

Drink in hand, I turned to see who was there. The bar was crowded and I could see from the variety of lanyards and badges that there were quite a few events that weekend. I walked around the perimeter of the room but couldn't see anyone I knew. Trying to quell my disappointment, I realized most people would probably just travel down the next morning rather than stay overnight. Usually these training sessions were a two-day event, with everyone staying over on the middle night.

I drank my gin and ordered another, and yes, it was another double. It was a hot summer night, just the right weather for gin and tonic, and I didn't have anyone I was responsible for. I felt if I wanted a drink, I'd damn well have one.

Just as I'd decided to go back up to my room, my phone beeped in my bag. I checked my messages, hoping Rory was ready for a chat before he went to bed. He'd been out to a friend's house earlier, so we'd agreed he'd call at bedtime.

Hey Gem, are you having a good time? Rory's just had a bath and fallen asleep. Sorry, he was going to call you. Fancy a chat? xx

I stared at the phone. That was the one thing I'd asked him to do tonight. He knew how much I missed Rory. I didn't want to talk to Joe now; I'd only get angry. And I'd had a couple of drinks; I knew he'd be able to tell. I didn't want a conversation about that. I was about to ignore his text but knew there'd be a flurry of others and I'd end up snapping at him, so I sent him a message:

In the bath then I'm going to sleep. Will call you tomorrow xx

In seconds he replied:

Oh ok. Night xx

I could sense his disappointment that I couldn't chat and felt bad almost immediately but stopped myself in my tracks. Whenever he went away for the night, I just sent the odd message, but when I went anywhere, he was never off the phone. I ignored the fact that I was usually really glad of this and drank some more gin.

After circuiting the bar, I walked into the lobby. Again, I knew nobody there. Then I saw a group of middle-aged men walk in through the revolving door, and my stomach sank. One of them, Liam Fossett, was one of the most boring people I knew. I should have guessed he'd be here; he worked up in the north-east, so he'd have to stay overnight. When he saw me, his face lit up. He waved and I let my eyes drift past him, as though I hadn't seen him. Out of the corner of my eye, though, I could see that he was pushing his way through the crowd towards me.

In an instant I decided to escape to my room. I turned quickly and bumped into a man standing in a group of other people behind me. He put his hand out to steady me.

'Careful!' he said.

'Oh, I'm so sorry,' I said. 'I didn't see you.'

I looked at his glass, which had spilled red wine onto the floor, then looked up at him.

'It's Gemma, isn't it?' he said. 'Gemma Brogan? David Sanderson. You showed me around some properties in Chester the other day.'

'Oh, of course! I didn't recognize you out of context,' I said, moving back from the spilled wine. 'I'm really sorry I knocked your drink. Let me get you another.'

'Don't worry,' he said. 'What are you doing here?'

'I'm on a training course,' I said. 'It's about new money-laundering regulations. It's easier to come on a course and get all the literature than try to figure it out myself.'

'Nice to get away for the weekend too, I bet?'

I laughed. 'Yes, sometimes it's good to have a break. It's pretty hectic with work and a young child.'

'Is your family down here with you?'

I shook my head. 'No. My son's only three. I didn't dare tell him I was going on a train. He'd have been harassing me for ages to come with me.'

He laughed. 'I was like that when I was a kid. The best part of any holiday was always the journey.'

I felt a tap on my shoulder, and flinched. I knew who that would be.

'Hi, Liam.' I tried to dodge his wet kiss on my cheek but didn't quite manage it. I felt David's arm brush against mine for just a second, and I knew he'd noticed my reaction. 'How are you?'

'Great, thanks, Gem,' he said. 'We're going in to dinner soon. Come and join us?'

I looked at him, at his red face with its slight glaze of sweat. I couldn't think of anything I wanted to do less.

'Oh, I'm sorry,' said David. 'Gemma's having dinner with me.'

I glanced at him. *I am?* I kept my face straight.

Liam looked at David, then at me. 'You want to join us too?'

David shook his head. 'Sorry, it's business. I need to ask her advice. I'm afraid she'll be busy for the next couple of hours.'

Liam nodded reluctantly. 'All right. Maybe a drink later?'

I smiled. 'Maybe.'

David and I watched as he made his way back to his friends. He leaned towards me and whispered in my ear, 'You owe me.'

I laughed. 'You have saved my life.'

He smiled. 'You're lucky I was here.'

'No kidding. But what are you doing here?'

'Oh, I've been in London for business.'

'With Barford's?'

'You've got a good memory! Yes, I'm meeting some suppliers. I've been staying here all week and need to see someone again in the morning. I'll go back north tomorrow.'

'Still looking for a house?' I smiled at him, hoping I didn't sound too cheeky.

He laughed. 'Yeah, sorry I haven't been in touch. There was a hitch on my mortgage because I was waiting for the money from my house sale in Boston, but it's all through now and the bank's ready to go ahead.'

'Well, get in touch whenever you're ready,' I said. 'I'll find you a good deal.' I could feel that my face was hot now and didn't know whether it was the drink. I put my empty glass down on a side table and turned to go. 'Thanks for getting me off the hook with Liam.'

'I don't suppose you *would* have dinner with me, would you?' He saw me hesitate and said quickly, 'You'd be doing me a huge favour. I've been sitting here on my own night after night.' He grinned. 'And I'd hate that guy to think you'd stood me up.'

I paused. I'd been about to go up to my room. I thought of my earlier plans to order room service and have a long bath in peace. I was so tired after this week at work.

And then I thought of the potential sale. Sure, he was a good-looking guy and he did make me laugh, but my business brain was the one I used when I said, 'Okay, but I'll pay.' He started to object, but I said, 'It's a business expense. You're a client.' It wasn't an expense I could afford, but if it led to a sale it would be well worth the money. An investment.

He laughed. 'Well, that would be very nice. Thank you.'

I saw Liam looking over at me. 'Shall we go now?' I gave him a little wave, and David and I walked through the bar to the restaurant.

7

That night seemed to fly by in a flash. It had been a long time since I'd been to dinner with a man on my own, and I was surprised at how comfortable I felt. The waiter came over and asked us about drinks.

I looked at the wine menu. 'You were drinking red wine, weren't you?' I asked David. 'Shall I get a bottle?'

'That would be great, thanks.'

I ordered a bottle of Barolo and David poured us a glass each while he talked me through the menu, telling me which meals he'd had while he was down there. He told me about the places he'd lived abroad: Boston, Dallas, and Hong Kong.

'You're in sales, aren't you?' I asked.

'Yeah. It's not for everyone, but I'm happy in that kind of environment. As long as the company's reputable. You've got to believe in the products.'

'And Barford's is a good company?'

'They've been great. Sent me all over the place. I love that.'

'I wish I'd worked abroad in my twenties,' I said. 'I don't think I realized when I was child-free that I should do as much travelling as I could then.'

'It can be hard work moving around, though. You lose

touch with your old friends and you can be relocated at any time. It's hard to fit in sometimes.'

'I suppose so.'

'Still, you're in a great position now. You have a family and it looks like your business is going well.'

I hesitated, not wanting to admit that in this economy people were avoiding buying property. Of course in any climate people wanted to buy low and sell high, but I was noticing it now more than ever. In the end, he was a potential client, so I just said, 'Yes, it's going well. I'm very lucky.'

'You look tired. Busy week?'

I nodded. 'Always.'

'Why not forget about work for a while? Have a night off.' He picked up the wine we'd ordered. 'Fancy a top-up?'

I looked at the bottle and then back at David. I already had a buzz on and could feel my skin tingling. I'd reached my limit with the drinks I'd already had; I knew better than to drink more, but suddenly the lure of a couple of glasses and some carefree conversation with another adult – okay, another man – was too great.

I pushed my glass towards him. 'Why not?'

We stayed in the restaurant for a few hours, enjoying our meal and some drinks. He was great company, talking about his life overseas and living in London as a student. I felt completely at ease with him; he was entertaining and funny and I felt sure he'd come back to the office in the next couple of weeks to see some more properties. I made a mental note to get everyone at work onto looking for a suitable place; after talking to him I had a good idea of the sort of lifestyle he wanted.

It took a while at the end of the night for our bill to arrive, and then when it did, the waiter stayed at the other side of the restaurant chatting with a waitress and, despite my waves, didn't meet my eye. I sighed and went over to him to ask him to bring the card machine. When I got back to our table, David was pouring the last of the wine into our glasses.

'Thanks for the meal,' he said. He picked up his glass. 'Cheers!'

Automatically I raised my glass to his. 'You're welcome,' I said, and drank the wine. I looked at my watch. 'I have to go; I've got an early start tomorrow.' I felt unsteady when I stood. 'Gosh, I've drunk far too much!' I looked down at the table and frowned. Two bottles of wine were empty – I didn't think I'd had much more than a couple of glasses. 'Did we drink all that?'

He laughed. 'I'm afraid so. But it's Friday night, time to let our hair down,' he said. 'It's my fault, I think. I drank far more than you did.'

I blinked hard. 'Ugh, I'm going to have such a hangover.'

'Make sure you drink lots of water,' he said. 'Do you have any painkillers? Perhaps take a couple before you go to sleep.'

I nodded. 'I will.'

We walked over to the lift. There were still crowds of people in the bar, and just one elderly couple was waiting for the lift.

David stood next to the lift buttons. 'Which floor would you like?' he asked the couple. He pressed a button for them, then said to me, 'How about you?'

For a moment I couldn't remember, and searched in my bag for the little envelope containing my key card.

He glanced at it and said, 'The ninth? I'm on the tenth.'

The couple got out at their floor, and David and I stood in silence. In the few seconds it took for the lift to take us up to the ninth floor, I felt as though I could sleep for a week. I wondered what would happen if I didn't go to the training. Would it matter? I could hardly remember the name of the training event at that point. Was it in this hotel?

The Girl I Used to Be

When the doors opened onto the ninth floor, I stumbled out. David grabbed my arm.

'Steady!' he said, laughing. 'Steady on, sweetheart.'

I stared at him, confused.

'What's your room number?' he asked.

I couldn't answer. I tried, I tried to say something, but I couldn't think straight and my tongue felt thick and swollen in my mouth.

He took the key card envelope out of my hand. '912,' he said. He laughed again. 'You've really had too much to drink, haven't you?'

I tried to smile but I couldn't. All I could think about was getting into bed.

He stopped abruptly outside one of the hotel-room doors. I lurched into him. I tried to apologize but nothing came out.

My back was to the door and he reached out and touched my hair. 'Time for bed,' he said, and suddenly the atmosphere seemed to change.

He leaned forward. I twisted my head away and saw a woman standing at the far end of the corridor. She reached out her hand to press the button on the wall to call the lift. I tried to move away from David, to keep the distance between us, but I bumped against the door and then his hand moved to the side of my face and he turned my head towards him. I couldn't take my eyes off him.

And then he kissed me.

8

Saturday, June 24

The next morning I felt as cold as if I'd spent the night sleeping on a stone floor. I opened my eyes to find a beam of sunlight glaring through the gap in the curtains. My eyes hurt just to open them. A glance at my watch told me it was nine A.M. I had to get up; I'd slept through my alarm. I knew I had to go down to the conference room, but my head was pounding mercilessly. My mouth was dry and foul. I needed water.

I hauled myself up out of bed and staggered into the bathroom, kicking aside my dress, which I'd left on the bedroom floor the night before. For a moment I thought I'd be okay, but the sun was shining through the window onto the bathroom tiles and they were such a brilliant, vivid white that they made my head hurt. Immediately I was sick in the toilet. Afterwards my head throbbed so badly I saw stars. I rinsed my face at the basin but avoided looking at my reflection. I knew I'd look awful. There was a minibar in the bedroom, and I took a bottle of water out and drank it down in one, my hands shaking. I brushed my teeth vigorously, but my mouth still tasted disgusting. I couldn't go downstairs like this.

Outside the door the cleaner's trolley squeaked its way down the corridor, and I winced at the sound. Surely it shouldn't be so loud. I wanted to take some painkillers and go back to bed, but the conference was due to start at nine thirty, and in any case, checkout was ten A.M. so I had to get going.

I had no choice: I had to go down to the conference. I took off my underwear – clearly I hadn't bothered getting fully undressed last night, never mind putting on my pyjamas – and stepped into the shower. Every movement seemed a huge effort, as though my limbs were heavy and weak. Eventually I was clean and dry and dressed, but I knew I looked far from well. I spent longer than usual on my make-up, trying to make myself appear sober and smart, but I doubted I'd be fooling anyone. My eyes were red-rimmed and sore, and I put my sunglasses on to try to hide the fact that I was hungover. I was so furious with myself for drinking like that; it was as though I hadn't had a filter, a gauge to tell me when to stop.

Downstairs I took a cup of coffee from the buffet table and picked up a couple of bottles of water too. There was no way I could eat anything; just the thought made me feel ill. I bought some mints and a newspaper from the kiosk. I had no intention of reading the paper, but I wanted something to hide behind. When a text came through from Joe to wish me a good morning, I winced with shame. When would I ever learn? I hadn't drunk like that for years, not since the old days at university. He'd never known me like that, though he knew I'd been through a tough time there. When I'd met Joe I'd felt comfortable with him immediately and had told him everything about my past. I was ready to move on then, ready to make a new start, and one of my promises to myself was that I wouldn't drink too much. I'd stuck to that promise, too, until now. I flinched. I couldn't tell him I was hungover;

I'd told him earlier in the evening that I was going to bed early.

'Bad night?' Helen, a woman from Cornwall who I met occasionally at these events, sat down next to me. Her expression was sympathetic. 'You look really tired.'

'I feel awful,' I said. 'I had far too much to drink last night. If I have to dash out, will you make my excuses?'

She smiled. 'That bad, eh?'

'Worse.'

'Want some painkillers?'

'Thanks, I've run out.' Grateful, I took them from her. I swallowed a couple with a drink of water; my hand was shaking so much I spilled it on my newspaper.

'Wow, you have got it bad!' she said. 'You can keep the rest of those tablets; you might need them later.'

'Thanks,' I said, embarrassed. 'I don't drink much normally. Haven't for years. I overdid it last night.'

The room started to quieten as Philip Doyle, the tutor, moved to the front of the room and tapped his microphone. The sound made me flinch.

'Were you here overnight, then?' she whispered. 'I was staying with a friend in Surrey. Who else was here?'

My mind went blank. Who had been here? I turned to look around the room and saw a sea of faces. I couldn't recognize anyone at first, and then I saw Liam sitting with his colleagues, laughing at something one of them had said. He looked pretty rough too, though he was managing to eat a huge sandwich. Like me, he must have missed breakfast. I turned away, unable to watch him.

'It was pretty busy,' I said. 'Liam Fossett was here, though. I know I saw him and all his gang.'

'Ugh, you didn't have to spend much time with them, did you?'

'No,' I said. 'One of my clients was here. I had dinner with him. He's been here for meetings all week.'

She smiled at me. 'Nice?'

The thought of David's face as he lowered his mouth to mine came into my mind then. I shuddered. How drunk had I been? I shook my head to try to force the image away. 'Yeah, he's okay. Better than Liam, at any rate. We had too much to drink, though. I'm paying the price now.'

'It's our age,' she said. 'Remember when you could drink whatever you wanted and it didn't make a difference the next day?'

'I don't miss that at all, though. Halfway through a night out I tend to wish I were in my pyjamas, in bed.'

Just then Philip Doyle started to introduce the day's events. I couldn't concentrate on what he was saying; it was like trying to think through fog. I drank more water, then tried to eat a biscuit that was on the coffee cup's saucer, but as soon as I felt the dry, sweet crumbs in my mouth, I had to leap up and run for the nearest cloakroom.

Later, at Euston station, I took one look at the crowds of people waiting for the train back to Chester and upgraded my ticket to first class, where it was quiet. I spoke to the attendant just before the train pulled out and told her that I wasn't well and needed to sleep. She put me at the far end of the carriage, away from the other passengers, and gave me a blanket to wrap around myself. I slept all the way home.

Joe and Rory picked me up at the station.

'Mummy!' Rory shrieked, running towards me and leaping into my arms. 'I've missed you!'

I kissed his head, smelling the fresh scent of his apple shampoo. Just pulling him to me made me feel better.

'I've missed you too,' I said. 'So much.'

Joe looked at me oddly. 'Are you okay?'

'I'm not well,' I said. I couldn't bear to tell him I'd had too much to drink. 'I haven't felt well all day.'

He put his arm around me. 'How come, sweetheart? You're not hungover, are you? I thought you had an early night.'

I thought about the text I'd sent him, telling him I was in the bath. Worried in case he smelled alcohol on me, I said, 'I had a couple of drinks in my room. It's probably just that. I drank them too fast and went to sleep. I'm so tired, though.'

'You'll be fine,' he said. 'Have another early night. I'm out with Mike, remember?'

That had been our arrangement when Joe had agreed to stay at home with Rory, that he'd have the chance to see his friends every week. Mike was a guy that Joe used to work with. He lived half a mile from us and often they'd go out for a run or a drink. I'd understood that: I spent all day with other adults and I knew he needed to see his friends. I'd forgotten, though, that he was planning to go out that night.

Rory leaped up and down, pulling at my arm. 'Just you and me, Mum! And you promised you'd play swingball with me before I went to bed!'

My head thumped at the thought of that. I looked up at Joe, hoping against hope that he would offer to stay home, but his eyes were fixed ahead. He knew exactly what I wanted, but he knew I wouldn't ask, either. It was our agreement, after all.

'Swingball it is,' I said weakly, planning already that the moment Rory got into his bed, I would get into mine.

9

Friday, July 21

I was in the office a month later when the post arrived. We have the same postman every day and of course Sophie has a crush on him. I don't think I've seen any guy under twenty-five that she hasn't had a crush on. Fair enough with this one, though; he's tall and tanned, with a surfer dude look about him, despite being quite a way from any waves. She'd been anticipating his visit all morning and I'd noticed the surreptitious smudge of lipstick and the smell of her new perfume. She bounced up as he entered the office and passed me the mail. The day was hot already and a soft breeze came through the open doorway.

There were no clients in the office. Rachel was working at her computer and Sophie fetched the postman a bottle of water from our fridge. She held on to it while she chatted to him, a ploy to stop him from leaving. It was just an ordinary day.

I glanced through the mail. There were a couple of letters from solicitors confirming that they were acting for clients. There was another letter from a solicitor confirming completion on a sale. A vendor had returned a signed and approved

49

set of property details. Mostly, though, as usual, it was junk mail and takeaway menus.

'Coffee?' asked Rachel.

'Great, thanks.'

I was just gathering together the junk mail, ready to throw it out, when I saw there was another envelope underneath it. I checked that it was for me, then opened it just as Rachel came over to my desk with a mug of coffee. 'Biscuit?' she asked, and put the tin on the desk beside my coffee.

'No, thanks,' I said. In the envelope was a sheet of paper, folded in half. I opened it up, thinking it was a flyer, but it was a photocopy of a receipt. I looked inside the envelope again to see if there was a compliments slip, but there was nothing.

'What's that?' she asked.

'I don't know,' I said slowly. 'It's a receipt for something.' I squinted at the logo. 'Oh, it's from the Shaftesbury Hotel.'

'The Shaftesbury Hotel?' she said. 'That's not around here, is it?'

I shook my head. 'No, it's the hotel I stayed in when I was in London.'

She picked it up and looked at it closely. 'It's from the restaurant. Steak. Barolo. Two bottles? Very nice.'

I took it back from her, exasperated. There was never any privacy at work. Everyone always wanted to know exactly what was going on.

The postman had left now and Sophie was back with us. She tried to look at the receipt too, but I turned it away from her. She said, 'I thought you were going to have room service and an early night?'

'I was,' I said. 'I changed my mind.'

'There are two meals there,' said Rachel. 'Did you pay for someone else?'

Struggling to keep the irritation out of my voice, I said, 'I met a client there. I paid for the meal.'

Out of the corner of my eye I could see Sophie and Rachel staring at each other and then at me.

'Why have they sent it to you?' asked Sophie.

'Tax reasons,' said Brian. I hadn't even known he was taking an interest. 'You have to keep your receipts so that you can claim the tax back.'

'Well, then,' I said, 'that was very nice of them.' I put the document into the folder I used to store receipts for my tax returns.

But later, when everyone was busy and I had a few moments to myself, I took the receipt out and looked at it again. Why had they sent this to me? And why send a copy? It wasn't as though they needed to keep the original for themselves. They would have a record of it on their system. But in any case, surely if it was just left on the table, they'd throw it away?

I'd tried not to think of that night with David in the restaurant. I'd thought those days where I'd drink too much and get into situations with strange men were over. By the time I hit my mid-twenties and met Joe, I was past all that. But the night I'd met David, I'd drunk so much I couldn't remember much of it. Why had I done that? While Rachel dealt with a client and Sophie spoke on the phone to a solicitor, I forced myself to think about it.

I could remember bumping into David and his drink spilling on the floor. I remember realizing it was him. He'd saved me from talking to someone else, too. I thought hard. Liam, that was it. I was glad he'd done that. And we'd had a meal. I'd had a couple of drinks before the meal, I knew that. I could remember ordering gin and tonics from the barman. Then an image flashed into my mind: two empty bottles of red wine on our table. I never drank more than a couple of glasses, maybe half a bottle, normally, and not as much as that if I'd had gin beforehand. How much had I drunk? I couldn't bear to think about how ill I was the next morning. Being sick from drinking was something teenagers did, not adults. Surely I hadn't drunk that much? But my head hurt so much the next day . . . I must have been completely out of it. I winced with embarrassment. I hadn't had a drink since that night and planned to keep it that way.

But I kept coming back to the question: why would the hotel send the receipt to me? I'd never known that to happen. Even in a shop, if you walk off without the receipt, the assistant just throws it into the bin. Why spend money and time returning it to me?

Just then the door opened and Joe's sister, Caitlin, came in. I put the receipt back into the folder and stood up to hug her.

'Good holiday?' I asked. The weekend before, she'd come back from a holiday in Italy with her husband, Ben. 'Lovely tan.'

'Thanks. It was tough going to work this week, though.'

'Ben's back in Dubai now?'

'Yes. I won't see him for another couple of weeks.' She looked lost for a moment, then pulled herself together. 'I've just been to Wrexham for a meeting. No point going back to Liverpool now, so I thought I'd call in and see what you're up to.' Caitlin worked in recruitment and was in charge of a number of offices in the north-west of England. 'Are you okay? You looked worried when I came in.'

'I'm fine, thanks. All okay.'

'And Joe? Rory?'

'Yes, they're great.'

'I called in to see them before I went away,' she said. 'You were down in London. Rory and Joe were having a good time.'

'I meant to call you about that,' I said, immediately feeling guilty. 'They said you were there. Did you get roped into cooking for them?'

'Oh, Rory persuaded me to make him an apple pie,' she said. 'He said he hadn't had one for ages.'

'You've been had,' I said. 'Joe makes them for him all the time.'

She laughed. 'He was very convincing. Said it was years since he'd had one.'

I laughed. 'He has no idea of time.'

'I didn't mind, though; it was nice to see them. Did you have a good time?'

I grimaced. 'The course was okay, but I wasn't well on Saturday. I had to keep running out to the loo.' My face burned at the memory of the swift dashes from the room and the knowing looks of some of the guys who must have seen me in the bar the night before.

'Ugh, that sounds horrible. Did you have too much to drink? Weren't you just going to have a quiet night?' We'd talked about it the week before the training day, how I was looking forward to a relaxing night on my own.

I hesitated but luckily she didn't seem to notice. 'I think I just had an upset stomach.'

I don't know why I didn't confide in her. We told each other everything, right from our first night in halls when we were students. We'd always been close, and I loved the fact that she was Joe's sister. His family became mine and mine his; it was perfect for us. But this . . . I couldn't talk to her about this. I hated the thought of her thinking of me drunk and incapable, stumbling and incoherent as I knew I must have been. As she'd seen me so many times before.

10

Caitlin came back to our house with me that night. I knew she was bored and a bit lonely at home since Ben had started to work away. They'd moved up to Liverpool a couple of years after we moved to the north-west and now lived thirty miles from us. We usually saw her at least once a week, particularly when Ben was away.

She came upstairs with me and we sat on the bathroom floor as Rory played in the bath. It was a Friday night and Joe had gone out to pick up some pizzas. I sat with my back against the tiled wall and closed my eyes. The late-summer sun was coming through the coloured-glass window, and the air smelled of Rory's bubble bath. He was singing a little song to himself, one that he'd learned in nursery that week.

I patted Caitlin's hand. 'Watch out for Rory, won't you, if I doze off.'

'Of course I will. He's the one I came here to see! But why don't you go and lie down for a bit? He'll be fine with me.'

I shook my head. 'I don't see enough of him as it is.'

'You look really tired. Are you working tomorrow?'

I grimaced. 'Yeah. Not until the afternoon, though. I've got to be there for twelve.'

'And Sunday?'

'I'm working the morning. Well, until two.'

'So when are you getting time off?'

'I'm not. I can't afford to. But I'm not working nine to five every day. Occasionally I'm working half-days. Well, more like three-quarter-days. I go in mid-morning sometimes, or finish early and then go back to lock up. Or I come home for a longer lunch.' I stopped, confusing myself.

'So you're in work every day?' Her voice softened, and immediately my eyes filled with tears. 'That must be exhausting.'

'It's not that,' I said. 'I am tired. I'm tired all the time. I just miss seeing Rory. Some weeks I'm working until seven for a few nights on a run, if people need to view later on or if I have to value someone's house. He goes to bed at half past, so I hardly see him.'

'Eight o'clock on a Saturday!' piped up Rory.

I hadn't realized he was paying any attention to us and shook my head at Caitlin. *Pas devant l'enfant.*

'Did you know I can speak French?' Rory asked Caitlin. 'That means "Not in front of the child."'

She laughed. 'Come on, mister,' she said. 'I've just heard Dad come in; let's go down and have that pizza.'

Later that evening Caitlin and I sat on the patio with Joe. They were drinking wine, but I poured Perrier for myself.

'How come you're not drinking?' asked Caitlin, and then she laughed. 'Oops, sorry, I shouldn't have asked that.'

'What do you mean?' asked Joe.

She shook her head. 'It's none of my business whether she has a drink or not.'

'She's wondering whether I'm pregnant,' I told Joe. 'That's always a clue, if someone refuses a drink on a Friday night. She's being discreet.'

'I was trying to be!'

Joe said, 'You're not, are you?'

I laughed. 'Of course I'm not. Don't you think I would've told you?'

He reached out and put his arm around me. 'I'd hope so!' He kissed my cheek. 'Maybe one day.'

I smiled at him. 'Maybe.' I drank some more Perrier, then said, 'I haven't felt like a drink for the last few weeks. But yes, we've been talking about having another baby, though not yet. Next year might be good. Nothing's guaranteed, though, obviously.'

'You lucky thing,' said Caitlin. For a moment she looked glum. 'No point in my getting pregnant, with Ben being out of the country all the time.'

'You could always go with him.'

'What, and be a trailing spouse? He'd be out of the house for fourteen hours a day and I'd have nothing to do. No thanks.'

Ben was an engineer who worked away for months at a time. On the one hand they were rapidly paying off their mortgage, but on the other I wasn't too sure how long they would last with hardly seeing each other. I was always grateful to have Joe, when I thought of her relationship with Ben. It was so hard for her not being able to spend much time with him.

We talked then about her trip to see him in Dubai in August, and the issue of my not drinking didn't arise again.

When I went up to bed, I thought how different that night was from the Friday I'd spent in London. I hated that feeling of being out of control. I knew I'd drunk those gins that night far too quickly, and again I got a flash of the two empty bottles on the table. I shook my head. I should never drink like that again.

While Joe was in the bathroom, I went back downstairs to find my bag. In the zip compartment was the receipt for the meal at the hotel that I'd received in the post. I took it out and looked at it again.

Pâté and smoked salmon. Those were the starters. Then steak and chicken.

I closed my eyes. What had I eaten? I had no idea now. How could that happen? No matter how many times I looked at the items on the receipt, I couldn't remember eating any of them.

When I saw the two bottles of Barolo, I winced. Two bottles. What would that be, twenty units? And I'd already had gin. I couldn't remember how many of them I'd drunk. Quickly I took out my phone and found the bill for the hotel. They'd sent an automatic receipt once I'd paid my bill on the Saturday morning. I knew I'd put the bar drinks on my room tab. The receipt showed I'd had a double gin with tonic at seven fifteen P.M. and another at seven forty-five. I'd also had three bottles of water from the minibar. At least I hadn't drunk anything more when I got back to my room.

I frowned.

One thing I could remember was drinking a bottle of water when I woke up that morning. Red wine always makes me so thirsty. I'd taken another bottle downstairs with me and I'd drunk it by the time I got to the conference room. There'd been a table set out with hot and cold drinks and I'd picked up a couple of bottles then to last me the morning.

Had I drunk another in the night? When I woke that morning, light was streaming through the gap in the curtains, so I could see everything quite clearly. I'd been desperate for water then. Surely I would have noticed a bottle of water on the bedside table?

I remembered standing by the door holding my overnight bag as I left the room. There was a waste bin by the door and I remembered throwing the glass bottle into it and flinching as it hit the metal. I'd looked into the bin, to see if it had smashed. There hadn't been another bottle in there.

But then I saw sense. My clothes from the night before had been strewn around the room and my handbag had tipped over. I'd probably had a bottle of water when I got in and left it on the floor.

I switched my phone off and put it in my bag and tucked the receipt back into the inside pocket. I was so glad I hadn't drunk anything since that night. I didn't want to ever get in a state like that again.

11

Saturday, July 22

Caitlin stayed over that night in the spare room, which had virtually become hers since Ben was away so often.

When I woke automatically at seven o'clock, the house was dim and quiet. Joe lay beside me, his body heavy and unresponsive. I knew he'd lie there like that until I got up with Rory; I was well used to that. When I heard the familiar sound of Rory jumping out of bed and coming onto the landing, I sat up to call him into my room, then heard Caitlin say, 'In here, sweetheart. Let's give Mummy a rest, shall we?' and quickly lay back down again.

I love that woman.

Caitlin said, 'Anyone for pancakes?' and the sound of Rory's cheers rang through the house. I snuggled down next to Joe, who hadn't woken at all, and tried not to think about the fact that he hadn't had to wake; he'd known Caitlin or I would take care of Rory. I had to grab whatever time I could with my son.

I forced myself to stop thinking like that. I knew that resentment corroded a marriage. I closed my eyes tight and made myself think happier thoughts, and the next thing I knew, sunlight was streaming through the curtains and my bedside clock showed it was ten o'clock. I could hear Rory in the garden and the sound of Caitlin calling to him. Joe lay beside me, silent and still, as though he was determined not to be the first to get up. True to my suspicions, when he felt me get out of bed, he yawned and rolled over, stretching out across the bed.

'I won't be long,' he said, and gave me a lazy smile. 'Unless you want to come back?'

'Right,' I said. 'Because ten o'clock isn't late enough?'

'Oh no, is that the time?' He got out of bed and stumbled into the en suite. 'I'm meeting Mike for a run.'

'Don't forget I'm working later.'

He nodded, though I didn't think he was taking much notice, and turned the shower on.

I put my dressing gown on to go downstairs. Caitlin and Rory were in the garden, watering his little patch of vegetables. He was earnestly showing her the pots of herbs he was growing and she was admiring his work.

She looked up and waved as she saw me. 'Good sleep?'

'You're an angel,' I said. 'Thank you so much.'

Rory rushed over to me, planting a huge kiss on my cheek. 'Sit down, Mum, we're making you breakfast!'

I didn't need much persuasion. By the time Joe came downstairs, I was sitting at the patio table eating pancakes with strawberries and drinking coffee and orange juice, all courtesy of Caitlin and Rory.

'Look at you with your servants,' said Joe. He leaned over and kissed me. 'You're a lady of leisure.'

'Yeah,' I said. 'I'm living the dream. You'll be back by eleven thirty, won't you?'

He looked at his watch. 'Why?'

'Because I'm going to work! I said I'd be there before twelve.'

'Oh, for God's sake,' he muttered. 'That only gives me an hour.'

'It's okay,' said Caitlin. 'I can stay with Rory till you get back. I'm not doing anything.'

I bit my lip, determined not to say a word. Caitlin was aware of this and Joe must have been too, because he crashed around the kitchen, getting all his gear together, then gave a brief 'I'm off, then,' before slamming the front door behind him.

'I don't get it,' I said. 'I've got to go to work – it's not as though I'm just off enjoying myself.'

'It's because he's always gone for a run with Mike on a Saturday morning,' said Caitlin tactfully. 'It does him good. You know that.'

'Well, I used to go shopping in town on a Saturday afternoon and have cocktails afterwards,' I said. 'And that did me good, too.'

She grinned. 'I remember. Those were great days.'

'Things change when you have children. And he has plenty of free time when he could go running. Rory's in nursery three afternoons a week.'

'I suppose Mike's not free then,' she said. 'It's different going on your own.'

'I know,' I admitted. I did want to be fair to Joe. 'And it's what we agreed when we had Rory. Joe doesn't know any other stay-at-home dads and he doesn't feel part of the women's groups. He needs to see his friends every now and then.'

Caitlin nodded. 'You do have to stick up for yourself a bit more, though,' she said. 'We've talked about this, Gem. You need to be more assertive with Joe. You can do it at work; you have to make sure you do it at home, too.'

This was something we'd discussed many times. She was right; I had no problem being assertive at work. I knew what had to be done and I did everything I could to make it happen. I felt in control of things there. But at home ... I still found it hard to say what I wanted, at times. And I knew why I struggled with it, but that didn't make it any easier to deal with.

She moved her chair closer to me, so that Rory couldn't hear us. 'It's still working for you, isn't it, having Joe at home with Rory? It's much easier than if you had to rush to nursery to pick up Rory every night. Imagine that if you had a client you needed to talk to. If Joe was working in Liverpool or Manchester, the pressure to be there for Rory as well as be in the office would be horrendous.'

I nodded. 'I know, and it does work well. It's just . . . I know it's easier having Joe at home, but it's tough at the moment. I'm working every day and any free time I spend with Rory, but it means I don't have a minute for anything else.'

'What about the evenings? Fancy doing something then? I could stay over. Or I could babysit and you could go out with Joe.'

'I'd love to. It's just I'm usually working till late. I don't think I could cope with going out.' I laughed. 'I don't even know what I'd do if I had some spare time. I don't seem to have any interests or hobbies. I can't remember the last time I finished a book.' I saw the worry on her face. 'Sorry, Caitlin, I don't mean to complain so much. I'm just tired.'

The sun was high now, burning us. I was still in my dressing gown and it was eleven o'clock. Time to go and shower and get ready for the day.

'You weren't this tired before,' she said. 'I know I haven't seen you for a few weeks because I've been away, but you seemed okay then. Is everything all right?'

I looked over at her, at her kind, concerned face. We'd been through so many things together and had always pulled through. She'd been there for me during my darkest time and until now I'd thought I could tell her anything.

I desperately wanted to tell her about the weekend in

London, about how drunk I'd been and how David had kissed me, but something stopped me. When I married Joe, Caitlin and I had become sisters-in-law, and though this had brought us nothing but happiness, I realized with a lurch that her loyalties would be with Joe, not me.

That thought was too much to cope with just then. I jumped out of my seat and started to clear away the plates from the table. 'Everything's fine. Don't worry.'

'Leave this,' said Caitlin. 'I'll do it. You go on up and have a shower. I can keep an eye on Rory while I sort the kitchen out.'

I kissed her cheek.

'And me!' Rory shouted, and he ran down the garden path on his stocky little legs. 'I want a kiss, too!'

I hugged him to me, breathing in the smell of strawberries and grass and milk. I glanced over to see Caitlin looking at me, an expression of yearning on her face.

'You're so lucky, Gem,' she said. She came over to us and put her arms around us. 'I'd give anything to have what you have.' When Rory wriggled away and went back to his tent on the lawn, she said, 'I love you and Joe, you know. And Rory, too, of course. You're my favourite people in the whole world.' She kissed my cheek and whispered, 'I'm so glad you two got together.'

I smiled and hugged her, the guilt of keeping secrets from her and from Joe nearly overwhelming me.

12

Thursday, July 27

The following week was even busier at work. Sophie phoned in sick on Monday morning, and for a day or two I thought we'd manage without her, but after an eight P.M. finish on Tuesday night, I admitted defeat and called Lucy when I got home to ask whether she could help us out. Lucy used to work with us, but after her daughter, Maisie, was born four years ago, she decided to stay at home with her. We remained in touch and over the years Lucy stood in whenever I needed help. We agreed she'd work school hours for the rest of the week.

On Thursday morning I was out with a newly retired couple, showing them properties a little further out of town. We went from house to house and they loved them all. I knew instinctively that they wouldn't be buying anything. They seemed to treat it as a bit of a day out, a chance to have a look around people's homes. They came back to the office to pick up a bunch of other details and went off for lunch, happily chatting about the places they'd seen.

'No luck?' asked Rachel.

I shook my head. 'Sightseers.'

She grimaced. 'Are they selling, too?'

'They are, but not here. They're from Nottingham and their son's up here with his family. I get the feeling this is something they do now and again for a bit of fun.'

'To torment their son, more like.'

'Yes, they took the brochures home to show him and his wife. She's probably threatening divorce right now.'

We laughed.

'Poor things,' said Lucy.

I made some coffee and sat at my desk. I checked my e-mails, then pulled the tray of post that had been delivered to the office towards me.

'I've dealt with most of that,' called Rachel. 'There's something addressed to you personally, though. Obviously I didn't open it.'

I picked up a large white envelope. It had a typed label on it with *Private* written above my name. I ripped it open. Inside was a piece of paper, about four inches by six. It was a photo, glossy and full colour: a photo of David kissing me against the door to my hotel room.

My hand jerked and my mug of coffee went flying over the desk. I grabbed the photo and threw it into a drawer as Rachel and Lucy hurried over with paper towels.

'Are you okay?' asked Rachel. 'You didn't burn yourself, did you?'

'No. I'm fine.' I took the paper towels off her. 'I'll do this, thanks.'

'Did it go on your papers?' asked Lucy.

'No, I got them in time.' I sounded curt but I couldn't help it. I wanted to take the photo out of the drawer and look at it again, but I couldn't do that while they were here. We only had this one office, with a little kitchen behind a partition at the back. There was no privacy at all; this hadn't been a problem until now, but at that point I would have done anything to have my own room so that I could try to work out what on earth was going on.

That afternoon I sat at my desk and answered the phone and spoke to new clients and arranged appointments, all the while aware of the photo that was sitting in the drawer next to me. Who had taken it? Why would they send it to me?

For the last few weeks I hadn't let myself think about what had happened at the door to my hotel room. It had been both expected and unexpected. If I'd been single, I suppose I would have known he was going to kiss me. It was just the way the conversation was going. We were both drunk, laughing a lot, and very, very relaxed. But he knew I was married. I'd told him about Joe.

I was dying to talk this through with someone. I couldn't talk to Caitlin. Obviously I couldn't talk to Joe. My mum would be horrified I'd kissed someone else.

I looked over at Lucy. She was great fun and a good friend. Very understanding, kind and loyal. But I was her boss. Surely there was a limit to what I could tell her? Sometimes we went running together, and we'd joined a yoga class for a while, but although we had the odd moan about our husbands, it was never anything serious. And I worried that my judgement could be off: I imagined walking into the office and realizing that all the others knew about this and had been talking about it while I was out. My stomach knotted at the thought of that.

'Are you okay?' asked Rachel. 'Are you feeling all right?'

I forced a smile. 'Yes, I'm great, thanks. Just a bit tired.'

'It's nearly time to go home,' she said. 'Not long now.' She'd been to the cloakroom and come back looking as immaculate as she did when she arrived at work. Her hair was always glossy and pinned back, her make-up always fresh.

'You're looking very nice,' I said. 'Are you going out?'

She blushed. 'No, just going home. Another night in.'

'Me too.' I thought of going home and holding Rory in my arms. Just the thought of it was enough to lower my blood pressure. That was all I wanted to do, to hold him close, to make him laugh. To kiss him until he screamed for mercy. I relaxed at the thought. I looked at my watch. It was ten minutes to closing time. 'Come on, everyone,' I said, 'let's get out of here on time tonight.'

There was a sudden mad dash as people cleared their desks and washed up mugs. While they were in the kitchen I grabbed a folder and threw in the photo and the envelope that had arrived in the post.

'Taking work home?' asked Rachel when she saw the folder on my desk. 'You're tired; you should be relaxing tonight.'

'There's always something to be done.'

She held my bag and folder while I locked the door and pulled down the shutters. The others had walked off in the other direction, and she and I set off to the car park behind our office. In the quiet of the car park I stood next to her as she opened her car door, and for one crazy moment I thought, *Should I ask her what to do?*

Rachel always seemed so capable and sensible. She was quiet; although she'd join in if she was encouraged, she was more likely to sit on the edge of the group. Maybe that meant she'd be less likely to gossip. I desperately needed someone to talk to.

'Rachel?' I said as she got into her car and put her bag on the passenger seat. 'Can I have a word?'

She looked up at me, startled. 'What, now?'

Then common sense prevailed. I couldn't talk to her about David. She was too young and I was her boss.

I shook my head. 'It's okay. Nothing that won't keep until tomorrow.'

She looked relieved and I realized I wasn't the only one who wanted to get home early. I waved goodbye and got into my own car.

13

Although I'd intended to go straight home, I found myself driving in the opposite direction, down towards the River Dee. The car parks there were emptying now and I found a quiet spot in the castle car park. I needed to see the photo on my own.

I pulled it from the folder and looked at it again.

At the bottom of the photograph was the time and date it was taken: June 23 at 22:45. That was the Friday night I was in London. I remembered it had been so hot and humid when I arrived at the hotel that I'd showered and washed my hair before going down to the bar. My hair was gleaming, my make-up still in place. My eyeliner swept my eyes in a smooth line, untouched by the night, but my face was pink and had a sheen that I hoped wasn't normally there. It was easy to tell I'd been drinking.

My eyes were nearly closed and my face was upturned. I was being kissed by a man with dark hair who was touching my face as though we were lovers. His face was in shadow; unrecognizable.

I knew who it was, though. It was David.

And I thought: *What would Joe do if he saw that photo? Would he leave me?*

At the thought of that conversation, of living alone for half the week, of not being able to see Rory every day or to speak to Joe whenever I wanted to, I felt panic course through my body. I could lose everything over this.

I leaned my head against the car seat and closed my eyes. What was going on? Why would anyone take a photo of me that night, and why would they send it to me?

A band tightened around my forehead at the thought of Joe seeing that photo. He'd never believe me if I told him I couldn't remember doing it. He thought I was in bed, asleep, at that time. I'd *told* him I was! And I'd told him by text, too, so I couldn't even deny it. My heart thumped as I thought: *What happened that night? What happened after we kissed?* I was so frustrated. I couldn't remember anything. Had we slept together? Surely not! How would I not remember that? I was furious with myself for drinking so much; I should have learned my lesson by now, but every time I thought of Joe seeing the photo, of hearing what happened that night, I felt sick.

And then I knew I needed to get hold of David and ask him what the hell was going on.

Within minutes I was back at the office. I opened the shutters, unlocked the door, and turned on my computer.

It was nearly six P.M. and I'd told Joe I'd be home early that night. Quickly I logged into the database we kept of all our clients and searched for David Sanderson. I clicked on his name. I pulled my mobile out of my bag and saw I had three missed calls from Joe. I felt a stab of guilt and dialled David's number.

I held my breath as it rang out. I counted eight rings and then it cut dead. It didn't go to voicemail. I tried it again and then again. Why wasn't he answering? Was he monitoring his calls?

Quickly I called from the office phone and withheld the number, so that he wouldn't know it was me. Again it rang out. No reply.

On the database was his e-mail address, and I opened my work e-mail and sent him a quick note.

```
Hi David, this is Gemma from Chester Homes. Please
can you get in touch asap? I need a quick word.
Thanks.
```

I looked at his e-mail address again. It was a Gmail account. What if he didn't see it? I sent him a text with the same message, just in case. I needed to speak to him.

Joe was waiting at the front door when I arrived home.

'You said you'd be back early!' He pushed past me and grabbed his kit bag from the cloakroom. 'I'm late for football.'

'I'm so sorry. I've been at work. You'll be in time if you run now.'

'I called you there and there was no answer!'

'I was halfway home and realized I'd forgotten something,' I said. 'I had to go back. I'm sorry. I forgot about football.'

He snatched my car keys from my hand. 'You've blocked me in. I'll take your car.'

With a bang of the front door he'd gone. It was only when I was bathing Rory that I realized I'd left the folder with the photo of David kissing me on the front seat of my car.

That night Joe came back late, long after I was in bed. I guessed he'd gone to the pub with his friends after playing football. I couldn't sleep when he was out; I always struggled to relax if I knew I'd be woken up.

That night, though, there was no chance of sleep. I lay for hours, rigid with worry. I hadn't expected him to take my car and couldn't remember whether I'd put everything back into the folder, or whether the photo and envelope were just lying underneath it. Would he see it? Would he come storming in, demanding to know what was going on?

I nearly jumped out of my skin when I heard the front door open. There was a clink as he put my car keys in the bowl on the hall table, then the soft creak of the stairs as he came up to bed. He looked in on Rory first, and by the time he came into our room I realized that of course he hadn't found anything. He never looked at my files at home unless I asked him to. He wasn't very tidy and wouldn't even move them out of the way if I'd left them on the coffee table or pick them up if they were on the floor. There was no way he'd bother to look at one when he was in a hurry to get to football.

'Hey,' he said, and smiled, his earlier temper forgotten. 'Sorry I'm late. I didn't realize the time.'

'Good night?'

'Yeah, it was great. We won, two-nil, then we went to The Crown for a couple of pints.' The Crown is the pub at the end of our road. 'I brought the car back after football and walked down with Mike.'

I could have kicked myself then. I hadn't heard him park the car earlier; if I had, I could have run out to see whether the photo had been moved.

When he eventually got into bed, we chatted about Mike and his family and then Joe said, 'He was telling me about someone he knows who's moving over to Ireland.'

He gave a deep sigh and my heart sank. Joe's from a huge, close Irish family and a couple of his brothers and sisters still live over there. Whenever he has a couple of drinks he talks about moving back home.

'What will he do there?'

'He's transferring his business,' he said. 'He's a plumber

The Girl I Used to Be

and says he can do that there as well as anywhere. He said there are lots of opportunities in Ireland now.'

One of the things I loved and hated about Joe was his absolute and complete optimism. The trouble was that he was also able to talk all night.

I yawned. 'Can you tell me about it tomorrow? I'm half asleep.'

'Sorry, sweetheart. It's just that I was thinking – we could do that.'

I was losing track. 'Do what?'

'We could go back to Ireland.'

'Back? I've hardly been there!'

'You know what I mean. Everyone goes back home in the end, don't they?'

'But it's not my home.' I wriggled away from him. 'And what about my business? And the rentals?'

'Oh, you could do that anywhere,' he said confidently. 'Everyone needs to buy houses. And you could get someone to manage the rentals. You could even get someone to manage the office and start another one there.' He turned to me, all excited. 'We could make it work, Gem!'

All of me, every cell in my body, told me not to ask the question, but I couldn't resist. 'And what would you do in Ireland?'

'Me?' He sounded puzzled. 'I'd look after Rory, of course. And hopefully we'll have another baby soon. Or more than one.' He stroked my belly. 'Who knows, we could have a football team!'

He snuggled close to me, dreaming his happy dreams. My happy dreams involved being able to take the whole day off for once in my life. Slowly I slid away from him and made a vow not to get pregnant until we were sharing the same dream.

And then, as I lay there feeling the familiar weight of Joe's arm around my waist, his warm breath on my neck, I thought of that photo again and the lies I'd told him. If Joe saw it, he might go to Ireland anyway, without me. He might take Rory with him.

14

Sunday, July 30

On Sunday Sophie was back at work. Her boundless energy made me doubt her illness earlier in the week, which, according to her, had made her think she was dying. I found I couldn't drum up the energy to care. While she managed to type up her notes and kept up a stream-of-consciousness monologue, I sat at my desk and tried to work out what was happening. In the end I couldn't think straight and sent her out to the corner shop for milk, a job that I knew would buy me twenty minutes' peace.

As soon as she'd gone, I called David's number. There was no reply and it didn't go to voicemail. I tried again and again. Frustrated, I sent a few texts, each one more hysterical than the previous one, but then had to stop myself. I was making an idiot of myself.

Sophie returned and made coffee. Surreptitiously I moved my computer monitor slightly so that she wouldn't be able to see what I was doing on my screen, then opened my personal e-mail address. I'd disabled it on my phone the night before, in case a message came in when Joe was with me. I'd felt grubby then, as though I were having an affair. There was no reply to the e-mail I'd sent David. I looked around: the office was quiet. I picked up my phone and car keys and went out to my car. I looked up the hotel where I'd stayed in London and called them.

'Hi,' I said. 'My name's Gemma Brogan. I stayed at your hotel on Friday, the twenty-third of June.'

'Hi,' said the receptionist. 'How can I help you?'

'I met a potential client that night. I believe he was staying with you for a few days around that time. He gave me his business card but unfortunately I've lost it. Would you be able to give me his contact details?'

'I'm sorry,' she said. 'We're not allowed to give out personal details.'

My heart sank. I'd guessed she'd say that. 'I don't suppose you could pass on a message, could you?'

'Yes, of course, I could do that for you as long as he's given us his details,' she said. 'Just let me check. What was his name?'

'David Sanderson.'

'And when did you say you were here? The twenty-third of June?'

'Yes. That was a Friday night; he'd been there all week.'

'I'm sorry,' she said after checking her computer, 'I'd love to help but he must have been staying somewhere else. There's no record of him staying here.'

And then I remembered him saying, *I'm on the tenth floor.*

I thanked her and ended the call, then sat back, confused. I remembered him saying he'd been at the hotel all week. He'd told me he'd tried most things on the menu in the restaurant.

I frowned. I knew he'd said right at the beginning that he was there on his own, that he'd been bored every evening. Did he simply mean he'd been in London? I'd certainly understood him to mean he'd been staying at the SHAFTESBURY.

There was a knock on my car window and I jumped with fright. Rachel stood there.

'Sorry to bother you,' she said when I got out of my car. 'Paula James is on the phone. She says she's thinking of backing out of the purchase. Can you speak to her?'

I went quickly back into the office to reassure Paula, who called nearly every day, that everything was going well and that you couldn't buy a house without the process taking a bit of time. All the time I was working, right at the back of my mind, niggling away, were questions upon questions.

Why did he tell me he was staying at the hotel when he wasn't? Who had taken that photo? Why had they sent it to me? Had the same person sent me the receipt?

I was desperate to talk to someone about it, but who? While Sophie was occupied with clients, I opened the desk drawer and took the folder out. I reached up and took a box file from the shelf behind me and used it to block the folder, then slid the photo out and stared down at it.

I thought back to the times I'd gone out with Caitlin when we were students. She didn't drink much, but I'd keep going as long as we were out. The next day I'd feel 'the shame', as she put it, where I'd lie on the sofa in our student halls and remember stupid things I'd said or done when I was drunk. I seemed to lose all inhibitions at the time, but afterwards I'd curl into a ball, cringing at the memories as they flashed back into my mind, and she'd say how glad she was that she'd stayed relatively sober. She tried to keep me safe, though, keeping tabs on me when we went out, making sure I didn't go off and do something crazy on my own. She didn't always succeed.

And now here I was again, years after I'd calmed down, married to one man and kissing another while I was drunk. I couldn't even remember doing it. David was nice enough, but I hadn't wanted to kiss him when I was sober. Joe was the only man I'd wanted to kiss since the day I met him, and I was happy with that. He was everything to me. He was my family. I loved him.

But there was no denying it: here was the evidence that I'd betrayed him. When I looked at the photo, I felt a greater shame than I'd experienced before wash over me. I couldn't bear to think of Joe seeing it. It was something we'd agreed on right from the moment we fell in love, that we'd always be faithful. That there would only be him and me. And now it looked as though I'd destroyed our relationship and – worse – done it so casually, too. As though it was worthless.

I looked at the details that had been put onto the system when David had first come into the office. He'd given an address twenty miles south of Chester. I frowned when I saw the location: why would he live there when there were so many rentals in the city centre? I was just about to enter the street into Google Street View when Rachel came back from showing potential buyers around a house nearby, and I took the chance of everything being quiet to go and find out. It was Sunday afternoon; it was likely he'd be home.

'I need to go out for a bit,' I said. 'You're in charge, Rachel, okay? I won't be long. Call if you need anything.'

I had no doubt that as soon as my car had left our car park, Sophie would be at the shop buying magazines and sweets for their leisurely afternoon, and I found I didn't really care. All I could think about was getting hold of David and asking him what he thought he was doing.

As I drove, I thought of what I'd say to him. Would he answer me? Would he deny all knowledge? My stomach clenched at the thought of a confrontation, but I needed to know who'd taken the photo. He'd been with a group of other men when I first met him, but would they have taken a photo of us together? Why would they do that? And had he been at the hotel with them or was it merely casual chat? I just couldn't remember. I hadn't known them. He hadn't introduced us or even mentioned them; once he turned to talk to me, his focus was on me alone.

I'd always prided myself on my memory. Before we had Rory, Joe and I used to go to The Crown every Thursday night for a pub quiz and he'd laugh as I would remember the most ridiculous facts, things I'd heard once, years before. It was a curse as well as a blessing, of course; some things I really didn't want to remember and I had no choice, so I'd had to learn to block them out. Yet I couldn't remember parts of that night as well as I could remember others from years ago. I was more tired now, though. Maybe that was it.

As I drove to David's house, I remembered that he had said he worked for Barford's on the outskirts of Chester. Just then my phone rang. I saw that it was Rachel and parked in a lay-by to speak to her. She had a quick question about a sale I was involved with, and just before she hung up, I asked, 'Are you busy?'

'No, apart from that query it's fine. Do you want me to do something?'

'Remember that client who came in a couple of weeks ago? David Sanderson. I took him to view the flats down by the river. Can you call his details up for me, please?'

I could hear the click of her mouse as she searched the database.

'Just a second,' she said. 'Oh, I think I remember him. Nice-looking guy?'

I winced. 'I suppose. Dark-haired. Tall.'

'Just a minute, the system's slow,' she said. 'I think I have him now. Do you want his number?'

'No, I've got that. Which company did he work for?'

'It says here he works for Barford's.'

I nodded. That was the name I'd remembered. 'Did he give their address?'

'No.' She was curious now and I could have kicked myself. 'Why do you need his work address?'

'It doesn't matter,' I said. 'I'm just trying to get hold of him. Did he give a number for Barford's?'

She read it out. 'Is there anything I can do, Gemma? Where are you?'

'Don't worry. I'll be back in an hour.' I clicked the phone off before she could ask any more questions. I knew she and Sophie would be talking about me now, wondering what I was up to.

My call went straight through to a recorded message. 'You are through to Thompson and Sons. All of our offices are closed today. Please call back between nine A.M. and five P.M. Monday to Friday.'

I stared at the phone and back down at my notepad. He'd said he worked for Barford's, but this company was called Thompson's. I looked them up online. They were a building company and yes, their number was the same as the one he'd given us.

I checked Google, found the real number for Barford's and called them. Luckily someone was on duty there and answered my call. Nobody by the name of David Sanderson was on their staff list.

15

The street David had said he lived in was a cul-de-sac, arching around a pretty piece of land planted with trees and flowers. The houses were double-fronted, with smart gates and bright, well-tended gardens. I stopped just short of the house and looked around carefully. I thought of what David had said about not being ready to live in a house, preferring a flat instead. These were family houses, exactly the opposite of what he'd wanted.

There was a red Toyota parked outside the garage and I realized I didn't know what car David had been driving when he came to see us. I have CCTV installed in our small private car park, ever since someone had parked there and scratched my car; I took out my notepad and wrote *Check CCTV* so that I wouldn't forget.

My stomach tightened as I rang the doorbell. I didn't know what I would say to him. What could I say? For a moment I thought of leaving, of running back to my car and going back to work, but then a figure appeared through the coloured glass of the porch door and I found I couldn't move.

A woman of about my age opened the door and immediately

I panicked. Was she married to David? How was I going to ask him about the photo if she was there?

She glanced up and down the road as though wondering why I was there and whether I was selling something. 'Hello?'

I pulled myself together and smiled reassuringly at her. 'I'm looking for David Sanderson,' I said. 'Is he at home?'

She frowned. 'Who?'

'David Sanderson.'

'He doesn't live here,' she said. 'I've never heard of him.'

For a second I wondered whether she was lying, but then she leaned into the hallway and shouted, 'Neville!' A few seconds later, a man appeared. He was about my height, fair-haired and stocky. 'This woman wants to find someone called David Sanderson. Do you know him?'

He shook his head. 'Sorry, never heard of him.'

'He gave me this address,' I said weakly. 'He said he lived here.'

They looked at each other, clearly puzzled. 'We've been here for more than ten years,' said the woman. 'And we know all our neighbours. There's no one in this cul-de-sac with that name, I'm afraid.'

The man agreed. 'Sorry. You must have the wrong address.'

They looked so earnest and honest that I didn't feel I could start quizzing them further, so I thanked them and went back to my car. I drove out of the cul-de-sac and back onto the main road, and then parked. I opened Facebook. There were quite a few men with the same name, but those with photos clearly weren't him and those without lived in other countries. I checked Twitter and he wasn't there either.

He'd said he was in sales. Surely he'd be on LinkedIn? I checked, but the only David Sandersons there were clearly not the man I'd met. I entered his name into Google, but it was quite a common one, and even though I scrolled through page after page, I couldn't find anything about him at all. I sat back and closed my eyes, trying desperately to think. His phone number had rung out; it was impossible to leave a voicemail. My e-mails to him weren't answered. He didn't live at that address and he didn't work where he said he had, that much was clear.

Just then my phone pinged in my hand, startling me. It was an Instagram message. I only use Instagram with a few people, and on the screen it said the message was from someone I didn't follow. I looked at the sender's name; it was WatchingYou. There was a little cartoon figure next to the name, rather than a photo. I frowned and clicked on the message.

There didn't seem to be anything there at first. I was just about to switch off my phone when a video appeared.

It was a video of me.

When I heard my own voice, I nearly jumped out of my skin.

'I don't know. I'm not sure I would have married him if I'd known.' My cheeks were pink and a glance at my eyes made it clear I was drunk. 'It's not that he's lazy,' I heard. My tone was confidential, as though I were telling a secret, and my voice was husky. 'Well, he is lazy sometimes!' On the video I laughed, just a bit too loudly, and covered my mouth to stop myself. 'God, he's so lazy at times.' I sounded irritated now, rather than fond. 'It's just that when he said he'd stay at home with Rory, I didn't think he meant forever! I just wish . . .' My voice became pensive then. 'I just wish I'd been able to stay at home, too. Instead of him. I wish I'd had that chance.' I looked up at the person I was speaking to. 'You only get one chance, don't you?'

On the screen I picked up my glass of wine and drank some. A little wine smile appeared around my mouth. I said, 'What?' and then laughed, using a napkin to wipe it away.

The person I was speaking to said something then. In the car I strained to hear it, but I couldn't. On the screen I replied,

'Well, that's what he wants. And he wants to try for another baby now. I'm just worried that he'll never go back to work.' Again, the other person spoke. I could see my own face in the video, drunkenly focusing on what was being said. Then I replied, 'I don't know. I just don't know if I would marry him again, knowing what it would be like.'

The video stopped there, frozen with my face in a grimace, my glass in my hand.

I stared down at the screen, my mind whirring. What on earth was this? I had no memory of saying it to anyone. I hadn't even thought it, or not for a while, anyway, and only then in a temper. I wanted to play it again, but now the list of messages I'd received appeared, and next to *WatchingYou* it said *Video Unavailable*.

I scrolled through the messages. The last one I'd had, prior to this, was from Caitlin the other day. She'd sent me some photos of toys and clothes that she wanted my opinion on for Rory's birthday. Those photos were still there.

I swiped the Instagram app so that it disappeared from my screen, then reopened it. I could still see that WatchingYou had sent me a video, but that it was unavailable.

I felt like I was about to hyperventilate. Where was the message? Who had sent it to me?

And then I realized. In the video I was wearing that dress I'd worn in London, the night I had a meal with David. Although most of the video showed just my face, there was a moment when I picked up my glass where I'd seen a flash of a dark green shoulder strap. One strap must have slipped down my arm – it was always doing that – and it had almost looked like I was naked.

I drove slowly back to Chester, my mind racing. When I got back into the office, all was quiet. A couple were leaving as

I entered, their hands full of brochures. I forced myself to smile at them, to ask them whether they'd got what they'd come for, and they promised they'd be in touch when they'd looked through the house details. All the time I was thinking about the video, the way I appeared. Drunk. Flirty. Betraying my husband without a second thought.

Brian was on the phone; it sounded as though he was talking to a tenant about rent that was overdue. I looked at him, knowing I should ask him what was going on, but I couldn't concentrate on anything else but my own fears. He gave me a thumbs-up so I let it go. I knew he'd manage without my input.

Rachel was typing on her computer and Sophie was washing up some cups in the kitchen. I took a bottle of water from the fridge, found some painkillers in my drawer, and sank into my office chair.

'You look tired,' said Rachel. 'Is everything okay?' I didn't know where to start. I looked over at her, just dying to confide in someone. She smiled at me. 'Rory okay?'

Rory was about the only thing that was okay, I thought. I wondered what Rachel would say if I said, *Yes, actually, he's fine, but everything else seems to be going wrong*. I pictured her face if I told her what was actually going on and I thought it would only be a matter of seconds before she told Sophie.

I knew that the only people I really trusted were Joe and Caitlin. The only people I wanted to talk to were the ones who mustn't know what was going on.

16

I let everyone at the office leave a few minutes early, saying I would be okay to lock up. I put the *Closed* sign on the door and clicked the latch down, then went through to the back and made sure the door to the small back yard was locked too. When I was certain I was the only person in the office and nobody else could get in, I sat back at my desk and downloaded the CCTV footage for the car park.

I own the tiny car park behind the office. Because of the security systems in place, we have to lock up and leave via the front door, then go round the corner into the car park. There was room for only six cars and the spaces were clearly marked. After the incident last year when my car was damaged, I'd installed a cheap CCTV camera to record vehicles entering and leaving the car park. I wondered whether David had left his car there when he'd come into the office. I couldn't remember whether I'd asked him when we drove off where he'd parked.

I set the CCTV to play. The grainy screen hurt my eyes right from the beginning. I tried to remember what time he'd come in, but decided to put it to run from eight A.M., just in case he'd arrived early and gone for coffee.

Nothing happened at all until eight thirty, when I arrived at the office.

On the screen I could see my car enter the empty car park. I watched myself get out of the car, lock it with my key fob, then leave the car park, turning in the direction of the office. Fifteen minutes later Rachel drove in and neatly reversed into the space next to mine. She sat in the car for a few minutes – I couldn't see what she was doing but guessed she was checking her make-up or on her phone – and then she jumped out and waved at someone on the street. I assumed that was Sophie; they usually arrived at about the same time. Two minutes later, Brian's car entered the car park. He parked nearest to the exit, as he tended to come and go all day.

Nothing happened for the next couple of hours. Then at ten thirty I saw myself walk into view, throw my bag into the back seat of my car, and drive off. It was clear that David hadn't parked there.

I closed down the CCTV and thought about what to do. My office is on a corner, with the car park behind it. We're opposite a restaurant, and I know they don't have cameras there. On the other side of the road is a charity bookshop – no cameras there, either. However, if you walk further up the street to the end of the block, there is a small shop that sells newspapers and groceries. The owner and manager, Michael, was a guy I'd known for a few years through our local small business association. I guessed he'd have a CCTV system because of the problem he'd had with shoplifters at times.

I locked up the office and walked down the street to Michael's shop. I had to wait a while behind people who were picking up groceries, then asked the assistant if Michael was free. When she called him, he came out of his office at the back of the shop and beckoned me over.

'Are your CCTV cameras working?' I asked. I explained that I was concerned about a client of ours but didn't say anything more than that. I said I wanted to see whether I could see him onscreen, as I wanted to go to the police about him. Michael raised his eyebrows at that, but ushered me into his office and switched on his machine.

'When did you want to check?'

'June the sixteenth,' I said.

Immediately he stopped. 'I'm sorry, Gemma, but we only keep them for a week. It's an old system and we store them on rewritable disks. Every week I erase everything and start again. There's no point in us keeping it any longer if there hasn't been any trouble. What's he been up to?'

I hesitated. I didn't want to tell him the full story, obviously, but I needed him to understand why I wanted to check.

'We had someone come in who was a bit odd,' I said. 'He freaked me out slightly. I checked out his contact details and he was lying about who he was. I wanted to see whether I could find a picture of him.'

'I don't blame you. Remember Suzy Lamplugh?'

I winced. Suzy Lamplugh was an estate agent in London who took a client to view a property and was never seen again. It was discovered later that the client had given a false name when he'd made the appointment. I was only too aware of her whenever I thought of David. The responsibility I had to my staff, sending them into empty properties with people we didn't know, was huge. I decided that the next day I'd tell the staff they had to ask for official ID before showing a client any properties. I'd make them take a photocopy of it, so that at least if something happened, the police would know who was responsible.

'That's why I need to know who he is,' I said. 'I need to protect my staff.'

And protect myself, too.

17

Monday, July 31

The next morning, I woke with a start. I thought someone had held me by the shoulder and hip and turned me over in my bed. It was the strangest sensation, as though I could still feel hands gripping me tightly and then letting me go as I landed face down on the bed. I couldn't resist, could only do what the hands were making me do. My heart thumped and I gasped.

I opened my eyes and saw that the room was light; it was nearly time to get up. 'Joe?' I touched his shoulder, but he grunted and moved away. 'Joe, did you move me just then?'

'Eh?' Slowly he wakened and turned over to face me. 'What?'

'Did you turn me over in bed?'

He looked bemused. 'I was asleep, Gem. I didn't do anything.'

'That was really weird. Are you sure?'

He closed his eyes. 'You must have been dreaming, honey,' he said. 'I was nowhere near you.'

My heart was pounding still from the sensation of being

moved, and I lay on my side, away from Joe, and tried to calm myself. It was a dream; it had to have been.

The bedroom door opened then and Rory came into the room. I lifted the quilt and he slipped in beside me. I held him to me and kissed his forehead. It was hot and damp.

'Are you all right, sweetheart?' I whispered.

He shook his head and put his hand on his throat. 'It's all sore.'

Just then my alarm went off. I reached out to switch it off, and Rory held on tightly.

'Are you at home today, Mum?'

I hesitated. 'I'm supposed to be going in, pet.' His lip wobbled and he clung tighter. I looked down at him and thought, *What is the point in working for myself if I can't take time off when my child is ill?*

'I'll stay home today,' I whispered. 'I'll stay home until you feel better.'

An hour later, Rory was lying on the sofa, covered in his quilt, with Buffy, his fluffy rabbit, by his side. He was dozing while his favourite cartoon was on television.

'Shall I call the office and tell them you won't be in?' asked Joe.

'I'll give Lucy a call and see if she can come in today.' I groaned. 'She's changed her number and I forgot to put it into my phone. I'll have to go into the office to phone her. I won't be long.'

'I'll go in for you, honey,' he said. 'You stay here with Rory and I'll get the number.' He picked up the keys to his car and the office. 'Where is it? On your desk?'

I froze. Lucy's new number was on a slip of paper in my desk drawer, and in there too was the photo and the receipt. No way was Joe going into that drawer. Luckily it was locked, so none of the staff would be able to get in either.

'It's okay,' I said. 'I need to have a word with them about a couple of things. I'll run in and be back in half an hour.'

Rachel was waiting outside for me. She was holding a cup of coffee from the café up the road and looked at her watch as I approached the door to the office.

'Sorry I'm late,' I said as soon as I reached her. 'Rory's not well. I need to phone Lucy to ask her if she'll stand in for me for a day or two.'

'Oh, the poor boy. But why didn't you call Lucy from home?'

'She wrote her new number down and I forgot to put it into my phone.' I opened the office door and went straight over to my desk to log on to my computer. Rachel stood next to me and I sat there, frustrated, wanting to open the desk drawer but not wanting her to see the photo that was inside it. My mind whirred as I thought of what to do with it. I couldn't risk taking it home, but I didn't want to leave it at work, either. Each of us had our own desk, but Lucy would be using mine that day and there was no reason why I would keep the drawer locked. 'Is everything okay?' I asked Rachel. 'Do you need something?'

She reached over for my computer mouse and clicked on the online diary we all shared. It contained nothing personal; we always checked each other's diaries if we were going to be out. 'I just wanted to see whether you had any appointments today,' she said. 'I don't have any until later this afternoon, so I can share yours with Lucy.'

'Thanks.'

I was so glad it was Rachel in that day instead of Sophie. She had a calm manner that made everything seem okay. I knew she and Lucy could be relied on to do a great job together. Brian would take care of the rentals; he knew exactly what he was doing, and now I felt safe leaving Lucy and Rachel to deal with the sales.

'Do you know how long you'll be off?' she asked. She scrolled through my diary. 'There's an appointment with the accountant that you might want to postpone if you're not going to be in. Lucy's okay to do any valuations, isn't she?'

'I'll be off until he's better. Probably a couple of days.' My dream of having time away from work was coming true, at the expense of poor Rory's tonsils. 'I'll sort out the accountant; I can call her from home. Lucy can do any valuations and you can split the other appointments between you. Let me know if you get stuck; I'll have my laptop with me and I can deal with any problems. I'll probably just be on the sofa all day.'

'Lucky you,' she said, and then added hastily, 'but poor Rory, of course. Have you got Lucy's new number? I can call her for you.'

'It's okay; I'll do it, thanks,' I said. 'I've got it here somewhere.' I unlocked my desk drawer and took out the slip of paper that had her number written on it. Surreptitiously I took out the photo and the receipt and slid them into an envelope. I jumped as I realized Rachel had come back over to my desk, and slipped the envelope under a file. 'That's just something I need to sort out later.'

'Is it for the post?' She held out her hand. 'I'll send it for you.'

I waved her away impatiently. 'No, it's okay. It's private.' And then, because I didn't want her to wonder what it was, I said, 'It's just something I need for the accountant.'

I called Lucy; she'd just dropped Maisie off at school and was only five minutes away. She agreed to come in and said she'd ask her mum to do the school run that afternoon.

I put the envelope into the zip compartment of my handbag, then thought of Joe finding it. Panic rose inside me. I couldn't let him see either the photo or the receipt. I pulled the envelope out of my bag and took it over to the shredder, pushing it in so hard the engine roared.

When I turned to go back to my desk, Rachel's eyebrows were raised, but she said nothing. The door opened and Lucy came in.

'Is Rory okay?' She sounded so concerned that immediately my eyes prickled. 'You go home and stay with him now.' She put her bag into the drawer in my desk – I was able to leave it open now that I'd destroyed the evidence – and said, 'I've just been into the newsagent's. Michael said you wanted to look at his CCTV footage.'

'CCTV footage?' asked Brian, who'd just come in and caught the tail end of the conversation. 'What's up? Has there been a burglary?'

All of them stared at me. I could have kicked myself. Kicked Michael, too. Why did he have to talk about it to my staff?

'There wasn't any sign of something wrong this morning,' said Rachel. 'What do you want to look at CCTV footage for?'

Frustrated, I glanced at Lucy, trying to tell her to shut up without having to say the words aloud. She took absolutely no notice. 'He said something about the car park,' she said. 'He was busy, though, so couldn't tell me much. Have you had trouble here?'

I picked up my bag and headed towards the door. 'No, no trouble. I thought I saw some teenage boys hanging around my car the other night. I was asking if he'd seen them too. He hadn't seen anything, though. It doesn't matter; I doubt they'll be back.'

'I'll keep an eye out for them,' said Brian.

'Me too,' said Rachel. 'If anyone touches my car, I want to know about it.'

I said goodbye, then paused in the doorway and said casually, 'Oh, and by the way, if anything arrives addressed to me personally, just hold on to it, will you? No need to open it; just put it into my drawer and I'll deal with it when I get back.' They would never open personal mail, but I couldn't take any risks. The thought of them seeing anything incriminating gave me a cold sweat. 'If it's got a company mark on it and it's clearly for a client, then you can open it, otherwise just put it aside for me.' They looked at me, bemused, but I just gave a big smile and said, 'Great, thanks!' and left the office.

18

Tuesday, August 1

I took a couple of days off work, grateful for the rest and the time spent with Rory. He was pretty lethargic, and I stayed on the sofa with him, reading him stories, watching films, and lying with him as he slept. Joe made the most of my being at home and went out for runs or to the gym, leaving me plenty of time to worry. All I could think about was the photo of David kissing me and the video I'd seen of myself criticizing Joe. Why had I done that? I must have been so drunk. And yes, everything I said about him was true, but I loved him. I loved our family. I couldn't bear it if Joe found out what I'd said and done.

My head ached as I wondered who had sent them to me. Was it David? But who had recorded us? How had that happened? I did remember David taking out his phone and checking his messages at one point. Did he film me then? But then I remembered that when he was on his phone, I took out my own and sent Joe a message saying I was in bed, ready for sleep. I winced as I thought of that message. Why had I lied to him? When I put my phone away, David had already slipped his into his pocket. He couldn't have filmed me then. And he couldn't have photographed me when he was kissing me.

He was definitely involved, though. He'd lied about everything. It was likely he'd even lied about his name. He might not have photographed me, but I was willing to bet he knew who had.

It was only when Rory woke and Joe came into the living room with a tray of cold drinks in his hands, calling, 'Room service!' that I realized the significance of the receipt.

I had told Joe that I was going to order in food that night in the hotel. I remembered saying in the week before I went there, 'I can't wait to have an early night. Room service, something on television and a long sleep. That's all I want.' I'd been so excited at this little treat that I'd talked about it more than most would, but once I was in London I realized I didn't want to hide away in a hot bedroom. The clinking glasses on the terrace below had called to me, and I'd remembered just how long it had been since I'd gone out at night.

That receipt showed I'd lied to Joe. It showed, too, that the sender knew I had.

As I was playing upstairs with Rory on Tuesday afternoon, I heard a text alert ping downstairs, and a minute later Joe came into the room holding his phone.

'My mum wants to know if we want to go and stay for a few days.'

'What, now? Did you tell her that Rory's not well?'

'I'm feeling better,' said Rory.

I looked at him; his skin had certainly lost its earlier clamminess and pallor. 'Not well enough to go to Ireland, sweetheart.'

'I reckon by Thursday he'll be fine. My mum says the weather's beautiful and Brendan will be there with their boys.'

Brendan, Joe's older brother, lived near Glasgow, and we usually saw him two or three times a year.

'Can we go, Dad?' asked Rory.

Joe laughed and ruffled his hair. 'I'd love to. Let's see what Mum says.'

Oh great, make me the miserable one.

'I don't know,' I said. 'I can't take the time off work just like that. Are Sarah or Caitlin going?'

'No, Caitlin's going over to see Ben, remember? And Sarah's got to work. Come on, Gem; it'll be great.'

Frankly, it wouldn't be a great holiday at all. Or it would for Joe, but not for me. When we were at their house, I wouldn't see Rory at all; he'd want to spend every minute with his cousins. I wouldn't see Joe, either, because he'd be with his dad and his brother. I'd be stuck with his mum, who was very nice, but it meant we'd be cooking and cleaning all day for her 'boys'. I think she thought it was an honour to do that for them. If Caitlin or Sarah were going I'd have someone to talk to and go out with, but with just Joe and Brendan there I'd be at a loss for something to do.

Joe looked at me and laughed. 'You don't want to go, do you?'

'Not really. It wouldn't be much fun for me, would it? I'd just be stuck in the middle of nowhere on my own, cleaning up after you lot.'

'Oh, come on now! We'd be there. We could help you.'

I raised my eyebrows at 'help' and he had the grace to look embarrassed. 'You'd be off playing golf with Brendan,' I said. 'You and Rory should go, though. Have a boys' holiday.'

'Would you like that, Rory?' he asked. 'Just you and me on a little holiday?'

Rory looked confused. 'Not Mummy?'

'Just you and me and Brendan and the boys. And Grandad.'

'And Nanny would look after you,' I said. 'She'd love that.'
'Come on, Rory, let's phone Nanny now and tell her.'

He sat down next to Rory on his bed and I heard Joe's mother's excited voice as she realized her boys were going to be back home.

I sent Brendan's wife, Sarah, a text. Seems like the boys will have a nice time at home.

She replied straight away. Mammy will be delighted.

I laughed. We both got on with Joe's mum, but I knew she loved it when she just had her sons home. This would be the first time she'd have sole charge of her sons and grandsons; it was probably the biggest gift we could give her.

Within minutes I got a text from Caitlin. Sarah's just told me. You're not daft, are you? What will you do when they're away?

Work.

She didn't answer for a while, and then I got a text. Sorry, I'll be away visiting Ben in Dubai, otherwise I'd come over and keep you company.

I had mixed feelings about that. If she were here, I knew I would probably tell her everything. I mustn't do that.

That afternoon I went back into work for a couple of hours at the end of the day. All was quiet; Lucy was there still at my desk, and Rachel and Sophie were in the kitchen, chatting, when I walked into the office. Brian was out; they told me he was showing a new tenant around a couple of flats in the city centre.

'How's Rory?' asked Lucy.

'Getting better, thanks. Joe's taking him to Ireland on Thursday for a few days. They'll have a great time there.'

'You didn't want to go?' asked Lucy.

I shot her a look and she laughed.

'Joe's brother will be there with his boys, so Rory will have a great time playing with them. He loves his cousins. I'll probably have them pressuring me for another baby when they come back.'

'You can't always have what you want,' said Lucy.

I nodded, embarrassed; I knew she would have liked more children. 'I know; if only it were that easy.'

'My sisters drive me mad,' said Sophie. 'I wish I were an only child.'

Rachel got up and collected all the mugs on a tray. 'You don't,' she said.

Lucy and I talked then about the new rota. 'I'll be here full time while Joe and Rory are away,' I said, 'but I'll take a day off when they get back.'

'That's fine. As long as I can take Maisie to and from school, I can work whenever you want.'

We agreed on the shifts for the next week and I booked myself in for all day every day, thinking I might as well make the most of them being away.

19

Thursday, August 3

In the couple of days before Joe and Rory left, there was a flurry of activity with washing clothes and gathering together everything they needed for the journey, but pretty soon it was Thursday morning, the car was packed up, and I was waving them off. I took a photo of them as they sat in the car ready to go, huge smiles on their faces. We usually went over to see Joe's parents a couple of times a year, but we hadn't visited since New Year and they were both excited about the trip. Rory was fully recovered now and sat strapped into his car seat in the back, diagonally from the driver's seat, so that Joe could check at a glance that he was all right. The front passenger seat was loaded up with a cooler full of drinks and snacks, and Rory had some headphones and Joe's iPad, ready to watch films if he got bored. I knew they'd have a great time; they always did.

Before Joe got into the car, he put his arms around me and kissed me goodbye.

'You have a good rest,' he said, seemingly oblivious to the fact that I'd be going in to work every day and he'd left behind a house in chaos. 'We'll call you every morning and every night when Rory goes to bed.' He kissed me again and I clung to him, wishing they would stay.

On hearing that Joe had left our house in a state, Sophie was outraged. 'You need to get some cleaners in,' she said. 'There's no way you should be going home and sorting out Joe's mess for him!' She took out her phone and sent her mum a text. 'I'll give you the phone number for our cleaners. They'll do a great job.'

'And,' said Rachel, 'you can tell Joe that you did it yourself.' She laughed. 'Unless you don't believe in lying to your husband.'

'That's a good idea, actually. He's pretty good at feeling guilty. I wouldn't lie normally, but sometimes . . .'

'Sometimes you lie to him?' asked Sophie, wide-eyed.

'No,' I said, impatient now. 'Of course I don't lie to him. But . . .'

'But you don't always tell the whole truth?' said Rachel.

I laughed. 'It's complicated. Marriage is complicated.'

'You're telling me,' said Brian.

Sophie's phone pinged then. 'Here's the number,' she said, 'just in case you want it.' She forwarded it to my phone and I saved it in my contacts list, determined to call them as soon as I could.

Later that day I escaped into the car park and called the cleaning service. They were happy to be recommended and the owner promised to come round to my house later that evening to see what I wanted done. They would be able to fit me in the next day, so I only had one more night of squalor. Before I went back into the office, I sent Joe a text wishing them a happy holiday. While I was waiting for his reply, I scrolled up, looking at the messages we'd sent back and forth over the months. When I saw the texts I'd sent the night I was in London, I paused.

There it was, clear as anything. At six thirty P.M. I'd written:

`Just got to hotel. Going to have a bath and relax! Kiss Rory for me xx`

He'd replied: `Will do and kisses to you from me. Hope you have a good night xx`

I'd replied: `Don't worry, I will! I'm going to order a meal and watch TV xx`

That had been my intention. That wasn't the problem, though. Anyone can change their mind. I'd looked at the empty room, heard the sounds of people out on the terrace through the open window, and decided to go down for a drink instead of staying alone in my room. That was okay. But then at nine thirty P.M. he'd written:

`Hope you've had a good night. What did you watch? xx`

And there in black and white was my reply:

`I decided to read instead. Ready for sleep now. Night xxx`

I felt cold as I looked at the message. Why had I sent that? I remember sitting chatting to David and having a good time when my phone beeped. Often when I'm out with friends, Joe will start to text and want to carry on a text conversation with me. If I'd said I'd gone down to the bar, he would've asked who I was with, what we were talking about . . . He wasn't possessive or jealous, he was just interested, but often it would spoil my night out because his texts would fly in while I was trying to talk to someone. And I'd known he'd be bored and lonely in the living room while Rory slept. He loved company, loved to chat. A night on his own after a day looking after Rory wasn't his idea of fun.

I could have gone back to my room and chatted to him, but I hadn't. I'd carried on drinking with someone I hardly knew.

I'd even paid for his dinner. I'd chosen to do that rather than talk to my own husband.

I thought of the photo that I'd received, the photo of me kissing David, or of David kissing me, whichever way it had happened. And I thought of the bill, the proof that I'd been for a meal with someone else when I'd said I was alone in my room. Then I realized: that was a photocopy.

Where was the original?

20

That night, Janet Boyd, the manager of the cleaning company recommended by Sophie's mum, came round and we had a bonding session over the state of my house. She was a quiet, efficient woman and I was immediately won over.

'We'll sort this out for you,' she said. 'Don't worry about it. Go to work in the morning and when you come back it'll be as good as new. If you give me a spare key now, I'll make sure it's left with the bill.'

It cheered me up to hear that. It was bad enough clearing up my own mess, but everywhere I looked I could see where Joe had been over the last couple of days. Everything was half finished, half eaten, half drunk. He had great intentions, but as far as housework was concerned, he seemed to have the attention span of a gnat.

Rory phoned me and told me about meeting his cousins; he was breathless with excitement as he described their adventures, and he said his dad would call me later that night.

I worked into the evening at home, then dialled out for a pizza and, feeling guilty about eating badly, took a vitamin pill. While I waited for the food to arrive, I lay on the sofa just staring at the television; I couldn't have said what was on.

The landline rang. Startled, I jumped off the sofa and picked up the receiver.

'Mum?' I said. She was the only person who called on the landline.

There was silence. I said, 'Hello?' but there was still no reply. I looked at the handset and saw that it was a withheld number. I sighed. It was likely to be from a claims company, trying to persuade me to claim for an accident I hadn't had. For a second I listened for the background sounds of a call centre, but there was no sound at all. Frowning, I put the phone down. Immediately it rang again. I picked it up and said, 'Hello?' again, but no one answered.

I glanced at the clock. It was after nine P.M. Surely call centres weren't allowed to ring at this time of night? Then the doorbell went, making me jump. I looked through the peephole to check who it was, something I rarely did when Joe was home, and saw it was just the pizza delivery guy. I took the box into the living room and turned back to the television again, but I was no longer hungry. Despite the fact that it was still early, I wanted to sleep, so I put the rest of the pizza into the fridge, filled a glass with water, and went upstairs.

The house felt weird without Joe or Rory in it. I stood in Rory's room and looked at his toys, at his little wooden bed, and his bookcase overflowing with the books I remembered from my own childhood. I would have given anything to have him there then, to kiss him as he slept, to feel him wriggle and then settle under my touch. I sat for a moment on his bed and held his pillow to my face, breathing in the familiar smell, holding it close in lieu of him. When I stood to put it back and straighten his quilt, I saw that his little toy rabbit, Buffy, was still there, stuffed down between the bed and the wall. Rory had slept with that rabbit every night of his life; I thought Joe must have had a nightmare putting him to bed without it tonight.

After I'd had a quick shower and was ready for bed, I switched on the lamps on either side of my bed and curled up under the quilt with Buffy in my arms. I called Joe but he didn't pick up, and I guessed he'd be down at the local pub with Brendan and his dad by now, his happy mum left with all the children. I took a photo of myself holding Buffy close and sent it to Joe via text, with a message saying, Tell Rory I'm taking good care of Buffy and we can't wait until you're both back home xxx

I wasn't expecting a reply that night. He hadn't seen Brendan for months and they'd be talking all night. I opened my Kindle and started to read, knowing I'd be asleep within minutes.

I was just on the brink of sleep when my phone gave a loud beep, making me jerk back to consciousness. Thinking it was Joe replying to my text, I reached over to grab the phone, hoping he'd sent a photo back.

He hadn't.

On my screen was another Instagram message. As soon as I saw the name, my stomach sank. *WatchingYou*. Again it said the person messaging would only know I'd seen their request if I chose Allow.

I sat up in bed, my stomach tight with panic. I held my breath as I selected Allow. I couldn't *not* see the message.

An image appeared on the screen. It was a photo of me, lying on a bed. My eyes were shut and I looked as though I was asleep.

I had a sheet wrapped loosely around my waist and legs, and I was wearing no clothes – nothing at all.

* * *

I think the photo must have been on my screen for about five seconds before it disappeared. All that was left was *Watching You* and *Photo Unavailable*.

My hands started to shake. When had that photo been taken? It wasn't my bed at home, I knew that. We have a white wrought-iron bedstead and the bed in the photo was completely different.

And then I knew. I think I knew right from the moment I saw it, really, but had tried not to believe it. I lay back down on the bed and buried my face in the pillow. It was the hotel room I'd stayed in while I was in London, I was sure of it. That bed had had a brown suede headboard, and I knew the one in the photo was the same.

I had no memory of that photo being taken. How much had I drunk? How much would I have had to drink to expose myself to another man? Fidelity was so important to Joe and me. We'd both been burned by people in the past; it was the one thing we agreed on.

Once that's happened, the relationship's over anyway, whether the other person knows or not, Joe had said, and I had agreed.

Did this mean my marriage was over?

The thought of that whipped me into action. I wasn't going to let my marriage die without putting up a fight. I needed to go down there. I needed to go back to that hotel room and see what I could remember.

21

Friday, August 4

The next day I was at work early. I'd been awake most of the night worrying about what was going on. Everything that had happened kept rolling around my head. The photocopy of the receipt. The photo of David kissing me. The video of me saying horrible things about Joe. And now the naked photo. I felt like screaming.

I'd called Lucy at eight A.M.

'Lucy, it's me, Gemma. I need to ask a huge favour. Are you free today?'

'Do you want me to come in? I can ask my mum to have Maisie after school. I can be there by ten if that's any good.'

'Would you? That would be great. Brian will be in, but Sophie's off today and I don't want to leave Rachel on her own with sales.'

She agreed to that and sure enough she was there just after ten, ready to start the day.

'I've got to go back home,' I told them once everyone was

in. 'My mum's got a hospital appointment so I said I'd go with her. I'd forgotten all about it.'

'Back to the Wirral?' asked Rachel. 'Which hospital?'

Rachel and I had grown up in the same town, though I hadn't known her as I was eight years older and we'd attended different schools. When she'd come for interview six months ago, I'd read her application form and recognized the school she'd gone to. We'd talked for a while about the area. She'd gone on to university in Liverpool but I'd been desperate to leave, and only went back on occasional visits.

'Arrowe Park.' I couldn't think of another one offhand.

'Do you know that area, Rachel?' asked Lucy.

Rachel nodded. 'We're both from New Brighton.'

'Really? I didn't know that. Did you know each other before you started work here?'

'No,' I said. 'Obviously I'm older and we went to different schools.'

'Do you go back often?' she asked Rachel. 'Are your mum and dad still there?'

'No, my mum . . .' All of a sudden Rachel's face was bright red and she looked as though she was going to cry. 'My mum died a few months ago.'

'It wasn't long after Rachel's mum died that she came to work down here,' I said to Lucy. I didn't want Rachel to have to say anything about it if she didn't want to. 'It's still so recent.' I looked at Rachel sympathetically. 'It must have been really tough.'

'It was.' She met my eye, looking proud and vulnerable at the same time. 'Nobody knows what it's like.'

Lucy made a move as though she was going to hug her, but Rachel dashed off to the cloakroom.

'What about her dad?' Lucy asked in a low voice.

'Her mum and dad divorced and he's living abroad with his

new wife now,' I whispered. 'He's in New Zealand, I think. She doesn't see him.'

Lucy winced. 'I don't know how a parent could do that. Poor Rachel, she's only in her twenties.'

I nodded. 'She told me at the interview. I don't think she was going to say anything but when we were chatting afterwards, I asked her what it was like living at home when she was a student. She told me she had been a caregiver to her mum, who'd died a couple of months before.' I thought of Rachel that day. She was so young, only twenty-four, and was all dressed up in a business suit and heels, and I could tell she was frightened of breaking down. My heart had ached for her then, having to cope without her parents. She was a great fit for the job and I offered it to her there and then. I felt really guilty now that I hadn't talked to her more about her family life, but she was so reserved that it had never seemed appropriate. 'I have to go, Lucy. Will you make sure she's okay?'

She nodded. 'Don't worry, you can go now. I'll deal with it.'

I called goodbye to the others and left, feeling guilty that I'd lied to them about where I was going. Once I was in my car, on my way to the railway station, however, I forgot about them immediately. I had a job to do.

22

It was like a repeat of the day six weeks earlier when I'd taken the train from Chester to London. The train to Euston was just as crowded and I was squashed alongside a mother with two children. Those children wriggled more than any child I'd known. Looking at the mother read a book to them, watching them cling onto her arms so she could hardly turn the page, made me long for Rory. I needed him to see him.

I sent Joe a text. Missing you both. Are you having a good time? Take a photo of Rory for me, will you? xx

Immediately he responded. Miss you too. Just about to go out with Brendan. Mum's minding the kids. She's taken them into town and then to a café for lunch. Will send a photo later xx

I looked at my watch. I wouldn't be back home until seven P.M. or so. I'd call his mum when the children were in bed. I didn't want to disturb her while she was having some time alone with them. I tried to quell the thought that I seemed to be the only person who wasn't having time alone with Rory.

Tears pricking my eyes, I sent another message: Is Rory OK? Is he happy? Did he sleep last night? xx

In a few seconds my phone vibrated. Happy? He's ecstatic. Have to run, talk tonight xx

I closed my eyes and thought of Rory running around with his older cousins. Joe was right: Rory would be in his element.

And then I thought of Joe's face if he knew what had happened to me in London. Panic raced through me at the thought of his expression if he saw that photo from last night. I couldn't let that happen.

From Euston I went straight to the hotel, walking down Tottenham Court Road again just as I had weeks before. This time my mood was different. I knew that whatever happened today, I was going to have to do something with the information I had. I knew I should talk to the police, but then Joe would hear about it. That was inevitable. I'd do anything to avoid that.

The hotel reception was busy when I got there. I hovered by the entrance, then decided to look into the bar before speaking to the receptionist on duty.

The bar was open to the public. There was no table service, just one huge mahogany counter lining one wall. I looked to see whether there were any staff I recognized but couldn't see anyone, and besides, they wouldn't have recognized me anyway. There must have been a couple of hundred people crammed into the bar when I was last there; there was no reason why they should remember me.

Today there was plenty of space, with small groups of business people and tourists dotted around the room. I ordered an orange juice and sat at a table by the wall. I remembered that night I'd come downstairs to see whether there was anyone I knew. I'd already bought a couple of drinks by the time I saw Liam, and I remembered trying to hide away from him. I wished now I'd talked to him, stood with his colleagues and listened to them brag about sales, rather than get drunk with David. What was I thinking?

When I'd finished my drink, I walked over to the restaurant, which was on the other side of the hotel's reception area. I stood in the doorway and looked in. I thought I could remember where I'd sat but realized I couldn't be too sure. I frowned. How could I not remember that? Clients could come into the office and I'd remember which house I'd sold them and for what price even several years later. How could I not remember which table I'd sat at just six weeks ago?

I picked up a menu from a vacant table next to me and read it. It was as though I hadn't seen it before. I thought of the meals on the receipt, the chicken and the steak. I couldn't remember which I'd eaten and which David had had. I felt like ordering both just to see if I could remember when I saw them, but the thought of seeing them made me feel sick.

I left the restaurant and waited at the reception desk until the receptionist was free.

'Please may I have a word with your manager in private?' I asked.

She raised her eyebrows but went through a door at the back of the reception and came out a few minutes later with a woman with an elegant silver pixie cut and a harassed look on her face. She greeted me and ushered me into a small office to the side of the desk.

'How can I help you?'

'I've got an unusual request, I'm afraid. I wondered whether it would be possible to view your CCTV. I stayed here a while ago and I need to identify a man I had dinner with.'

She looked surprised. 'Identify him?'

I swallowed. I couldn't think of any way around this. 'I thought I knew who he was, but it seems I don't.'

She looked completely confused by now.

'I was here for a training conference on the twenty-fourth of June,' I said. 'I stayed here the night of the twenty-third and I bumped into a man I knew from home. I'm an estate agent and he's a client.' I hesitated. My face was burning. 'And I think something happened that night. I think he was in my room.'

'Without your permission?'

'The thing is, I was very drunk. I don't usually drink much but I was really, really drunk. I felt terrible the next day.'

She winced. 'And you think he came back to your room afterwards? Were you hurt?'

'No, not hurt. I just had a hangover the next day. It's just . . .' Suddenly I wanted to tell her. I wanted to tell someone. I was sick to death of having these thoughts racing around my head. 'He sent me photos,' I said quickly. 'I need to contact him to tell him to delete them.'

'Photos?' She saw my face then, and understood. 'Incriminating photos?'

I nodded, humiliated. 'I was naked.'

'And you didn't consent to that?'

'God, no,' I said. 'I can't even remember him taking them.'

She looked horrified. 'You know he's broken the law? You should go to the police.'

'I can't. I can't do that.'

She glanced down at my wedding ring. 'They can be discreet, you know.'

'It would be different if I could show them a picture of the man. Everything he told me was a lie – his name, address, phone number . . . If I had a photo of him it would really help. And that's when I wondered – do you have CCTV from that night?'

'From the twenty-third of June?' She shook her head. 'I'm sorry, but that's over a month ago. We keep records for thirty-one days, and then they're destroyed. That's what we're advised to do by the police. Our system's automatically set up to delete anything after that time.'

My mind raced. He'd sent me the photo and the video over a month after I came back from London. He must have hoped I wouldn't be able to find CCTV records by then.

'I'm so sorry,' she said. 'Really I am. What he's done is shocking. Illegal. I can understand your reluctance not to get the police involved, but really I think you should.'

'I'll think about it.' I stood up to go. 'Thanks anyway.' I picked up my bag, then remembered something. 'I'm not sure you'd know about this. I paid for a meal in the restaurant here and must have forgotten to pick up the receipt. I was sent a photocopy of the receipt four weeks after I was here.'

As soon as I heard myself say that, I knew that of course the hotel hadn't sent it. Why would they wait four weeks to send a receipt to a guest they didn't even know?

She frowned. 'Who sent you that?'

'I assumed you had,' I said, feeling foolish.

'The restaurant is a franchise,' she said. 'It doesn't belong to us. We simply rent them the space here. We have no connection to them. If someone left their receipt behind in the restaurant, we wouldn't know anything about it. And besides, the restaurant's open to the public. The staff wouldn't know if you were staying here or not. We certainly wouldn't pass on your address.'

So he sent it to me. Why would he do that?

I stood in silence for a moment, trying to work out what was going on.

'I know this sounds odd,' I said, 'but if the room I stayed in is empty, would I be able to have a look at it?'

She looked a bit surprised, but clicked her mouse at the computer on the desk and said, 'Which room were you staying in?'

'I don't know. I'm sorry; I can't remember.' I frowned. 'My memory's been really bad lately.'

She looked up, a concerned expression on her face.

'It's just work,' I said. 'I run my own business and it's stressful at the moment.'

'Oh, that must be tough.' She asked for my name and scrolled down the screen, searching the database. 'The room's empty, though someone's booked into it for tonight. They're not due in until late as they're coming in to Heathrow on an evening flight.' She picked up her keys. 'Come on, I'll show you around. You were in room 912.'

As soon as she said that, I remembered. We went up to the ninth floor in the lift, and as we came out, I had a sudden jolt of memory.

I tripped here, didn't I? I remembered reaching out and grabbing the rail. I flushed, embarrassed at the thought of making a fool of myself. Then, as though he were here with us now, I heard David's voice as he laughed and said, 'Steady on, sweetheart.'

Sweetheart? *Sweetheart?*

We walked down the corridor towards my room. Memories were coming back, though they were of my arrival there earlier in the evening rather than later that night. I felt distinctly uneasy as we approached the room.

The manager touched the door plate with her card, then, as a green light flashed, she turned to me. 'Okay?'

I nodded reluctantly.

She opened the door. I stood in the doorway and looked at the room. The curtains were half drawn and it was dark and cool. She flicked on the light switch and I stepped inside. It did look familiar. I saw the brown suede surround of the bed and winced.

'Are you all right?'

I nodded again. 'It's the same bed that was in the photo.' The bed was a divan; there was no room for anything to roll underneath it. I walked over to it, then turned, looking at the rest of the room. The minibar sat underneath the desk. 'I was charged for three bottles of water but I'm sure I only had two.'

'Oh, I'm sorry. You should have told us and we would have adjusted your bill.'

'It's not that. I'm just trying to figure out what happened. Can a mistake be made with that sort of thing?'

'It shouldn't happen,' she said. 'It's an automated system, but we ask the staff cleaning the room to check, too.'

'I must have made a mistake,' I said, but I knew I hadn't. I turned towards the door. 'Thanks for showing me the room. I really appreciate it.' I stopped in the doorway and looked around again.

'Everything okay?' she asked.

There was something at the corner of my mind, nudging me, that didn't seem right, but I couldn't work out what it was. The room was clean, tidy, and neutral, just like any other hotel room. I shrugged and said, 'Yes, it's fine, thanks,' and she switched off the lights and we left.

23

It seemed a long train journey home. Luckily the seat next to me was empty, so I was able to sit quietly and look out of the window and think about what had happened since I was last in London. It had been good to talk to the manager, but it made me realize how alone I was now. Joe would find out straight away if the police got involved. I really wanted to talk to Caitlin, but she was away visiting Ben, and besides, she might feel she had to tell Joe. And I couldn't tell my mum. I shuddered. I couldn't think how she'd react if I told her.

I drove back home from the station feeling so weary. I was desperate to know what David was up to, but frightened too. Part of me thought of telling Joe, of calling him while he was safely in Ireland and just telling him everything. It wasn't the kind of thing I should tell him over the phone, but how could I do it face to face? My throat burned as I thought of the video where I'd said I wouldn't have married him. I couldn't let him hear that. I was so ashamed of myself. Everyone loses their patience with their partner from time to time, but I wouldn't normally talk like that about him.

By the time I reached my house, I was so exhausted I didn't

know what to do with myself. I opened the front door and stopped dead.

The house smelled different; there was an artificial lemony smell that would have had Joe reaching for his inhaler if he'd been here. And then I saw my spare key and a bill on the dresser in the hall and remembered the cleaners had been.

I walked from room to room, opening windows to get rid of the smell but admiring how lovely it looked. The house was polished and cleaned to a much higher standard than Joe or I did it. The kitchen was spotless, the dishwasher emptied. In the bedrooms the drawers were tidied, and clean laundry had been put away.

I wanted to marry those women. I glanced at the receipt and blanched. I'd asked them to do whatever it took and they had, but it had cost me. When I looked around at the scrubbed kitchen, the spotless living room, and the vases on the windowsills full of flowers from the garden, though, I knew they were worth every penny.

My phone pinged with a message from Joe. He'd sent a photo that his brother had taken, of Joe on a sun lounger with a glass of beer and a huge plate of sandwiches, his mother in the background playing tennis with Rory. How're things? We're missing you. Can't wait to see you again.

I couldn't wait either.

After locking up the house and making a quick snack, I went straight up to bed. It was so lovely to see the house clean and tidy, like being given a huge present. I got under the freshly laundered quilt determined to have an early night and called Joe and Rory from my bed. Rory was in bed too, as he told me all the things he'd been up to. It seemed strange to be going to bed at the same time as my three-year-old son, but it felt wonderful, too, to think of a long night's sleep. I switched the lamps on, though the room wasn't yet dark, then settled down with my Kindle. I sent Lucy a text to say that I should be okay to work in the morning, set my alarm for seven A.M., and soon I was asleep.

I woke in the early hours with a terrific jolt. My heart banged and for a moment I didn't know where I was. It wasn't a dream; it was as though a memory had come back to me when I was asleep.

I remembered then that I'd switched the lamps on in the hotel room before I went down to the bar, so that the room would be lit when I came back. I could remember it clearly. Each lamp was on a built-in bedside table, either side of the bed, and had a little silver chain that I'd pulled to switch them on. I could actually remember that physical act of reaching over and pulling each chain. One of them stuck a bit and I had to hold the lamp steady so that I could tug it sharply. The main light switch next to the door only controlled the overhead light. I'd noticed that again when I was shown the room the day before.

When I woke in the hotel bed that morning in June, with a crashing hangover and a thirst worse than I'd ever had before, those lamps were switched off. I hadn't done that. I would never do that. It was the one thing I couldn't help. I just can't sleep in the dark, no matter where I am. It was something Joe and Rory had had to get used to, though of course I'd never told Rory why.

I looked around my room. The two bedside lamps were lit and the door to the en suite was ajar; I always left the light above the mirror switched on there. On the landing outside the light was permanently on at night, even though I slept with my door shut tight when Rory was away from home.

It was the way it always was. It was the way it had to be.

24

Saturday, August 5

Back at work the next morning, it was hard to keep up the pretence that everything was all right.

'You look tired,' said Rachel as soon as she arrived. 'Was everything okay with your mum?'

For a second or two I wondered what she was talking about, then I remembered the lie I'd told the day before. 'I'm fine, thanks. She's okay.'

I saw her give me a sidelong look but I ignored her, busying myself at my computer. She came over to my desk and I thought for a second she was going to ask more questions, but she just said, 'Can you add Mr and Mrs Hudson to the viewing requests? I've put their details in the system.'

I'd just started to answer when my phone vibrated in my handbag in the desk drawer. 'Sorry,' I said. 'I need to check it's not Joe.'

She went back to her desk and I took out my phone.

My heart sank. On the screen was an Instagram message from WatchingYou. I closed my eyes for a second. That name was so apt. I struggled to think about anything else.

I glanced over at Rachel. 'Won't be a minute.' I touched the Allow button.

Our Internet connection was always pretty slow, and it seemed to take ages for the photo to download onto my phone. I held my breath. Slowly, almost a pixel at a time, the full photo was revealed.

I was lying on the hotel bed again and this time I was completely naked. There wasn't even a sheet or blanket to cover me. There was no expression on my face; I wasn't smiling or frowning, just staring straight at the person taking the photo.

As I looked at it in disbelief, it disappeared from view and immediately another message came up, causing the phone to vibrate again.

It was a screenshot of my Facebook page, just as it was when I'd seen it earlier that day. Within a couple of seconds, that too had disappeared.

I slammed the phone into my drawer.

'What's up?' asked Brian. He came over to my desk. 'Gemma, are you all right?'

I couldn't answer. All I could think of was how I would feel if someone put that photo of me on Facebook for all my friends to see. For my mum and dad to see. For Joe to see.

'You're shaking,' said Rachel. 'What's the matter?'

I shook my head. 'It's okay. It's just . . .'

They looked at me expectantly, but I couldn't think of a thing to say. What could I say? And I remembered they were friends with me on Facebook too. I took my phone from my drawer. 'Just give me a few minutes, will you?' I went out the back door to the car park and checked Facebook. I breathed a sigh of relief. The photo wasn't there. Quickly I looked through all the notifications; there was nothing unusual there. I deactivated my account. I started to come back into the office but then went back outside and deactivated my Twitter and

LinkedIn accounts, too. I hesitated over the Instagram account. I didn't know what to do; should I get rid of it and have him find another way of getting in touch? I hovered over the screen, trying to work out what to do, but then Brian called my name, asking again whether I was okay, and I slid the phone back in my pocket. I'd decide later.

When I got back to my desk, Rachel went to the fridge and took out a bottle of water. She passed it to me but didn't say anything. I was grateful for that; I couldn't tell her why I'd reacted so badly. My head thumped and I realized I was stupid to take it all on myself.

'Rachel,' I said suddenly, 'will you take over the meeting?'

'Me?' She looked dumbfounded.

'It will be good experience for you. You could stand in for me then, whenever I'm off work.'

She blushed, and I could tell she was feeling proud. 'Yes, of course.' She called over to the others, 'We'll have our meeting in ten minutes.'

She sat at my desk with me and I went through the viewing requests. I talked her through the order in which we should work, then suggested who should take which lead. She photocopied the documents and made quick notes.

'Okay, everyone,' I said, when all of my staff were gathered around the table. 'Apologies for the late start. From now on Rachel's going to be in charge of these meetings. Rachel, it's over to you.'

I sat back and drank my bottle of water. I could hear Rachel reviewing activities from the day before and setting targets for the day with the staff, but all I could think about was the messages I'd received.

I've never, ever had a photo taken like that before. I've always thought that women who send men intimate photos of themselves are crazy; those pictures could appear anywhere, long after the relationship finishes. I couldn't imagine how drunk I must have been to let someone do that. My stomach curled up in fear at the thought of it appearing on Facebook. I was so glad I'd deactivated my account, even though I knew some of my friends would question why. I'd have to think of some reason; I'd been on there for years.

I don't know how I did it, but I kept my face expressionless throughout the meeting, and all the while I was thinking, *I need to tell the police.*

As soon as the meeting ended, I thanked Rachel and quickly went back to my desk. I took my phone out of my pocket and looked at it again. The contents of both messages had gone. Disappeared into thin air. All that remained was the name *WatchingYou* and the notification for each: *Photo Unavailable.*

And then I realized, of course, I could send a message back. I hadn't thought of that before, because the actual messages had disappeared. I clicked on the Message button and typed, What is it you want?

I turned the sound on my phone up high and put it into my desk drawer. My heart still racing, I tried to work, though I was alert for the ringtone all morning.

There was no reply.

25

Joe called later on in the afternoon. I was in the middle of speaking to a couple of first-time buyers and had to ignore his call. He didn't leave a voicemail, just a text that said, All OK; he knew how I panicked if he called and I couldn't get to the phone, in case something was wrong with Rory. When I left the office, I sat in my car and thought I'd call him then instead of waiting until I got home.

'Hey, sweetheart,' he said, and my heart softened.

'I've really missed you.' I could hear my voice wobble.

He laughed. 'I've missed you too. It's been great seeing Brendan, though. And hey, guess what? He's planning to move back over here.'

'To Ireland? Really? With Sarah?'

'Of course with Sarah! All of them. They want to come back to the old country.'

'Sarah's not Irish.'

'I know, but since her mum and dad emigrated to Spain when they retired, she's not got the ties in England any more.'

My heart sank. I knew the pressure would be on me now.

'So, I've been okay,' I said, in a passive-aggressive attempt to stave off the inevitable discussion about moving to Ireland.

'Sorry, Gem! It isn't that I'd forgotten you. I just wanted to tell you the news about Brendan. So what have you been up to? How are you feeling?'

'Oh, okay. It's been busy here.'

'You poor thing. Make sure you get an early night.'

My mind flashed to the night before when I'd woken at midnight to remember the lamps in the hotel room. I'd hardly slept afterwards, my mind racing about what was going on. 'I will,' I said.

'Anything interesting happen?'

I was silent for a moment. How on earth could I begin to tell him I thought I was being blackmailed? 'Oh, not much,' I said instead, and scrabbled around for something I'd done that I could tell him about. There wasn't anything. 'Just sorting out the house.'

'Oh, I'm sorry, sweetie. It was a bit of a mess before I left, wasn't it? We were in a rush.'

I knew it was grossly unfair, but there was no way I was going to admit to the cleaning service. Not yet at any rate. I reckoned that was worth a good few months of ammunition.

'So you'll be back in a couple of days?' I asked.

'We will. What is it now, Saturday? We'll be back on Wednesday.'

'Okay. I'll miss you.' I could hear someone saying something in the background, and then Joe said, 'My mum says why aren't you on Facebook? She wanted to send you a message there but you'd disappeared.'

'Oh,' I said, frantically trying to think up an excuse. 'I was reading an article about how social media uses up too much of our time, and I thought I'd get rid of it for a few weeks.'

'Good idea. I know it's easy to waste hours on there. I'd better go, sweetheart.'

'Call me tonight, will you, if you get the chance? And is Rory there?'

'He is. Hold on; I'll call him. I love you.'

I heard him call Rory's name, and then my boy was on the phone to me, breathless with excitement about a game he was playing with his cousins that involved chasing and water and Nanny's dog.

I sat in the car for a few minutes after the call ended. I wanted to feel happy for them – I *did* feel happy for them – but I really missed them. I wanted to be the one running around the garden with Rory, or drinking beer and flipping burgers with my family. I started the car, feeling really sorry for myself.

And then my phone beeped and I switched the engine off again. A new e-mail had come through to my Gmail account. I opened the app and saw a message from WatchingYou. My stomach tightened. How had he found my e-mail address?

The message heading was *Soon*.

My fingers shook as I opened it. At first I thought it was junk mail, the kind that usually goes automatically to my spam box, where you're sent a link to a website and asked to enter your bank details and password for a prince in a kingdom far, far away. But the link in this e-mail, the only thing in the message, wasn't to a fake bank and it wasn't asking for a password or my life savings. It was a link to a website and it was clear from the URL that it was a site for voyeurs.

I leaned back, unable to believe my eyes. What did it mean? And then it dawned on me. I'd closed my Facebook account; had he tried to post the photos there? And now, finding that he couldn't, was he going to post those photos of me naked, identifiable, on that website?

Immediately I tapped out a response, What do you want? Is it money? and waited ten minutes, my heart pounding and my mind reeling, but of course the only reply was to tell me that the e-mail address did not exist.

I had no choice. I had to speak to the police.

26

Sunday, August 6

I decided to go to the police first thing the next morning, rather than on a Saturday night. I knew they wouldn't have time to talk to me then.

I waited outside the police station, trying to gather my nerves, then took my phone out of my bag and looked at it again. I scrolled through the messages I'd sent Joe, telling him that I'd had room service. I looked at the Instagram screen with the blank messages, all from the same person. And then I looked at the e-mail with the web address of a voyeur site, and my own pathetic attempts to get in touch with this person. Clearly he'd shut down his account immediately after e-mailing me.

It was so hard to control my anger towards David. How dare he treat me like this? No matter what had happened that night, no matter what I'd done, he had no reason to send me those messages.

At the police station I asked to speak to a female officer. When I was asked for my name, I said I was Gemma but didn't want to give my surname. I also didn't want to tell the guy at the desk why I was there. He looked at my face; I knew it showed signs I'd been crying, and he said that was all right, that the female officer could take details. I sat down to wait, automatically feeling I'd done something wrong just because I was there.

Ten minutes later a woman came to the desk and ushered me into a small interview room. She introduced herself as Stella Barclay and was a bit older than me. I was nervous enough before I went in there, but that room, well, I thought I was going to have a panic attack. I think she saw that, because she fetched me a glass of water and told me to sit there and drink it and not speak until I felt better.

'How are you feeling?' she said. 'Are you all right to talk?'

I nodded. 'Sorry. I'm a bit nervous.'

'That's okay. Now can you tell me what you're here about?' She had a notebook and pen on the desk, and somehow it helped that she was writing it in there and not staring at me as I spoke.

'I'm an estate agent,' I said. 'I have my own office.'

'What's the address?' she asked.

I hesitated. 'I'd really rather not at the moment. Is that okay? I'm just looking for some advice.'

She closed her notebook. 'That's fine. What's troubling you?'

I nodded. 'A while ago, on the sixteenth of June, a man came in. He wanted me to show him around a few properties.'

'He just walked in off the street? No booking?'

'No, he'd e-mailed us about some properties. I check all the e-mails and voicemail messages and allocate the jobs between us. With the amount he was prepared to spend, I decided to take on the job myself, rather than give it to one of my staff.'

'And do you have that e-mail address?'

I nodded. 'I do, but I've written to him there since and the e-mails have just bounced back.'

She grimaced. 'Go on.'

'So I spent a few hours driving him around. He seemed fine. Very chatty. Charming.'

I think she thought I was going to say he'd assaulted me. She became very sympathetic. 'What happened then?'

'Nothing happened. Not then. I drove back to the office and he went off somewhere after that.'

'And then?'

'A week later, I was in London at a training conference. I was staying in a hotel in Covent Garden and went down to the bar for a drink in the evening. And I bumped into the same man again. It was completely coincidental. We had a meal together. A nice conversation.'

'And then? Did something happen?'

I shook my head. 'I don't know. I just don't know.' I looked up into the officer's eyes and saw nothing but kindness there. I knew she was used to hearing a hell of a lot worse than I was going to tell her. 'But since that night, I keep being sent things. Photos. A video.'

'Can I see them?'

I shook my head again.

'Honestly, Gemma, you wouldn't believe the things we see. There's really no need to worry.'

'It's not that. He's using Instagram and withdrawing the messages immediately afterwards.'

'So they're not there now? How's he doing that?'

I showed her Instagram on my phone. 'All you can see now is the names he used and the fact that the message has been withdrawn. And he sent a screenshot of my Facebook page, too. I've got rid of Facebook now. I deactivated it as soon as he sent that screenshot. And yesterday I received an e-mail. I know it's from him.'

'What does it say?'

'Nothing. There's just a link there to a voyeur website.'

I opened his e-mail on my phone. 'Look.' I passed it to her, and when I saw the expression on her face, I felt my eyes prickle with tears. 'I think he's going to post my photos to the site.'

'Have you opened this link?'

I shook my head. 'I was worried in case it contained a virus.'

'You're right not to open any attachment he sends you,' she said. 'Unfortunately, this is a real site. If you do want to look at it, just type in the address manually, though, rather than clicking on the link he gave you.'

I couldn't imagine wanting to look at it, but agreed that was what I'd do.

'But how is it legal for a website to show photos like that?'

She said patiently, 'Well, no one can police the Internet. If they've set up a site in another country then they have to abide by their laws, even though the site can be viewed anywhere in the world. You can imagine the problems it's caused us. But you can usually get a photo pulled down off a site if you make a complaint; most webmasters will do that. They're not usually after a lot of aggravation, and if you ask, they'll oblige. You can also ask Google to prevent a page appearing in their search results if you are nude or shown in a sexual act, so anyone searching for images of you online wouldn't see the pictures of you naked. They'll do that as long as the act was intended to be private and you didn't consent to the photo being publicly available.' It was clear she was used to reciting this. 'The most important thing, though, is to ask the webmaster to remove the image from the site as soon as you see it.' She must have noticed the stricken look on my face. 'If you see it,' she added hastily.

'But if someone sees it before me,' I said, 'the damage is done then, isn't it?'

She nodded sympathetically. 'We'll do as much damage

limitation as we can. Don't forget to delete all your social media – Twitter, LinkedIn, that sort of thing. Don't give him a platform for posting images that your friends could see.'

'I've done that already. I did it as soon as he sent the screenshot of my Facebook page. But what about Instagram? Should I delete my account?'

'I would. I'd cut off all the ways he can reach you.'

I did it there and then. She asked more questions about David, and I told her how I'd called the numbers he'd given me, and discovered he didn't work for Barford's or live at the address he'd given us. I was getting more and more agitated as I told her everything I knew.

'Look, he's given you a false name,' she said. 'When he came to your office, he knew in advance that he was going to do something. Whether he knew exactly what, who can say now? But he created a fake e-mail address to book an appointment before even seeing you. I don't think he was targeting you at that point. You have a number of staff. Any one of them could have become his victim.'

I shuddered at the thought of the other women in the office being put in this position.

'So you need to increase your precautions,' she said. 'And speak to the other estate agents in your area. No house visits with anyone unless they've shown photo ID. I'll get our community police officers onto it too.' She looked at me sympathetically. 'So when you had a meal with him, you didn't get an inkling anything was wrong with him? No red flags?'

'No, nothing jarred at all. He was really nice. Great company. I drank far too much, though, and had a terrible hangover the next day.' I grimaced. 'I don't usually drink more than a glass or two. I have a three-year-old son and I have to keep my wits about me. But that night I was away from home and I drank more than I usually did.'

'Do you remember going to bed?'

'I remember going down the corridor to my room. I remember stumbling.' I winced. 'I'm mortified now, just thinking about it.'

'And was David with you then, do you remember?'

'Yes. Yes, he was. He pulled me upright.'

'And did you invite him into your room?'

'No,' I said. 'I wouldn't do that. I'm married. Happily married.'

All the while I was insisting on this, the thought was there, though. How did he take a photo of me on my bed? Had I actually invited him in?

'Do you remember brushing your teeth that night? Washing your face? Or did you decide not to bother?'

I stared at her uncertainly. 'I can't remember. I'm sure I did. I always do – it's automatic, isn't it?'

'But can you remember doing it?'

No matter how hard I tried to remember, I just couldn't. I shook my head.

'Think about those moments before you first went into your room,' she said. 'You were walking down the corridor. How would you normally open the door to the hotel room, do you remember? With a card?'

'Yes,' I said. 'It was one of those contactless cards that you hold next to a metal plate on the door. It was a white card, no markings on it. The room number was on a little envelope.'

'And later on Friday night, when you were going back to your room . . . do you remember opening the door then? Putting the card next to the door?'

I closed my eyes and tried to remember, but I couldn't. I shook my head, frustrated with myself. 'I don't know. I must have done.'

'What about your clothes? What were you wearing?'

I described my green silk dress.

'And when you woke up the next morning, what were you wearing?'

I frowned. 'I was wearing my underwear. Bra and knickers.'

She was quiet for a while then, before she said, 'Were they the same ones that you'd worn the night before?'

I stared at her. 'What do you mean?'

'Well, when you arrived at the hotel, did you change before going downstairs?'

I nodded. 'It was a really hot day, so I had a shower and changed my clothes.'

'And do you remember which underwear you put on after your shower?'

I thought hard. 'Yes, I can remember. I bought it when we were in Italy last summer. It's black silk. I always wore that set with my green dress.'

She leaned forward. 'Gemma, when you woke up, can you remember which underwear you were wearing then? Was it the same set?'

I closed my eyes, panic coursing through me.

She spoke gently and I knew she was used to coaxing hidden truths from women in situations like mine. 'What did you do when you first got up? Did you go into the bathroom?'

'I went into the bathroom,' I said. 'I was sick. It was the drink.'

'And did you look in the mirror? What colour was your underwear?'

I felt the blood drain from my face as I remembered seeing my reflection in the mirror as I dashed over to the toilet. My face had been pale and sweaty. The mirror was about three feet square, placed at waist height. In my mind's eye I could see myself as I passed through the room. My underwear was white.

27

As soon as I got home, I raced upstairs to find the underwear I'd been wearing the night I'd had dinner with David in London. I'd come home and tipped all my clothes from my overnight bag into the laundry basket on the landing. That was empty now, thanks to the cleaners, and all of the clothes there had been washed and put back into drawers. I searched my bedroom looking for the set, but knew I wouldn't find it.

I checked the utility room, hoping against hope that they would be there, left in the dryer by mistake, but no, all was spotless, not a thing out of place.

'You told me that you were naked in those photos,' Stella had said. 'So your underwear was obviously off at one point. This sort of man often likes to keep something. A kind of trophy. I wonder whether he took it with him and put your other set on you so that you wouldn't notice.'

Or so that I would *notice. So that I'd remember one day, later, after he'd gone.*

I sat at the dining table and tried to control my breathing. I couldn't let myself think about this. I just couldn't.

All of a sudden I was overwhelmed with the desire to talk to Joe. I sent him a text to ask if he was free, but I didn't get a reply. I could phone their house, of course, but guessed his mum would answer, and I just couldn't bear to talk to her now. She'd know something was wrong and she really, *really* mustn't find out what I'd done.

What *had* I done, though? I just couldn't remember a thing. Something had happened and I was being punished for it. I thought again of those photos appearing on social media and sites for voyeurs and just wanted to collapse in a heap.

I picked up my laptop and opened Chrome in Incognito mode. There was no way I wanted Joe to see this. I typed in the address of the site. As soon as I saw the content, I started to cry.

The whole site was devoted to images and videos of women who were unaware they were being recorded. It showed them in the shower, in the street, asleep in bed. There were unsuspecting women on crowded trains, unaware that some creep was holding a camera up their skirt. There were even women on the toilet, completely oblivious to the fact that they were being filmed. I clicked on link after link, feeling more sick by the minute. Most pictures had a stream of comments underneath, congratulating the bastards who'd filmed these women. I felt dirty just reading those messages. There were Like buttons, too; any idea I'd had that this was a niche market was quickly quashed by the sheer number of people who liked these photos.

Tears pricked my eyes as I realized that could be me on there. Next time I looked, there could be comments next to my photo, telling other men what they'd like to do to me. And it was no comfort to think the men I knew wouldn't go on there, wouldn't dream of looking at photos taken by a hidden camera in a woman's bathroom; I knew these things had ways of getting out.

It didn't take long to get a full grasp of what the site was about, and then I started to look for someone to e-mail. There were thousands of photos posted there since the date I was in London, and I couldn't face looking at them all. I wanted to ask someone what I could do if I found a photo of myself there, but try as I might, I just couldn't find any contact details. I suppose that on a normal site the owners are keen to be identified with it, whereas here they weren't. Then I realized that there was a Report button next to each of the photos and videos. Perhaps I could leave a message that way?

Still in Incognito mode, I created a new e-mail address for myself, using a fictitious name, then reported one of the posts:

```
Hi, I need to talk to someone about privacy and
can't find an e-mail address. Someone is threat-
ening to post explicit photos of me on this site.
Obviously I don't give permission for that. If I
see a photo of myself and report it, will it be
taken down? Thanks.
```

I added my new e-mail address to the end of the message and clicked Send. I doubted I'd get a reply, but I couldn't think what else to do.

Stella had asked me if I wanted them to take things further but confirmed I shouldn't hold out too much hope. 'What with throwaway phones being so cheap, and as it's more than a month after you met him in London, I really doubt whether there's anything we can do now. I do want you to keep in touch with us, though.' She gave me a contact number and I put it into my phone. 'If you think of anything else, you must tell me straight away. Don't try to contact this man.'

I nodded but she wasn't convinced.

'I mean it,' she said. 'If you want us to investigate, come back and I'll do what I can. But in the meantime, don't try to find him.'

'Right.'

We sat for a second while I got myself together, and then she said, 'I need to ask you something but I don't want to upset you further. Is it possible that you had sex that night?'

'No,' I said immediately. 'No, it's not possible. I would know, wouldn't I?' She said nothing and so I said again, 'No. I would know if I had. I would have noticed.'

28

Monday, August 7

By Monday morning I was desperate for Joe to come back, if only because I was taking a couple of days off when he returned.

'Are you feeling all right?' asked Sophie. She startled me; I must have been miles away, thinking about seeing Joe and Rory again. I looked up and saw her standing by my desk, a look of concern on her face.

'I'm fine, thanks.'

'Can I get you some water?'

'I'd love some.'

She fetched a bottle out of the fridge and passed it to me. It was only when I went to the cloakroom afterwards that I saw why she was worried: my face looked pale and tense, my eyes showing the strain of staying up late searching the voyeur site for naked photos of myself.

At the morning meeting I sat back while Rachel took control. She'd clearly watched me closely at those meetings and followed the same routine that I did. She seemed so much more confident now. I had a notebook on my knee to make notes to go through with her later, but I was too distracted and worried. While I made a pretence of listening to her, I made note after note of what had been done to me and what I had to do to make things right.

Lucy came into the office just as the meeting was about to end. I'd sent her a message asking her to call in when she dropped her daughter off at school. She sat down at the meeting table with us.

'Now that we're all here,' I said, 'I want to bring up the issue of safety. I don't want anyone to meet a client outside the office unless we have seen some form of ID. Check it carefully, then photocopy it and keep it with your files in the office. If you're unsure, ask me.'

'Why's that?' asked Rachel. 'Has something happened?'

'I'm just looking out for you,' I said. 'You've all heard about Suzy Lamplugh disappearing. In those days they just had to write the client's name in the diary. We do more than that since we collect their address, e-mail, phone number, et cetera, but it's still not enough. If we're taking clients to a property, we need to make sure we're safe. And if you have any doubts about a client – any at all – then make sure you don't go anywhere with them. I'll deal with them myself. If I'm not in, tell them they have to wait until I'm back. And when I'm not here, I want two of you to lock up together. If that's not possible, I'll come back to the office or send Joe to do it.'

They looked a bit subdued.

'Everyone still remembers the code word, don't they?'

'Anne-Marie Thomson,' said Sophie.

'That's right,' I said. Anne-Marie had been a friend of mine when I was in school and I'd chosen her name as our code word, which acted as a distress signal. If any one of us used it in a call, it was a signal that we needed help. 'Don't forget, it doesn't matter what you say, as long as you mention her name. You can say she'll be coming into the office later than planned or that you need to meet with her. Anything at all. Rachel, can you remind us what happens when Anne-Marie's name is mentioned?'

'We have to ask questions where the answer's yes or no,' she said promptly. 'Like "Are you where it says you are in your diary?" If the answer is no, we have to phone 999.'

'And don't forget, you must never go out without your panic alarm. If you leave it at home, let me know. There are spares in the cupboard, but I need to know if someone's taken them out. Do you remember the rule about always walking behind the client?'

Lucy said, 'That's quite a hard one to stick to. Some people are quite insistent that I go into the house first.'

'If you get any bad feeling about that, as though they're trying to make you do something you don't want to do, then don't go into the house with them. Always have an excuse prepared, like you need to get something from your car.'

They were in a pretty sombre mood by then.

'Has something happened?' asked Sophie. 'You've told us all this before, but . . .' She looked up at me and her face appeared so young and scared. 'I know I'm here in the office all the time, but it frightens me to think that someone might attack one of you. I'd hate to get a call where someone spoke about Anne-Marie.'

I could see that Rachel looked pale and scared too, as though she were panicking about what she'd do if someone frightened her when she was on her own. Lucy seemed more confident, though she was much more experienced and more likely to see trouble coming. I knew, though, how easily something could come out of the blue and destroy your sense of self.

'No, there's nothing for you to worry about,' I said. 'I was reading an article about personal safety the other day. A woman in Bolton is running courses; I'll get in touch with her later and ask for some advice.'

The Girl I Used to Be

After the meeting Rachel and I sat together and I went through some points she hadn't raised in the meeting.

'Thanks for not bringing them up in front of the others,' she said. She sounded a bit embarrassed and relieved. 'That was really nice of you.'

'It's okay,' I said. 'I remember what it was like when I first started holding the morning meetings.'

She looked at me, curious now. 'What, you were scared?'

I laughed. 'I was petrified. I used to work in London when I first left university. It was so competitive there, especially in the estate agency business.'

'I would have thought you'd like that. You're pretty competitive, though, aren't you?'

I shook my head. 'Not really. I just wanted to run my own business. In London . . . well, it got a bit cut-throat. All sorts of tricks were pulled. You used to work for Bailey and Harding back home, didn't you? That's the sort of place I want here.'

She nodded. 'I worked for them every weekend when I was at university, and then for about a year afterwards.'

'They gave you a great reference.'

She blushed. 'How was your mum when you went back the other day?' she asked. 'Did everything go well? She was at Arrowe Park, wasn't she?'

'What?' I'd completely forgotten that I'd told them I'd been up to see my mum when I'd really been in London. 'Oh yes, she was fine, thanks. It was just a checkup.'

We sat for a few more minutes. I could hear Sophie busy with the photocopier in the back office, and Brian was washing up the cups from our meeting.

'Do you ever go back there?' I asked Rachel.

She started. 'Back where?'

'Back home.' I smiled. 'I don't know why I call it home. I haven't lived there since I was eighteen.'

'There's nothing for me to go back for,' she said. 'And I was glad to get away. It doesn't hold very good memories for me.'

'Me neither.'

Rachel put all her papers back into her file and stood up. For a moment I saw her mouth tremble, and I felt guilty. Her mother had only died last year; it was obviously still raw. I watched her as she sat at her computer and drank some water. She was soon typing really fast, focused on her work, and I hoped she'd be all right.

Before I started work, I e-mailed the personal safety adviser and asked her to contact me. A reply bounced back saying she was on holiday until August 18 but that she'd be in touch, so I set up a reminder on my diary to make sure I contacted her then if I hadn't heard from her.

The morning went quickly, with a sudden rush of clients calling in around lunchtime, so we all had to abandon any hope of lunch. At three P.M., as usual, the office grew quieter. Everyone set about their routine jobs so that everything was arranged for the next morning. Sophie was in the window, stocking up the brochures, while Brian was on the phone to a plumber to fix a leak in a tenant's flat.

'Sophie, do you fancy running out for some cakes for everyone?' I asked. 'My treat.'

'Cakes? It's not your birthday, is it?'

'No, I just wanted to treat everyone. We need a sugar hit.'

While Sophie went off happily to the shops, I went over to Rachel's desk. 'I wanted to talk to you alone for a minute,' I said. 'How long have you been here now? Six months?'

Rachel nodded, her expression wary.

'You've worked really well. I've had this place for over seven years now and you've picked things up quicker than anyone else who's worked here.'

She blushed and looked down. Her hands played with the

rings on her fingers. 'I'd been working for Bailey and Harding, don't forget. I learned a lot there too.'

'Don't undervalue yourself. You've done really well here. And I've realized that I need someone who can stand in for me. I want to cut down my hours a bit; I want to spend more time with Rory. So, I thought I'd promote you to senior negotiator and look for someone new for your role. What do you think?'

She looked up, astonished. 'But you can't do that!'

I laughed. 'Why not?'

'But . . .' Her face was pink with embarrassment. 'What about Lucy? I thought she'd be coming back soon. I don't want her to think I'm taking her job.'

'Lucy's great, really great, but she only wants casual work for the next couple of years. Even then I think she'll just want part time. Anyway, I'm offering you a promotion; you shouldn't say someone else would be more suitable!'

She looked awkward and I realized just how young she was. She dressed older than her years and always looked well groomed, as though she wanted to be taken seriously at work, but she was still very young. I knew I'd done the right thing; she deserved this promotion.

Just then Sophie returned with the cakes and I stood to go back to my desk.

'Please would you make us some coffee, Sophie? We've got something to celebrate.'

29

Tuesday, August 8

There was just one day to go before Joe and Rory returned, and the house was lonelier than ever without them. As soon as I got home from work that night, I put the chicken and salad I'd picked up from the local deli into the fridge and went upstairs to have a bath. I poured bath oil into the running water and found my Kindle. I locked the bathroom door firmly behind me – something I rarely did when Joe and Rory were at home – and put my phone by the side of the bath. I wasn't going to take any chances.

    I lay in the bath and thought of Rachel and her pride in her promotion – she seemed embarrassed that her skills had been noticed and hardly met my eye after I told the others. Sophie was the opposite: she was very keen that I should know she was progressing well, and I half expected her to ask whether she could have Rachel's job, despite the fact that her only experience was a year in administration, but luckily she didn't.

    I sent Joe a text asking when Rory would be free for a chat, and he replied immediately, asking me to call in an hour. Perfect. I picked up my Kindle and started to read. The room was steamy now and the late-summer sun shone through the window, making it hard to see the screen. I jumped out of the bath to open the window, then sank back into the warm water to read some more.

I was just drifting into a nap when I heard a ping from my Kindle and jolted awake. My phone pinged then too, a second later. I clicked on the notification on my Kindle and my e-mail box opened.

I didn't recognize the sender's address. I frowned. Was this junk mail? The heading was *Are you ready?*

My stomach fell. I knew this was meant for me. I clicked on the e-mail. There seemed to be nothing there and then I saw a link. Should I click it? I thought of what Stella had said, that I shouldn't open any attachments or links, but I couldn't resist. I touched it lightly and held my breath.

An image appeared. A gif. It was a timer and it was counting down in seconds. The time left on the image was five hours and forty minutes. I stared at it as the numbers clicked over, then looked up at the clock on the bathroom shelf. It was now six twenty P.M.

It was counting down to midnight.

In a panic I clambered out of the bath, pulled a towel around me, and sat on the chair in the bathroom with my Kindle and phone. The same message was left unopened on my phone; it hadn't yet registered that I'd opened it on my Kindle.

My heart was thumping hard. What was going to happen at midnight? I would be here alone. Suddenly I was so scared I just didn't know what to do.

As quietly as I could, I slid open the lock on the bathroom door and peeped out into the bedroom. Everything looked the same as when I'd left it to have my bath. I pushed a chair against the bedroom door and dressed hurriedly. My mind worked frantically – what was going to happen? I couldn't stay here, that much I knew. I had to get out.

I checked my messages to see what Caitlin had said about when she was returning home. It was as I thought: she wouldn't be back for another week, so I couldn't go to her house. My mind raced as I tried to think where I could go. I thought of my other friends, but quickly abandoned that idea. Freya was a friend I'd made while I was on maternity leave with Rory; we still met up every now and again, but she'd had twins a year after her son was born and her life was really hectic now. Besides, she didn't have a spare room; I knew she wouldn't be able to put me up. It was only until tomorrow, when Joe was back, but even so I couldn't just turn up there; I hadn't even seen her for a few months, though we'd kept in touch on Facebook. And my friend Grace's husband had been unfaithful last year and had walked out when he was confronted; he'd been meeting the other woman in hotels all over the place, so I didn't want to tell her what I might have done in case she thought I was the same as him. Really, I wanted Caitlin, but she was Joe's sister – how could I tell her I might have been unfaithful to her brother? I'd lose her. I'd lose him.

I started to panic. If I lost Joe, I could lose Rory too. Joe was the one who took care of him each day, and yes, he could only do that because I worked all the hours I did, but the fact remained that he was Rory's primary caregiver. If Joe left me, he might take Rory with him. They might go and live in Ireland.

I felt dizzy at the thought of that. I was not going to lose my son. I wouldn't do anything that would put me in that position. But what could I do?

I had no choice. I grabbed an overnight bag from under the bed and crammed some clothes and toiletries in it for the next day, then picked up my handbag and car keys and left the house.

30

An hour later, I was in a hotel five miles from home and on the phone to Joe. It was only when I was safely in the room that I remembered I was supposed to be calling to speak to Rory. I'd decided not to say anything to Joe while he was away, and still couldn't figure out whether to *tell* him, or even what to tell him.

'Is Rory there?'

'I'm so sorry, Gem. He's flaked out already. I gave him a bath and brushed his teeth and went downstairs for his cup of water and by the time I came back up he was flat out.'

'Can you take a photo of him? I really want to see him.'

'Okay.' I could hear him smiling and my heart just reached out to him. I wanted to be near him, to hold him. Both of them. I shouldn't have agreed to them going away without me. I could hear Joe walking upstairs, then heard his mother's voice. He said, 'Won't be long,' and I didn't know whether he was talking to her or to me, but then a few seconds later my text alert sounded and Rory was on the screen. He was lying in a double bed with his two little cousins, his blonde hair tousled, his Spider-Man pyjamas pulled up to show his plump belly. All of them were asleep, snuggled up against each other, their faces pink and scrubbed after their bath.

I enlarged the photo so that I could see only Rory's face. Tears welled in my eyes and I brushed them away. 'He's grown since I saw him,' I said. 'He looks more like a boy than a toddler.'

'Oh now, we've only been gone a few days!'

'So you'll be back tomorrow?'

He laughed. 'Have you missed me?'

'Put it this way, you're not going away without me again.'

'What, ever?'

'No,' I said. 'I miss you too much. I need you here.'

'I promise. How's work?'

'I've decided to promote Rachel to senior negotiator. She's going to take over some of my jobs and in a while I'll take on a junior. It'll mean I can get some time off in the week.'

There was a silence, and then he said, 'That was a very quick decision.' He sounded hurt; we usually talked over staffing issues together. 'Won't it be expensive?'

'Would you prefer me to work every day?'

'No, no, of course not.' He sounded defensive. 'Stop putting words into my mouth. You know I didn't mean that.'

'There's no alternative.' Anger surged through me. He was on his holidays with his mum looking after him and he wanted me to carry on without any help! 'Either I work every single day or I take on someone new. One or the other.'

He was quiet and I guessed he was figuring out whether the business could afford more staff.

'I need to go,' I said, though actually there was nothing I needed to do. I hadn't brought any work home with me for a change, and I only had my Kindle for company. 'I'll see you tomorrow. Send me a text when the ferry arrives in Holyhead and I'll make sure I'm home to meet you.'

I sounded subdued, I knew, and he hated that.

'Oh, okay then, if that's how it is,' he said. 'I'll give your love to Rory.' He ended the call and I knew that if he could have slammed down his phone, he would have.

I didn't know what to do then. I couldn't go home. I could not be in my bed at home at midnight, waiting for something to happen. What if someone came into my house? I broke into a cold sweat at the thought of that. I put the television on and flicked mindlessly through the channels. I couldn't concentrate. I couldn't think straight. What on earth was I doing alone in a hotel? I was being chased out of my own house. I thought of calling the policewoman, Stella, but by now it was eight o'clock and I guessed she wouldn't be at work. And what could I tell her?

I looked at the e-mail again. What if Stella said that it was just junk mail? I knew it wasn't, but how could I prove it?

Quickly I sent a reply:

Why are you doing this? What is it you want?

Just typing that message made me feel pathetic. That didn't stop me from sending it, though. Thirty seconds later it bounced back: there was no such e-mail address. Of course there wasn't. He'd closed it now.

31

At nine that night my phone beeped with a message. My heart leaped as I thought it was Joe, apologizing for our argument earlier. No such luck. An e-mail had arrived from the voyeur site in response to my query.

We operate under DMCA law, it said. There was a link to Wikipedia's Digital Millennium Copyright Act. If someone makes an abuse request we process it and remove content from the site.

Well, that was a relief. Now all I had to do was to find the photos. I switched my iPad on and started to search the site again, trying desperately to find any photos David had taken of me. I dreaded seeing them, but at least I knew now I could have them taken off the site. As I scrolled through pages and pages of images of women – yes, all women – being photographed in intimate situations, without a clue they were going to end up on a site like that, I started to cry. What kind of person was I dealing with here?

I tried to sleep but couldn't. The hotel bed was comfortable, the room was warm, and I felt safe there, but I lay in bed wondering what on earth I was going to do. I had to admit everything to Joe, I knew that. Part of me thought I should sell up, move to Ireland as Joe wanted, and leave all my problems behind. I could change my e-mail addresses and contact numbers, go back to my maiden name, even, and just run away. And part of me really did think that was what I should do; it was the only thing I could do. But then I got furious, with David and with myself. Why should I do that? Why should I have to hide when I hadn't done anything wrong? Even if I'd invited him back to my hotel room in London, even if I'd *asked* him to take those photos, there was still no reason for him to torment me like that.

And then, just before eleven P.M., I thought again of the countdown gif. I opened the e-mail again and the timer was still ticking down. Seventy minutes to go now. Suddenly I was in a blind panic, wondering what would happen then. He would assume I was in my house, wouldn't he? What was he planning?

I jumped out of bed and got dressed. If something was going to happen, I needed to know about it.

I spent an hour driving around my neighbourhood. All was quiet; it always was late at night in that part of town. I didn't know what I was looking for or what I'd do if I found it. I drove past my house and watched as the neighbours' lights popped off for the night. The road was quiet; the only cars around were ones I recognized.

When it was nearly midnight, I parked near my house and took out my phone. I opened the e-mail and clicked on the timer gif and watched as the digits clicked nearer to their goal. In another window I opened the voyeur site and clicked frantically on the Latest Pickings section. Just the name of that made me feel sick. That last minute to midnight seemed to last an hour; I held my breath as the figures changed. What was going to happen? I had visions of my phone ringing, of a photo appearing online, of seeing someone approach my house.

Nothing happened.

I sat and watched the street, my hand clutching my phone, feverishly refreshing the screen, reassuring myself that if someone went into my house I'd see them and if something appeared online I'd see it. Nothing stirred on the street and the screen remained full of strangers. At half past twelve, I started the car. There were some parked cars by the side of the road, but nobody sat in them. The street was empty, the alleyways were clear, but still I drove quietly up and down, my eyes straining to see if anyone was around.

Finally, exhausted, I headed back towards the hotel. The receptionist greeted me and asked if I had my key card. I nodded, unable to speak, and took the lift to my room, where I collapsed into bed wondering what the hell that had been about.

32

Wednesday, August 9

I overslept the next morning and reached the office ten minutes after Rachel and Sophie, though as I'd given Rachel the spare key, they didn't have to wait around outside. When I walked in, I felt Rachel's eyes on me.

'What's up?' I asked.

'You look tired. Are you okay?'

I said, 'I'm fine,' but when I went into the cloakroom I grimaced as I saw what she meant. I always prided myself on looking groomed, but that day my skin was dry and patchy, its usual response to stress, and my make-up was all over the place. My eyes were red from lack of sleep and I quickly put on glasses to hide them. I locked myself in the cloakroom and spent a while tidying myself up, but I could still see everyone staring at me when I came out.

'We'll have the meeting in five minutes, shall we?' asked Rachel, sorting out the files on her desk.

I looked up, startled. Even though I'd happily promoted her, it was odd to realize that responsibility for that task would no longer be solely mine. 'Yes, just give me a moment.'

'It's just that it's now nine fifteen and I've a few things I need to get through,' she said. 'I got here early so I've made a list of all the overnight enquiries.'

That put me in my place. I bit hard on my lip and tried to stop myself from making a sharp comment.

'Okay. Let's start,' I said.

Rachel sat at the head of the table, just where I'd sat from the first day I opened the office seven years ago. I didn't mind; I wanted to pass it all on, but it felt strange and I could tell that Sophie and Brian were uneasy. They kept glancing over at me as I sat in Rachel's old seat, as though I was going to object, to oust her from her place.

I reached into my bag and pulled out my iPad, so that I could make a few notes on the meeting. When I switched it on, it opened at the voyeur site; I must have fallen asleep with it still open. Hastily I switched it off again, then picked up a pen and a notepad from the nearest desk. My face was hot with embarrassment. Had anyone seen the screen? I glanced up at the others. Sophie's expression was as plain as daylight; all she was thinking about was whether to have a cake with her morning coffee. I looked at Brian – was he averting his eyes? Oh God, what if he thought I was looking at porn?

Then I realized Rachel was looking at me closely. She was the one I really hoped hadn't seen my screen. She noticed everything; while that was great at work, I really, really didn't want her to know my private business. I gave her a questioning look and she avoided my eyes, then started the meeting.

We had a number of things to get through in a short time, and I watched Rachel organize everything that needed to be done that day. She was very efficient, and fair, too, I thought; in the past I'd worked with people who, once they were promoted, refused to take on any of the boring or awkward jobs themselves, but she wasn't like that.

'You did a good job today,' I told her, once the meeting was over.

She blushed. 'Thanks.'

'It'll be easier on the days when I'm not here,' I said. 'The last thing you want is me watching you.'

'Oh, that's okay,' she said, but I knew I was right.

Joe sent me a text at three P.M. telling me they'd just arrived at Holyhead. Within minutes I'd packed up my things, ready to go home.

'You're in a rush!' said Sophie.

'I'm just desperate to see them.'

She smiled. 'Have a lovely evening. See you on Friday.'

I'd picked up groceries in the supermarket at lunchtime, so I was able to dash back home to get dinner ready for Joe and Rory. It would take them a couple of hours to get home from Holyhead if the traffic was good, so I had time to cook for them. At the front door I took the post from the letter box and put it on the hall table. Everywhere still looked lovely after the cleaners had been there, and I wondered how long I'd be able to fool Joe that I'd done it.

They arrived home at five P.M. I heard the car pull into the driveway and ran out of the house to greet them. Rory gave a shriek of joy when he saw me and flung himself into my arms when I opened the car door. I held him close to me, rocking him as though he were a baby. I breathed in the sweet scent of his shampoo, felt his T-shirt rise up as my arms held him, so I could feel his skin, soft and warm and damp from the heat of the car.

And then Joe was behind him, his arms around both of us. 'We've missed you.'

My throat tightened. 'I've missed you too.' I thought of the loneliness I'd felt since he'd gone, the worries I'd had. *I'll tell him*, I thought. *I'll tell him tonight. Everything will be all right. He'll help me sort it out.* He hugged me tighter, and for that moment I truly believed it would all be okay. He was on my side.

In the house, dinner was ready for them. I took the roast lamb out of the oven and put it onto the counter ready to be carved. The gratin dauphinois was bubbling and golden and the air smelled of garlic and rosemary. The patio doors were open and the table was set for dinner, with roses in bud vases and our special-occasion glasses and cutlery shining on the crisp white linen tablecloth.

'Wow, this place is clean!' said Joe. He turned to me, a guilty expression on his face. 'I'm really sorry it was such a mess when we left. How long did it take you to clean up?'

'Oh, you know,' I said. 'I did it as I went along.'

'It looks brand new!' Rory said, and promptly tipped his biggest box of Lego onto the rug.

'How are you?' asked Joe. He held me tightly and kissed the side of my neck. 'Anything been happening while we were away?'

I hesitated. 'There'll be lots to talk about. Let's get Rory fed and bathed first, eh?'

We sat at the dining table to eat our dinner. Joe lit candles around the room, though it wasn't yet dark, and poured us a glass of wine and a cup of juice for Rory, and they told me what they'd been up to in Ireland.

After dinner I let them go upstairs ahead of me, as I wanted to hear their reaction to the rooms up there. The cleaners must have spent hours putting everything back in drawers – my husband and son were so messy and favoured the floor for everything. As they walked upstairs I noticed the mail that had arrived earlier in the day. There was a bowl of white roses on the hall table and a couple of petals had fallen onto the envelopes. I picked up the mail and gave it a cursory glance. A renewal for our car insurance. A takeaway food leaflet. A letter from a credit card company we'd never used; I assumed it was junk mail. At the bottom of the pile was a padded envelope addressed to me. I was just about to open it when something about it made me stop in my tracks. I knew I hadn't ordered anything lately. Was he sending something to my home? But how would he know where I lived?

Even as I raised that question, the answer was there. I knew that if I Googled myself, my home address could be easily discovered.

I heard Joe's exclamations as he saw how tidy and clean everything was upstairs and his footsteps as he came to the top of the stairs. Before he could come down, I shoved the envelope into my handbag and zipped it shut.

'Yes!' I called as I ran upstairs towards them. 'I've been really busy!'

33

It was hours before I could check the envelope. I left my handbag downstairs by the front door when I went up to Joe and Rory. I knew that otherwise I'd be looking at it all the time, willing them to go away so that I could open it. We stayed upstairs all evening. Rory had his bath; I'd so missed doing that each night, missed his warm, sweet body as he'd stand up in the bath ready to come out, his skin slippery with bubbles. As usual he soaked me as he leaped out, but that night there were no recriminations, just gratitude that he was back home. A little voice at the back of my mind kept saying, *This is how it would be, not seeing him for days at a time*, and the fear of that just kept me frozen, stopped me from saying anything to Joe. After I'd read Rory a record-breaking number of stories, he finally dozed off. By then I'd changed into my pyjamas as I was so wet after his bath, and Joe had had a shower.

'Shall we go downstairs?' he asked. 'Watch some television?'

I groaned at the thought. 'I'm going to stay up here, I think.'

'Good idea,' he said. 'You look like you need a rest. You must have been working so hard, cleaning the whole house.'

We lay on the bed, his arm around me, and chatted about his trip to Ireland.

'So Brendan and Sarah are moving back there?'

'Yes, they're planning to be there within the next few months. They'll rent their house out over here, to keep their options open. He's trying to persuade his boss to give him a leave of absence for a year, so they have the freedom to come back if they want.'

'Good idea. But what happens if one wants to stay and the other wants to leave?' I couldn't see Sarah putting up with her in-laws getting as involved in their lives as they'd like to be. 'Are they going to live near your mum and dad?'

He ignored the first question I'd asked. 'Yes, they're looking for houses now.'

My heart sank. I could tell from the longing in his voice that it was something he was really keen to do as well.

We were quiet then and I knew he wanted to talk about us going there. I was desperate to sleep, but I knew that if I didn't say something he'd be awake for ages thinking about it.

'You do know we couldn't do that, don't you?' I asked. 'My job's here. My business. I couldn't just pack up and leave here and start again in another country.'

He squeezed me tight. 'Nothing's impossible, sweetheart.'

'Seriously, Joe. We couldn't do it. I don't know the first thing about the property market in Ireland.'

'Oh, you'd be fine,' he said. 'Okay, so the laws are different, but essentially it'd be the same, wouldn't it?'

'Do you have a time in mind?' I asked, my voice tight with irritation. 'When would you like to go?'

He squeezed me tighter. I didn't know how he hadn't noticed my body was rigid. 'I was thinking maybe the end of the year?'

'What? You want me to close down my business, arrange management for the rentals, sell this house, move to Ireland, buy another house, and set up another company in the next four months?'

'We wouldn't have to do it all at once. We could get a manager in to do your job.'

'One manager?' I asked. 'I'm at work every day of the week!'

'Perhaps two, then, job sharing. We could rent out this house, too. Brian would look after it. And there's no rush with setting up over there. We could settle in and you could get used to the area.'

'But where would we live?'

'If we were renting this place out, we could rent somewhere over there,' he said. 'Just take a short contract at first till we found somewhere we liked.'

I was quiet. I hadn't realized he'd thought this through, and I wondered now whether he and his brother had cooked it up between them.

'Nothing's impossible,' he said again. 'You just have to want it enough.'

'But I *don't* want it enough!' I shouted, unable to hold back any longer. 'I don't want it at all!'

'You'd see more of Sarah,' he said. 'You like her.'

'And I wouldn't see as much of Caitlin,' I said. 'If I wanted to see more of Sarah, I would. It's my own son I want to see more of.' I could hear my voice wobble now. 'I need to spend time with him. I don't want to be left behind while you take him on holiday.' I could feel Joe's hostility; he was always like that when he felt guilty. 'And I especially don't want to have to clean up after you while you go on holiday.'

As I said this I knew there was no going back and I would never be able to admit to having the cleaning service. I felt so angry in that moment, it was as though I *had* scrubbed the house from top to toe.

We lay in silence. I was full of things I wanted to say, but I just didn't feel that I could. I never had; I could only say what I wanted, what I needed, when we were fighting, and then afterwards, when we'd made up, Joe would think the problem was resolved. I hated it; I hated being unable to assert myself. I lay there simmering, thinking of things I should have said to make him see my point of view, and then I realized his breathing had slowed down and that he was asleep.

I slid out of bed and took my dressing gown from its hook. At the door I paused. Joe didn't move; his breathing didn't alter. I pulled the door closed and went downstairs to get a glass of water.

Once Joe got hold of an idea, he found it hard to let it go. Obviously he'd guessed I wouldn't want to go to Ireland to live, but if his brother and sister-in-law were going, then he must have thought he'd have a bigger chance of persuading me. It wasn't Ireland that bothered me. It wasn't as though I had an emotional connection to Chester. My friends now were mainly from university and were scattered all over the world. My mum and dad were still on the Wirral and I saw them every few weeks, but the flights to Ireland were cheap and they had just retired, so were young enough to travel.

It was work that was the problem. How could I set up a business over there? It was a completely different country! I felt a surge of anger at the thought of his suggestion. I knew, too, that I'd struggle to talk this through with him in the cold light of day.

And then I remembered the padded envelope. The argument forgotten now, I sat at the table and opened my bag. I took out the envelope and looked at the label. It was neatly typed and addressed to me, and it reminded me then of the envelope that had arrived containing the photo. Suddenly I was scared. I didn't want to open it. I didn't want to see what else this nutcase had sent me. But I had to. I had to know. He'd upped his game now, sending something to me at home.

My hands shook as I ripped it open. I kept hoping that it would be nothing.

When I saw what was inside, it took me a minute or two to comprehend it. It was a piece of black silk. Black silk with pink embroidered roses on it. I blinked hard. Those were my knickers. What the hell were they doing here?

There was a thud from upstairs and I leaped up from my seat. Was that Joe? I stood in the doorway, my heart pounding, then heard Rory give a little wail. I shoved the knickers into my dressing gown pocket and put the envelope back into my bag, then ran upstairs to my boy, who was wondering where I was.

34

Thursday, August 10

The next day was pretty quiet. Joe seemed to find plenty of excuses to leave me alone with Rory, which suited me just fine. Rory was tired after his trip and was happy to potter around with me. We spent the morning doing some gardening, and in the afternoon I took him swimming and to the park. Later we had a barbecue in the garden and invited one of his friends from nursery; they played on the lawn in a little tent, while I relaxed on the sun lounger. This was as close as I was going to get to a summer holiday, and the jealousy I felt as Joe planned what he was going to do over the next few weeks with Rory was overwhelming. I felt a band tightening around my head at the thought of having this conversation with Joe again.

He hadn't talked any more about going to Ireland but had seemed pretty distant. Normally he'd be all over me after a trip away, but now he seemed cautious, as though he was tiptoeing around me. That wasn't what I wanted, but it gave me an excuse not to confide in him about David. I didn't know where I'd stand with that now. Ever since I'd found my underwear in the mail I'd had trouble breathing whenever I thought of David.

That evening, after Rory's friend had gone home, I was going from the garden into the house to get the bath ready for Rory, and as I walked into the hallway, I saw the shadow of someone through the coloured-glass panels of the front door. The figure seemed to hesitate, and then slowly something was pushed through the door.

Without time for the thought to process, I'd collapsed onto the bottom stair. It was as though I were underwater; all I could hear was the sound of my own blood thrumming through my veins. Black splodges appeared in front of my eyes and whatever I looked at seemed to be moving.

'Gemma? What is it?' Joe ran through the kitchen to the hallway where I sat. 'Are you all right?'

I turned to look at him. It seemed to take hours. I couldn't see his face properly; it was blurred. Out of focus.

'Put your head between your knees,' he said sharply. 'Breathe in slowly. Come on, Gem, you can do this.' He crouched down beside me and put his hand on my shoulder.

I tried to focus, to breathe, but I had to see what had come through the door. If it was another envelope, I had to get hold of it before Joe saw it.

I pushed him away. 'Give me some space.'

He moved back and I could see a brightly coloured sheet of paper lying on the doormat. I felt weak with relief; it was just a pizza delivery leaflet.

Slowly my breathing returned to normal. Joe stood beside me, his face pale and concerned. 'What is it, sweetheart? I haven't seen you like that for years. Has this happened while I've been away?'

I looked up at him, feeling lonelier in that moment than I'd ever felt. Who could help me?

'It's okay,' I said, struggling to my feet. 'I don't know what happened. I felt a bit faint, that's all.'

He helped me upstairs, then insisted I lie on our bed while he went back down to get Rory.

'I'll sort his bath out,' he said. 'Just lie there and try to relax. And I don't think you should be going in to work tomorrow, either. Or not in the morning, at any rate. You need to rest. You've been working too hard, what with the office and cleaning the house.' He had the grace to look shamefaced at that. I knew I should have told him the truth; I knew he would normally find it funny, but I didn't want to. I felt he was in the wrong, leaving the place a mess. If he felt guilty now, there was a chance he'd up his game a bit.

'I can't stay off work tomorrow. Rachel's got a couple of days off. She's going with some friends to Amsterdam for a hen weekend and won't be in until Monday afternoon. She's been going on about it for months.' It showed how little Joe and I had talked lately that he didn't know this.

'What about Lucy?'

I shook my head. 'She can only do school hours. I need to be there to open and close if Rachel's not there.'

'Couldn't Brian do it?'

'It's his day off tomorrow. I'll be fine. Don't worry.'

He sat down on the bed next to me. 'I'm worried about you, Gem.' He reached out to put his arm around me, but I flinched. I don't know why, it was automatic, and the hurt on his face was plain to see. He went out of the room, closing our bedroom door tightly. I heard him in the family bathroom, calling Rory in to him.

'I want Mummy to do it,' I heard Rory say.

I couldn't hear Joe's reply, but a moment later Rory shrieked with laughter. I didn't think he was missing me.

An hour after Rory got into the bath, he came tumbling into my room, holding a big fluffy towel around him.

'You must be waterlogged,' I said, getting off the bed to dry him. 'I'll get your pyjamas. Just wait a minute.'

As I took his pyjamas from his chest of drawers, he shouted, 'Can I wear your dressing gown, Mummy?'

I laughed. 'Put your pyjamas on first, then.' I helped him into them, then said, 'Which one do you want tonight?'

'The blue one,' he said. 'The one with the flowers on.'

He climbed onto my bed and I draped my Chinese robe around his shoulders, just as he liked it, and he rubbed his face against the silk. I asked him which books he wanted me to read and went into his room to find them. When I took them back into my bedroom, I got onto the bed beside him and opened one of the books. Before I could read a word, he started to laugh.

'What's up, poppet?' asked Joe from the doorway.

Rory laughed. 'Mummy's knickers are in her pocket!'

My head shot round. 'What?'

Rory held up my black silk knickers, the ones that had arrived through the post yesterday. I'd completely forgotten that I'd shoved them into my dressing gown pocket. He waved them in the air. 'Look!'

I grabbed them off him and threw them into the laundry basket on the landing.

'Why were they in your pocket?' Joe's voice was both curious and wary.

I shrugged. 'I found them on the floor downstairs yesterday and put them in my pocket so I could put them in the laundry basket.'

'But there was nothing on the floor yesterday,' he said. 'Everywhere was pristine.' He tried to joke. 'I would have noticed a pair of knickers, believe me!'

I shrugged. 'They must have fallen out of the basket when I took it downstairs.' I didn't think I was going to be able to keep this up. 'Anyway, gentlemen' – I poked Rory in his tummy – 'never ask a lady about her knickers!' Rory shrieked with laughter. I could see that Joe was still looking confused, but I just said, 'I'll read to Rory now, then.'

'Okay.' He stood looking at me for a few seconds longer. I shot him a bright smile and opened Rory's book. The door closed gently behind Joe and I heard his footsteps as he ran downstairs. I breathed a sigh of relief. What an idiot I'd been, leaving them in my pocket like that. All the time I was reading to Rory, I thought of Joe and the lies I'd told over the last few weeks.

I could hardly recognize myself.

35

Friday, August 11

Work was quiet the next day, with just Sophie and Lucy around. Brian had taken a day's holiday and Lucy was covering for him. Rachel was on the seven A.M. flight to Amsterdam; she'd sent Sophie a text just before the plane took off to say a big crowd of men on a stag weekend had got onto the plane, all drinking cans of beer and causing general disruption.

After lunch, when Sophie was out and Lucy was busy with a client, a call came through on Brian's line. He had a dedicated line for rentals and I scooted across the office to pick it up.

'It's Zoe Hodge here,' said the caller. 'I'm a tenant at 50 Globe Street.'

'Oh yes,' I said, quickly checking our database. 'You're in flat three?'

'Yes. I've given in my notice and I'm leaving this weekend. Brian said he'd come round and do the inventory before I left.'

Those flats weren't furnished but were carpeted and came with a fully fitted kitchen. We had to check carefully when a tenant left, so that we could repair or replace anything for the next tenant. I looked up the property on our system; Zoe had been living there for four years. Then I looked at Brian's diary online and saw that he'd made a note to carry out the inventory the following afternoon.

When I told Zoe this, she said, 'I wondered whether it could be done today? I'd rather he did it while I was here, just in case there are any queries.'

'Just a moment,' I said. 'I need to look at my own diary.' I went back to my desk and checked. 'I'm not free until five P.M.,' I said, 'but I could come then, on my way home from work, if you like.'

'That'd be great,' she said. 'I'm moving my stuff all afternoon, but I'll try to make sure I'm back then. If you're there before me, do you want to just let yourself in and make a start on it?'

'As long as you're all right with that. Keep your phone with you so I can contact you.'

I made a note in Brian's diary and then in my own. When Lucy got off the phone, I asked her if she and Sophie could lock up so that I could make a head start on the inventory.

'That's where Rachel lives, isn't it?' she said. 'She's on the ground floor.'

'Yes, Brian was asking her if she knew anyone who wanted to move in to Zoe's flat, but she didn't. It's a shame she's away. She could have come with me and learned how to do an inventory.'

'You made the right choice promoting her,' said Lucy. 'She's a good worker, isn't she? Picks things up really quickly.'

'And calm, too,' I said. We watched Sophie hurry across the road to the office. She was ten minutes late back from lunch. There was no need for us to say a word.

Globe Street was very narrow, with only residents' parking, so I parked in a small car park off the nearby main road and walked around the corner to the property. At the entrance to the street there were workmen repairing a pothole, but apart from them there was nobody else about. There were six flats in the block, two on each floor. Zoe lived upstairs, on the same side of the building as Rachel. I remembered Rachel coming back to the office with Brian after he'd shown her around, her face lit up with happiness and relief. In that afternoon she'd got herself a job and a flat nearby and she looked a different woman from the nervous one who'd turned up to the interview.

'Did you like it?' I'd asked.

'I love it!' she said. 'I was expecting something like student accommodation, but it's great.'

'The landlady for that building is really good,' I said. 'She takes excellent care of it, but if you have any problems, you must let Brian know and he'll get it sorted. We're the managing agent, so everything comes through us.'

'And I can move in straight away?'

'Yes,' said Brian. 'It's empty now. Move in whenever you like and we'll start the tenancy from there. And if you go to work somewhere else,' he added, 'then of course that won't affect your tenancy at all, though you'll still have to come through us if there are any problems.'

'I hope that won't be for a while!' I said.

'Me too.'

She'd been in the flat for several months now and seemed happy there. As far as I was aware she hadn't complained about anything at all; I knew Brian would have told me if she had. Her living room faced the front garden and the street, and I could see she had photo frames and vases on the deep windowsill there. There were blinds at all the windows in the block, and hers were half drawn.

I stopped at the entrance to the building. There were six bells on the wall and an intercom grille next to them. I rang the bell for Zoe's flat, but there was no answer. I guessed she was taking her things to her new home, so I used the keys I'd brought with me and let myself in. Inside, the staircase and hallway were carpeted with a warm thick-pile carpet and the only furniture was a small table with a flowering azalea on it. The landlady paid for the shared area to be cleaned every week and I could smell polish in the air; presumably the cleaners had been in that day.

I ran upstairs to Zoe's flat and knocked at the door. When there was no answer, I opened it. I called, 'Hello,' just in case she was in the bathroom, but there was no reply. In the living room were a couple of suitcases and a pair of bedside lamps, and apart from a few boxes in the kitchen, nothing else was left there. She'd clearly been busy all day. I moved one of the suitcases to wedge the door open, so that she wouldn't panic if she heard someone in the flat when she returned.

The inventory she'd signed when she moved in was on my clipboard, and I searched for a pen in my bag. Just then I heard the sound of the front door downstairs opening. For a moment I heard the dull roar of the road drill outside, and then the door clicked shut and all was quiet again. I went out onto the landing and was just about to call out Zoe's name when I heard a cough. I leaned forward to look through the banisters into the hallway below and froze.

A man stood outside the door to Rachel's flat. In his arms were several carrier bags. He put his key in the lock and pushed the door open.

I held my breath.

I heard him dump the bags on the floor, and then he went back to the front door and opened the mailbox with a key.

Just then a mobile phone rang downstairs, making me jump almost through the ceiling. Instinctively I scrabbled in my pocket to find my own phone and muted it.

'Hey, babe,' the man said, and in that instant my head started to buzz. I took a step back from the banisters. 'Everything okay?'

There was silence while he listened to the caller, and then he said, 'Yeah, I've just got home.' He laughed. 'No, just going to get changed, then I'm off out.' Silence again. I couldn't breathe. 'Not sure. No, of course I won't. I'm meeting Danny in Liverpool.' More silence, and then he said, 'Hold on, just let me get in and you can tell me all about it.' I heard him walk into the flat and slam the door shut.

For a moment, I stood like a fool, unable to believe what I'd heard.

Why was David in Rachel's flat?

Part II

36

Rachel

Friday, August 11

It was so good to be sitting in a bar in Amsterdam with my old friends from university that first afternoon. We'd had lunch and then it started to rain, so we'd found the nearest cocktail bar and were steadily making our way through the menu. I was a lightweight compared to them, though, and had to alternate cocktails with soft drinks so that I didn't make a fool of myself.

I hadn't seen the other girls for three years, since leaving university, though it was clear they'd kept in touch all that time. They all lived in London now, had gone through graduate training, and were earning more than twice my salary. I was still friends with them on Facebook and kept up with their lives there, but I used private messaging to chat to them and never posted anything about myself.

There were six of us that weekend. I met them at the airport; they'd flown in from Gatwick and had waited around for my flight from Liverpool to come in. I know this sounds weird, but I felt like a normal person, meeting them. I'd had my hair and nails done, just as I knew they would have. I'd bought clothes and shoes and bags specially for the weekend, and spent a fortune on a cabin bag for the flight. I'd scoured Facebook for details of where they'd shopped and I made sure I went to the same places. I looked just like them when I arrived, and saw a couple of them glance at each other in surprise. I'd always been a bit of a mouse at university; I had so many responsibilities at home, making sure the bills were paid and my mum was fed and looked after, and I neglected myself a bit. I couldn't see the point in wearing make-up or fashionable clothes when all I did was sit in lectures and go straight home again. I was depressed – I can see that now – and it showed in the way I looked. Now, now that everything's going well, I look better. I spend a lot of time on my clothes, my hair. I go to the gym regularly. I feel great, really I do.

At university I'd never felt part of their gang; at least now I looked as though I was. I made so much effort to fit in that weekend, but by the time I came back, my face was strained with smiling too much, my head pounded with jokes I didn't quite get, and I knew that now, just as then, I didn't fit in. And I knew why – it was my secrets that kept me apart.

I'd never told them a thing about my mum when I was at university, and I didn't mention her now. They had no idea she'd died or even how she lived. I don't know why I said nothing; I knew they would have supported me, come to the funeral, helped me with the house. I couldn't bear them to set foot in my house, though, to see it as it was now. I couldn't bear to tell them about my mum and why she was the way she was. Our lives were too different and their pity would have been too much for me. It was easier to be alone, I'd found.

In those days at university, while they trooped off to a house party at the end of the night, I'd leave them to it and look for a taxi that would take me through the tunnel to the Wirral – not easy when the driver knew he wouldn't get a return fare. I'd tell them I was tired, that I had to go home, and they'd lose interest, sometimes going off without even saying goodbye. I got nervous if I stayed out too long; I had to check that my mum was all right, that she hadn't set the house on fire or done some drunk-dialling.

Now, when I look at it objectively, I can see that I have to take some responsibility. I could have forced her to see a doctor. I could have moved away and left her to it. I could have told my friends about her. Instead I got used to living two lives; one in public and one in private. That was good preparation for now, really.

My mum would always be awake when I got back. Not waiting up for me, nothing like that. We'd switched the mother and daughter roles long ago. She'd be awake because she was drinking. She'd go out to the taxi to pay my fare, no matter what time of night it was, and would try to spark up a conversation with the poor taxi driver, who just wanted to get back on the road. I'd hover around her, trying to usher her back into the house.

'It's a miserable night for you,' she'd say, and I'd hear the guy say, 'What?' and I'd realize that by now she was so far gone that nobody else knew what she was saying. And of course taxi drivers are used to drunks; it was a sign of how bad she was that they couldn't understand a word she said.

She'd stumble back into the house, having given the guy a huge tip or, once, a penny, and she'd look at me and my heart would sink. It would go one of two ways, then: either she'd cry and talk about the past, or she'd turn on me.

I don't know which I hated more.

But all that was over now and I knew I shouldn't dwell on it. That afternoon, as agreed, I called David and spent ten minutes giggling on the phone. I missed him so much; it was hardly worth my going away. I was sharing a hotel room with my friend Emma, so I wasn't sure how much I'd be able to talk to him at night. He and I had never been apart since the day we met. I wasn't sure how it would feel to be alone now, after being with him.

I must have looked miserable at that thought, then, because the bride-to-be, Laura, nudged me and whispered, 'Are you okay?'

I smiled at her. 'Yes, I'm fine. Having a great time.'

'Me too,' she said. 'I'm sorry you can't make the wedding.' This had been a bit of a sore topic within the group; we'd had over a year's notice, after all, but as David said, there was no way we wanted our photos on social media.

'Oh I am, too!' I said. 'I would have loved to be there. I'd already paid for the holiday, though.'

'That's okay. And thanks so much for the wedding gift. It arrived last week.' She looked so pleased, then, her irritation at my pulling out of the wedding assuaged by my choosing one of the more expensive presents she'd registered at a top department store. She put her hand on my arm and the diamonds in her engagement ring twinkled. 'It's so good to see you again. You look great. So much happier.'

I really didn't want to go into how I'd been in the past. As David said, there was no point in thinking about that now. So I shifted the attention back to her.

'That's a lovely ring,' I said. 'What's your wedding ring like?'

She curled up next to me and I was treated to a long, long description of her shopping trip with her fiancé for wedding rings. When she'd finished, she squeezed my arm and said, 'It'll be your turn soon. Maybe that guy you were calling just now?' She winked at me. 'Don't think I didn't notice.'

I laughed. 'Maybe.'

I'd never told any of them about David. None of my friends knew anything about him and none of his knew about me.

'We're the world's best-kept secret,' he'd say.

He was right; it was much more romantic that way.

37

Gemma

I stayed on the staircase for a moment after David went into Rachel's flat. I didn't know what to do. The late-afternoon sun shone through the hallway window upstairs and I stood, my face and body hot and sweating, as I strained to hear him in the flat below. If I leaned over the banisters, I could hear the deep rumble of his voice as he talked on the phone.

Silently I tiptoed into Zoe's flat. I hesitated in the doorway, wondering whether to shut the door so that she'd have to use her key, but I worried that she'd forget I was meant to be there and be startled by me. Instead I left the door ajar and moved as quietly as I could through the living room and into the kitchen. I stood to one side of the kitchen window and looked out into the yard below. It had been a hot day; I saw that the back door to Rachel's flat was opened out onto her patio, and thought, *So he must be staying a while, then*.

I looked at my watch. It was five twenty. He'd said he was going to Liverpool for a night out with his friend. It would take him an hour or so to get there. I guessed he'd be having a shower before he went, but couldn't be sure. I was terrified of bumping into him as I left the building; just the thought of that was enough to make my heart race. And then I remembered that the bathroom in this flat was above Rachel's; each flat was identical to the others in the block. I went into Zoe's bathroom and opened the window as wide as I could. Down in the yard below I could see steam coming from the drain. He was running the shower.

I grabbed the clipboard and my bag and left the flat, locking the door quietly behind me. I crept downstairs as fast as I could, then left the building, making sure that I went up the road away from Rachel's living room window, just in case he was looking out. At the end of the road I stopped and sent Zoe a quick text saying I'd been called away on an emergency but that everything looked fine. I'd get Brian to do the inventory. I had no intention of setting foot in that place again.

As I walked down the side street to get to my car, I tried to process what I'd seen. So Rachel was seeing David. When did that start? I knew she was single when she started work for me six months ago; we'd talked then about Liverpool and what it was like now, and she'd told me about being a caregiver for her mum and how it had been hard for her to go out at night. It sounded as though she hadn't had much of a life, and I'd felt really sorry for her. She'd said she was looking for somewhere to live and I'd asked her whether she had a partner; she'd said no, she hadn't, and she was quite happy that way. I hadn't thought anything of it; hadn't given it a second thought. I knew she'd made a few friends in the area and went to the same gym that Sophie went to, but I'd never heard her talk about a boyfriend.

Of course I'd never told them anything about what had happened to me in London two months before or anything that had happened since. She'd been in the office when David came in that day and definitely didn't seem to know him then. I remember her giggling with Sophie because he was a good-looking guy.

I frowned. We didn't have a rule about dating clients; there had never seemed the need, but we did have a rule about acting professionally around them. He was single and she was single. She wasn't dealing with his house purchase; she wasn't in a position to negotiate on his behalf.

Had he called her? How would he have known her name? Maybe he'd dropped in when I wasn't there, but why wouldn't she have said something? Or maybe they'd met on a night out. There wasn't really a reason why she couldn't date him – surely she would have told Sophie, at least? I thought about that. Sophie couldn't have known anything about it either. She would never have been able to keep that to herself. And yet Rachel and Sophie were good friends. Why would Rachel keep quiet about seeing a new man?

I felt responsible for Rachel, in a way. She had no family to talk to and she'd never mentioned any friends. I'd been surprised when she went on the hen weekend; she'd been so excited about that trip. I did remember that when she first started work she was always on her phone; I'd had to talk to her about that and she'd said it was just her university friends wondering how she was getting on.

I thought of the policewoman, Stella, then. I should tell her, I knew that, but I wanted to ask Rachel myself, speak to her face-to-face and give her the chance to tell me what she knew. And then I would call the police. I owed it to her to give her fair warning, though. I needed to tell her what her boyfriend had done to me.

The next morning I got to the office early and slipped the keys to Zoe's flat back in the key safe. When Brian and Sophie came in, I made a point of telling him that he needed to do the inventory for the flat, because I hadn't been able to go the night before.

'I thought you were going on your way home from work,'

said Sophie, who was looking worse for wear after her Friday night out.

'I was,' I lied, 'but Joe called and reminded me he had a doctor's appointment, so I had to go home to Rory.'

She accepted this without another thought and simply poured herself another coffee and hunted in her bag for more painkillers. But that morning I watched Sophie and wondered again what she knew. All the time she was photocopying house details and putting them on the racks in the window, I watched her and thought again about whether she knew about David and Rachel. Did everyone know?

And then I realized that if Sophie had known, she would also have known that Rachel wouldn't want me to find out. Surely she would have tried to put me off going there the night before?

When we stopped for coffee that afternoon and Brian had gone off to do the inventory at Zoe's flat, I said to Sophie, 'Did you have a good time last night?'

She smiled. 'A really good time! And I've got a date for tonight.' She whipped out her phone and showed us a photo of a young man who was beaming at the camera, his face flushed, his hair damp. He held a beer bottle; clearly it wasn't the first he'd had that night.

'Oh he's nice!' I said. 'Where did you meet him?'

She named a local club in the centre of Chester and told us how he'd singled her out from her friends and they'd talked all night.

'Is that where you usually go at weekends?' I asked casually.

'Yes, either on Friday or Saturday.'

'Does Rachel normally go with you?'

She shook her head. 'No, she doesn't like places like that. She likes to just go to the gym or to meet up for lunch or shopping. I go with my school friends or my sister.'

Lucy joined in. 'Maybe she's seeing someone.'

'No, she's not,' said Sophie. 'We were setting up dating profiles the other day.' A shifty expression crossed her face. 'Not at work, obviously.'

'And when you had that barbecue at Easter, she came on her own,' said Lucy.

I'd forgotten the barbecue. The weather at Easter had been great, so one Sunday evening I'd invited all the staff round to my house for a couple of hours. Lucy and I had watched Sophie chase Rory round the garden with a little bucket of water from his paddling pool, threatening to drench him with it. Both of them were almost crying with laughter.

'She's just a kid, isn't she?' Lucy had said. 'She seems so glamorous at times, but look at her now. This is the real Sophie.'

Rachel had arrived later than the others. She stood in the kitchen talking to Joe for a while, and Lucy had looked over at them and said, 'They're getting along well, aren't they?' I'd laughed. Joe got along with everyone. I don't think I'd met anyone who had a bad word to say about him. His Irish charm was obviously working on Rachel, though; I could see her laughing, her face pink and excited, as she talked to him.

'I think she's said more to Joe today than she has to us since we've known her,' Lucy had said that day. 'He's obviously charmed her.'

'He does have that gift,' I'd replied. 'It worked on me, anyway. Or it did.'

Lucy had looked at me sympathetically. 'It's always like that when you have a little child,' she said. 'You'll get back to normal soon.'

I'd nodded. I hoped so.

'Rachel seems to have settled in well, doesn't she?' Lucy asked now. 'I noticed you've been giving her more responsibilities lately.'

I said, 'Yes, she's been fine,' but I was too distracted to chat.

I couldn't stop thinking about David. Had he called in one day when Rachel was there alone? Had he liked her from the moment he saw her, that day he came to the office? Try as I might, I couldn't think of a spark between them. She'd blushed when she gave him coffee, but she was a nervous person at times. She hated attention drawn to herself. And when I'd met him in London, he hadn't mentioned her.

Had he targeted her since then? Had he seen another way to get to me?

38

Gemma

By the time it was five P.M., I was determined to go to the police there and then. I just had to trust Stella to do her best to make sure Joe didn't find out. I could hardly bear to think of the lies I'd told him. There were so many now. At night, unable to sleep, I'd go through them, my face burning with shame.

In the car park I got into my car and sat wondering what to do. My phone beeped with a message, and as I reached into my bag to read it, my heart sank. What was this going to be now? I relaxed when I saw it was from Joe, but when I read his message, I panicked.

What time will you be home? We need to talk.

Had he been sent something? David clearly knew our address, but did he know Joe's name? Why would he want to send him something anyway? Wasn't he content with making my life miserable?

My fingers were damp on the screen as I answered.

Just setting off. What's up? X

There was no reply at first. I panicked and had to stop myself from sending another message that would incriminate me. I had just started up the car and had reached the gate of the car park when I heard another message arrive.

Just come home now. I've sent Rory to Sam's house for a couple of hours.

I started to shake. What had happened? I sent a reply:

Don't just say that. Tell me what you're upset about. I don't want to drive home panicking.

I reversed back into my parking space and waited. I thought I was going to be sick with the tension and couldn't have driven then even if I wanted to. It seemed ages before another message came through:

I'm trying to think of a reason why you would stay in a hotel in Chester when I was away in Ireland.

My heart flipped. How did he know that? How did anyone know that? I'd left our house just before seven P.M. and I knew nobody had seen me. I'd been on the lookout for that. And yes, I'd driven up and down our street at midnight, just to check that David hadn't tried to burn the house down, but when I saw that everything was okay, I'd gone straight back to the hotel. Nobody had been following me. I'd driven at least two miles without anyone behind me at all. I'd never been to that hotel before, never mentioned it to anyone.

And then I thought, maybe he knows because of our bank statement? I took out my phone and went onto our online banking service. It showed that the last time it had been accessed was this afternoon, just an hour earlier. I scrolled down the list of credits and debits and saw that the hotel's charge was there.

I could have cried with relief. Nobody had told Joe, he'd just figured it out for himself.

But what could I tell him? Why would I go to a hotel when I could stay in my own house? There had to be a reason. I hadn't even thought about the hotel bill at the time; I'd been in such a state that I'd used our joint debit card to pay for it, without thinking he'd see it.

Then I had a flash of inspiration and sent him another message:

There was a mouse in the kitchen and I couldn't stand the thought of sleeping at home. Why do you think I had to clean up the house? I'm on my way now.

I started the car feeling dreadful. How many more lies was I going to have to tell him? And how on earth would I have got rid of the mouse?

Joe was waiting for me when I got in. He looked so guilty that I felt even worse. He came over to me and hugged me. I put my head on his shoulder, glad of the comfort but feeling terrible that I'd got it under false pretences.

'I'm so sorry,' he said. 'I know how you feel about mice. Why didn't you tell me?'

'There was nothing you could do about it from Ireland,' I said, hating myself for making him feel so bad. 'At the time I couldn't even speak about it without getting hysterical.' I've always been like that about mice; Caitlin and I had had them in one of our student houses and I'd had to go home to my parents' until some of the braver students had sorted them out. 'I meant to tell you when you came home, but then I didn't want to tell you when Rory was there. By the time he'd gone to sleep, I didn't want to think about it.'

I'd no idea that I could be so convincing.

'I thought the worst,' he said, his mouth against my hair. 'I remembered your knickers in your dressing gown pocket, and I thought you'd been seeing someone else.'

I knew that in the past I would have laughed at that suggestion. The idea of me having an affair would have been outlandish. I tried to laugh now and hoped it didn't sound forced. 'There's nothing to worry about.'

I wanted to say, *I wouldn't do that to you*, but maybe I had already. How could I know? The more I thought about that night, the less I knew.

'So where was the mouse?' he asked. 'And how did you get rid of it?' He paused. 'You did get rid of it, didn't you?'

'I got Neil to come round.' Neil was one of the handymen we used for the tenancies. 'He sorted it out. Don't ask me any more than that; all I know is it's gone. He put poison down, too, but that's under the floorboards; there's no need to worry about Rory finding it.'

'So that's why you cleaned the house? Oh God, Gemma, I'm so sorry. I know it was a mess.'

I did feel guilty about that, but you know what, it was his fault it was a mess. He and Rory lived like teenage boys; they had great fun but the house was always untidy.

'Forget it,' I said. 'It was nice to be in a hotel.'

'You're going to get used to that,' he said. 'That's twice in a couple of months you've stayed in a hotel.'

My cheeks flamed and he laughed. 'There's nothing to be embarrassed about. You deserve a break. You work far too hard.'

I just couldn't help it. 'But Joe, what's the alternative?'

'What do you mean?'

'I have to work hard,' I said. 'I don't have a choice, do I? I can't afford to pay for staff when I could do the job myself.'

He moved away, going over to the sink to fill the kettle. 'We agreed to do this,' he said. 'When you got pregnant we knew we couldn't both work. And you wanted to keep the agency going. That was important to you, remember?'

I couldn't speak. I knew that was what I'd said, but it was nearly four years ago, before Rory was born. How was I meant to know how I'd feel years later? I looked over at Joe; he was calmly making tea and he seemed so reasonable. It was as though I was at fault, as though I couldn't keep a promise. Tears filled my eyes. I knew I wouldn't say anything more.

I never did stand up to him. Not really. I'd shout sometimes and I'd get upset, but I never seemed able to sit down with him and talk about things honestly. Even now, I could feel myself backing off.

I muttered that I was going to fetch Rory and left the house. Rory was with Sam, a boy from nursery who lived nearby, and the walk there and the chat with Sam's mother helped me calm down.

Back home I changed into shorts and a T-shirt and we sat out on the patio to eat the dinner that Joe had made for us. Rory told me again all about Ireland and the lovely meals that Nanny had cooked for him and the adventures he'd had with Grandad and his cousins. It sounded as though Joe had hardly seen him all week; as though he'd reverted back to his childhood self. *No wonder he wants to move back there. No wonder he wants us to live with his parents.* I thought of how it would be if we did that, how I'd be the only one in the house getting up to go to work every day, while Joe and his retired parents and our child had a permanent holiday.

I had to get past this. I knew my resentment was poisoning our relationship, but I couldn't find the courage to stand up for what I wanted.

39

Rachel

Sunday, August 13

I know I'd told the girls in the office that I was coming back on Monday morning, but I actually flew back on Sunday night. David had persuaded me to tell a white lie so that I had more time to spend with him. He didn't have to be at work on Monday morning and he wanted me to be at home with him. I loved that about him. He always wanted us to be close, all the time.

So I drove back from Liverpool and parked in our residents' parking bay. I flicked on the car's interior light and took out my make-up bag. I looked okay, just needed to touch up my lipstick. I smoothed my hair, wanting to look my best, and sprayed perfume on my throat and wrists. When I was quite sure I looked good, I jumped out of the car. As I took my cabin bag from the boot, I saw Jennifer, the woman who lived in the other ground-floor flat, drive in. I waited for her to get out of her car and we walked towards the building together.

'Have you been away?' she asked. 'I noticed nobody was around this weekend.'

'I've just come back from Amsterdam,' I said. 'A hen weekend.'

'Wow, lucky you. What about David? Was he away on the stag weekend?'

'No, he's been here.'

She gave me a puzzled look. 'Really? A couple of lads were outside ringing on all the bells last night. Well, this morning. It turned out they were looking for Zoe, but she's gone now. I didn't want to go out to them, so I ended up knocking on your door, to see whether David would tell them to get lost.'

'He mustn't have heard you, otherwise he would've gone out to them,' I said. 'What time was it?'

'Oh, about three o'clock. Maybe nearer four. I was so annoyed; I had to be at work early today. He must be able to sleep through anything if he could sleep through that, though. I ended up shouting out of the window at them. They wanted Zoe's new address. As if I was going to give it to them at that time of night!'

We parted company in the hallway and I opened the door to our flat. It was pretty small, but it was a temporary arrangement. We made all sorts of plans about what we'd do when we sold my mum's house, and sometimes I did wonder how we'd manage in a much bigger house. So much space would be wasted. David liked to be with me, to be near me always.

My mum had left the house and her money to me. Well, there wasn't anyone else to leave it to. I was surprised she had so much, really. She certainly didn't spend a lot when she was alive, though to be fair, she'd paid for my university fees without a question, and for the year before she died, when I was looking after her, she used to tell me to use her credit card to get whatever I needed. She never bought anything for herself, though. Except alcohol. She never went out for the last few years; they delivered it to the house after I refused to buy it for her. I think she grew afraid of running out of money as she got older, though she would've been good for a long time.

David was a great help in sorting all that out for me. After she died I wasn't fit for much, really. On the one hand there was a sense of relief that that era of my life had ended, but on the other . . . well, she was my mum, and even if she hadn't prioritized me, it didn't mean the reverse was true.

When I opened the door to the flat, David was there waiting for me.

'Hey!' he said, jumping up from the sofa. 'I've just opened some wine.' He kissed me and I could tell he'd had a head start. 'Welcome back!'

I hugged him close. It was so good to come home to someone who loved me, and such a change to come into a house where there was warmth and fun. He'd lit candles in the hearth, and a bottle of white wine stood on the coffee table, wet with condensation. He poured me a glass, then went into the kitchen and came back with a tray of cheese and crackers and a bunch of plump, dewy grapes.

'Sit down, babe,' he said. 'I've missed you. Now tell me what you've done all weekend.'

We sat and chatted about Amsterdam. David had been there several times, but this was my first time. I hadn't really been to many places, but now that my mum's money had come through, I was determined to change that. I was going to live the life I knew she'd want for me, if only she'd been sane enough to know it.

'You're looking nice,' I said. 'New shirt? It looks great.'

'Yeah, I did a bit of shopping on Friday lunchtime,' he said. 'Got a few new things.'

'And you saw Danny on Friday night?' I asked. 'Where did you go?'

He told me about the bars in Liverpool that they'd been to, bars that he and I often visited, where he had a lot of friends.

'What about last night?' I asked. 'Did you do anything?'

'No,' he said. 'I was wasted from Friday night. I drank far too much.' He grinned at me. 'I was missing you! I need you to be the sober one when I go out.'

I laughed. That was always my role, to stay a few drinks behind him so that I could get him home when he'd had too much. He wasn't like my mum when he was drunk; where she'd just want to talk about the past, he liked to talk about the future: what we'd do, where we'd go. It was exhilarating hearing him discuss travelling around backpacking in Peru or bungee jumping in New Zealand. I'd never thought of doing these things before and, frankly, the thought of them scared the life out of me, but the prospect of doing them with him was exciting.

'So you stayed in?' I asked.

He looked up. 'What?'

'You stayed in last night? You poor thing. I'm sorry, baby,' I said. 'I hate to think of you staying in at the weekend.'

'No problem,' he said. 'I was too tired to go out. I had a takeaway and got an early night.'

I steeled myself, waiting for the body blow that I'd heard occurs when someone discovers their lover's lies, but it didn't happen. I realized then that I'd always known that he lied to me, that he'd probably been unfaithful, too, though this was the first time I had evidence of it.

I took a sip of my drink. I didn't know what to do. I couldn't ask him again, or mention what Jennifer had said. It would sound as though I didn't trust him, and I knew that wouldn't go down well. I thought for a second of her bumping into him and mentioning it; I just had to hope she wouldn't.

'But you're right,' he said. He took the glass from my hand. 'I've been lonely here on my own. Why don't you make up for it?' His eyes gleamed. 'Pay the price for your weekend away with the girls.'

I smiled and stood up. 'Good idea,' I said. 'I'll just put this food away and I'll be with you.'

'Great,' he said. 'I'll get a quick shower.' He started to take his shirt off, walking into the bedroom leaving a trail of clothes behind him. I quickly picked them up and put them into the laundry basket.

When I heard the shower start, I went into the bedroom. Quietly, I slid the wardrobe door open. A couple of new suits were on his side of the wardrobe. The labels were still on the cuffs: Paul Smith and Hugo Boss. Hanging next to them were several new shirts, and below, a couple of shoe boxes had been thrown in, as though they were nothing. They weren't nothing, though. In his lunchtime, in just one hour, he'd casually spent thousands of pounds of my mother's money, and there wasn't the slightest acknowledgement from him.

I closed the wardrobe door and went back to the living room. The tray of glasses and plates was still on the coffee table, and I picked it up and took it into the kitchen.

On Thursday night David had put the wheelie bin out, ready for collection on Friday morning. Just before I left for Amsterdam, I'd taken the bag from the bin in the kitchen and put it into the wheelie bin, then put a fresh plastic bag into the kitchen bin.

Now I held my breath as I pushed the bin's swing lid. There was nothing in there. No takeaway food cartons, nothing at all. It was completely empty. Quietly I opened the back door and lifted the lid of the wheelie bin, just in case he'd put it straight out there. Sometimes I did that if the food was very spicy, though I'd never known David to do it.

That, too, was empty.

I locked the back door and stood against it with my heart pounding. I knew it. He hadn't been here on Saturday night. I'd known from the moment Jennifer spoke to me that he hadn't.

I didn't let myself think about where he'd been or who he'd been with.

I couldn't. I couldn't afford to lose him. Not now.

I picked up the bottle of wine and filled my glass to the brim. I drank it straight down.

By the time David came out of the bathroom I had put on the lingerie he liked, sprayed the perfume he'd chosen for me, and put on the music he liked best.

'Come on, sweetheart,' I said. My throat was swollen with tears I knew I couldn't shed. 'Let me make it up to you.'

40

Gemma

Monday, August 14

I found it really stressful waiting for Rachel to return to work. I knew I was going to have to talk to her, but I couldn't think how I was going to say it and what she'd say in response. What if she denied knowing him? I had no right to go into her flat to prove he was there. And I had no evidence that David had actually done anything, apart from an e-mail that looked like spam.

And I was worried about her, too. What had she got herself into? She was so young and she had no family to help her. If he was taking advantage of her, would she be able to cope?

I knew that if I went to the police and this ended up in court, it was likely it would be in the newspapers. We were a small enough town that even minor events were written about as though they were global incidents. Our local newspaper certainly loved to report sexual misdemeanours; if they knew that a married businesswoman had been posing naked for her client, they'd be all over the story. And if it was in the newspapers, Joe would hear about it. I couldn't bear the thought of that.

The Girl I Used to Be

Rachel arrived back at the office after lunch. Sophie was surreptitiously putting on nail varnish, blissfully unaware of the fact that the smell was giving her away. Brian was on the phone to a plumber who was due to put in a new bathroom at a student house I owned near the university, and I was at my desk, working on an expenses spreadsheet for the accountant. Everything was normal, and as I saw her standing in the doorway, a breeze slightly lifting her hair, I knew that she thought nobody knew her secret.

She was wrong.

Ever since I'd seen David at her home, I'd wondered about him and how she knew him. I'd worried about her, too. This was a man who seemed hell-bent on destroying me. As she stood there, looking so young and so happy, I thought of how she'd feel when I told her about the things he'd done to me. I swallowed. She'd be destroyed.

Mid-afternoon, I received a call from Bill Campbell, one of the landlords I'd dealt with over the years. He'd bought up some flats in a dockside block and wanted Brian to have a look at them before renting them.

'Brian's at an auction this afternoon,' I said. 'I'll do it for you. Is later on okay?'

'Can you be there for four o'clock? Park up by the entrance and I'll buzz you in.'

He gave me the address and I wrote it down, repeating it after him. When I looked up from my call, I saw that Rachel and Sophie were looking at me eagerly.

'Are you going to that new development down by the racecourse?' asked Sophie. 'I walked past it last weekend. It looks amazing.'

'Yes, Bill Campbell's bought three flats there. He told me about them when I saw him last week.'

'I'd love one of those,' said Rachel. 'Do you know how much they're going for?'

I looked at her. She looked so calm and serene, the polar opposite of me right now. In an instant, the decision was made. 'I don't know,' I said. 'Why don't you come along with me and have a look at them?'

Sophie turned away, disappointed. She'd be even more disappointed if she realized what she was actually missing this afternoon.

Now was my chance to talk to Rachel.

Bill pulled up in his car ten minutes after we arrived. Rachel and I were in separate cars, so that we could make our own way home afterwards, and I pretended to be on my phone so that she didn't come over. I couldn't stop thinking that she would be going back to him and wondered what she'd say to him. And what he'd say to her.

'Sorry,' said Bill, when we met him at the door to the block. 'I'm running late.'

He tapped the code to get into the building and we exchanged pleasantries as we went up in the lift to the fifth floor. When the doors opened he ushered us out onto a landing that had a row of doors, each leading to a self-contained flat.

'So, I've just bought these three here.' He indicated those nearest to us. 'Got them at auction last week. I'm planning to rent them out for now, then see how it goes.'

We went into the first one and he said, 'You'll be able to deal with this for me, won't you? I want them rented as soon as possible, so can you get an advert out tomorrow? I've got painters coming in early next week. Nothing else needs doing; they're in good condition as far as I can see, but let me know what you think.' He told me the price range he was looking at, but said he wanted us to check around to see if more was viable. 'I can't stop, I've got to get to the council offices before they shut. Can you get the keys back to me?'

'No problem. I'll send Brian round with them tomorrow and I'll get him to place an advert, too.'

'Great.'

With that, he was off. The flats were empty and clean, ready for the decorators to start work before they were let. Rachel and I measured the rooms and made a note of any work to be done. We moved from flat to flat, careful not to miss anything.

'So Brian would normally do this, wouldn't he?' asked Rachel.

'Yes, but if you're going to take over in my absence, you have to know exactly what's involved in every job in the office.' Not that I had the slightest intention of even keeping her in the job, never mind promoting her, if she was going to carry on seeing David.

'This is the one I'd like,' said Rachel. 'Imagine seeing that view every day.'

We were standing in the last flat, looking out through its huge windows at the Welsh hills. Beautiful as they were, I hardly noticed them. All I could think was that now was my chance. There was nobody around.

It was time.

My stomach was knotted tight as I turned to Rachel. 'This would be a bit big for you, though, wouldn't it?' I asked.

She gave a little smile. 'Oh, that's okay. I like a lot of space.'

'But living here on your own,' I said. 'It's a lovely flat, but it's more suitable for a couple, isn't it?'

The difference in her was minimal, but I saw it. She stayed still, looking out of the window, and it was only because I was so fired up that I could see that her hands, which were touching the windowsill, now gripped it.

I took one step closer to her and watched as the tiny blonde hairs on her arms prickled to attention.

'I know,' I said.

She jumped then and turned. 'Know what?' Her voice was brave and strong; there was no sign of the nerves that had hit her earlier. She moved away from the window and gathered up the clipboard and laser measure that we'd brought with us, holding them against her chest.

I moved closer to her. 'How long have you known him for?'

'Who?' Her voice was uncertain then, and she swallowed hard after she spoke.

'You know who.'

She said nothing. I could hear her breathing, short, shallow breaths that made her face pink and damp.

'David Sanderson.'

She looked at me, her face defiant. Cool, almost. 'I don't know anyone called David Sanderson.'

She was probably telling the truth. I'd realized a while ago that it was unlikely he'd used his real name.

'I think you do. I don't know what he's really called, but I know you know him.'

She stayed very still and so did I, both so aware of each other, aware of every move. I wasn't going to be the one who broke that silence.

She caved. 'How do you know?'

'I saw him going into your flat.' The tension hit me and I gave a huge sigh. 'Did you really think I wouldn't find out? We manage that property. The chances of my discovering that you knew him were always high.'

She opened her mouth to speak, but nothing came out. I waited. It had worked before and I knew it would work again.

'It's my business who I live with.'

My stomach lurched. So he *was* living there. Ever since I'd seen him, I'd tried to persuade myself that maybe it was all innocent, that she'd only just met him and had lent him her key for some reason. Even now, I tried to give her the benefit of the doubt.

'I'm really worried for you, Rachel.'

She looked scornful. 'Why?'

'I don't think you realize what you're involved with. Your boyfriend . . .'

She cut in. 'He's not my boyfriend.' She looked me straight in the face then, and it was clear he gave her courage. 'He's my husband. We're married.'

41

Rachel

Last year

I've known David for years; he was one of my brother's oldest friends, but I hadn't been expecting him to turn up at my mum's funeral.

It was held in late October on such a grey, bleak day. My mother had distanced herself from so many of her friends over the years, and I hadn't had the nerve to get in touch with them at the end. When I say 'distanced herself', I really mean she'd phoned them up and screamed at them in the middle of the night, so I was reluctant to call them then.

The end of her life dragged out for over a year. A year when I wasn't able to work, wasn't able to do anything except look after her. Not that she was grateful, mind. I'd take her to hospital appointments where I'd hear mums talking about their daughters. 'I couldn't have asked for a better daughter,' they'd say. 'She's been such a comfort to me.' I would sit stone-faced when they'd talk like that. My mother had enough sense of propriety to pay lip service at times, though. Once I'd heard her saying she wouldn't have been able to cope without me. I was amazed, both by the sentiment and the idea that she was coping.

So her funeral was poorly attended. My dad wasn't there; that would have been one way to get my mother back from the grave. There was just me and a couple of neighbours who'd seen the ambulance come to the house and who'd called round later, when they saw I was home. She'd died in the ambulance, exerting her will right to the end. She'd been determined not to go into a hospital or hospice, but to die at home. When I'd found her unconscious one morning I called for emergency help, thinking she'd be furious when she came to, but that didn't happen. Ten minutes into the journey to Arrowe Park, she gave up the fight altogether.

I sat in the front row of the chapel at the crematorium, and our neighbours came to sit with me. An elderly cousin of my mum's turned up; she gave me a sympathetic look and touched my arm, but she hadn't been there when I needed her, so I was polite, but that was it.

The short service had just started when I heard the door to the chapel open. I wasn't expecting anyone else, but then I didn't know what to expect. The only other funeral I'd been to had been quiet, too. I was torn between looking at the minister and turning around to see who was there. The latter instinct won.

David stood in the doorway. I knew him instantly, though I hadn't seen him for more than ten years. He was taller than I remembered, and broader now, his hair still black and wavy. He turned to close the door, then walked up the aisle towards me. For a moment I felt dizzy, as though my brother was there beside him, just as he always was.

When he saw me looking at him, he winked, and that seemed so inappropriate but such a welcome diversion in all that misery that I winked back. As I turned back I saw that the funeral director had noticed and looked shocked. As well he might. I think that was the first time I felt like laughing in over a year.

He was waiting for me outside, after the service ended. 'Poor Coco,' he said, and suddenly it was like the old days. David had been visiting our house one day when I was little; I think I was four years old and the boys must have been eleven or twelve. I'd been playing with my mum's make-up and had made a right mess of myself. They'd laughed so much when they saw me and called me Coco the Clown. The nickname had stuck. I hadn't been called that for years, and as soon as David said it, it was like I had my family back. 'You've had a tough time, haven't you?'

For the first time since I lost my mum, I felt tears prickling the back of my eyes. I'd done everything – all the legal stuff, arranging the funeral, sorting the bills – on my own and I'd known that if I started to cry I'd never stop. Now at this hint of kindness from someone who'd known me as I was before, I could feel myself well up.

'It's all over now,' I said. 'Finally she's at peace.'

The neighbours said goodbye then, and my mum's cousin promised to keep in touch, though I wasn't going to hold my breath on that. They kissed my cheek, told me I'd been a good daughter, the very best, and they were off.

I was staring after them thinking I'd have to go back to the empty house, with no clue what to do with myself, when David said, 'You know what you need, don't you, Coco?'

'To sleep for a year?'

'You need to get drunk,' he said.

I laughed. 'What?'

'We should have a wake for your mum.'

'Wakes are usually held before the funeral.'

He shrugged. 'And did you have one?'

I shook my head.

'Well, then. Better late than never.' He smiled at me then and I couldn't resist. 'Come on,' he said. 'My treat.'

So off we went into Liverpool on the train, both dressed in

our sober black suits, on a Tuesday morning, to have our wake. We hopped from bar to bar and with each drink we had to toast my mum and say something nice about her. I struggled a bit with that, but he did well. He had the best memories. And then he went up to the bar to get more cocktails and when he came back I asked what they were.

'Between the Sheets,' he said, and he leaned over the little bar table and kissed me.

We were married within a month.

42

Rachel

Present day

Gemma stared at me, so shocked that her mouth fell open. She was clearly struggling to process what I'd said.

'You're married?' she said. 'To David Sanderson?'

I started to speak, to tell her that that wasn't his name, but stopped myself just in time. 'I'm married, yes.' I could feel myself flush. I hadn't told another person that I was married and it felt weird, as though I was pretending to be grown up.

'Since when?' she asked.

I bristled. What did it have to do with her? David and I had agreed I wouldn't go into detail. *There's no need for her to know anything*, he'd said. *Keep it to yourself. When in doubt, keep quiet.* So I did keep quiet, but it seemed Gemma could keep quiet longer than I could, as eventually I heard myself saying, 'A while.'

'And yet you said you were single,' she said. 'When you came to the interview I asked you and you specifically said, "I'm single. Never been married. Don't particularly want to get married."'

It sounded as though she was mimicking me, and I scowled at her. 'You've got a good memory.'

'Damn right I have,' she said.

I had to figure out how to play this. I'd known she'd find out sometime – that was part of it, knowing she would – but I'd thought we had time. I hadn't dreamed it would be today. One glance at her told me she wasn't going to leave here until this was sorted.

Oh well. So it was time. I was ready for her.

'Did you know him when he came into the office?' she asked.

I couldn't help it. I laughed at the thought of that day when I had to pretend I didn't know him and ask him how he liked his coffee.

Gemma looked shocked. 'Were you *married* to him then?'

I just looked at her. I wasn't going to tell her anything. I'd been preparing for this for a long time. *Don't incriminate yourself,* David had said over and over again. *Don't give her anything, not one piece of information, that she can hang you with.* I turned away and counted to ten. *Keep calm,* I thought. *Keep calm. She has nothing on you.*

'Rachel,' she said, 'there's something I should tell you.'

I readied myself. 'What?'

'He's trouble. David is trouble.'

I laughed again. 'I don't think he's the one I should be worried about.'

'He is!' she said. 'He's trying to destroy me.'

I was trying to keep quiet, trying to remember David's instructions, but I couldn't help it. It had to be said. 'Come off it, Gemma,' I said. 'You're making it sound as though you're a complete innocent here.'

She blinked. 'What? I am!'

The heat was rising now; I'd felt it simmering for years and all the time I'd tried to control it, to keep a lid on my feelings, but faced with her innocent expression, I couldn't control myself. 'Little Miss Perfect, always doing the right thing. That's how you portray yourself, isn't it?'

She looked at me as though I'd gone mad. 'Rachel, I have done nothing wrong. Nothing at all.'

I hardly heard her. I felt that if I didn't tell her then, I didn't know what I'd do. 'But you and I both know you have, don't we?'

She was staring at me. I knew my cheeks were red, knew she was wary now. I could feel anticipation rising in me. It had been dampened down for so long and now I was going to set myself free.

'We both know exactly what you are,' I said. 'What you've done. The question is, who else knows? Does Joe know, I wonder?'

She stared at me, her eyes boggling. She took a step back and I realized I was frightening her. Well, good.

'Did you tell him, Gemma? Do you tell him everything? Did you tell him what happened that night?' I gave her a hard, contemptuous look. 'Or did you lie, just as you always do?'

She looked like she'd been slapped. 'Are you saying that was my fault?'

'You and I both know the truth. That's what you can't stand, isn't it? You can say what you like, but I know the truth.'

'The truth about what?' she yelled. 'What your pervert husband has been doing to me?'

I flinched.

'You really know all that and you've the nerve to stand here talking to me?' she asked. 'You realize I risk losing everything because of him?'

And then the heat was in my face and I couldn't stop myself. Tears filled my eyes and I dashed them away. 'It's time you knew what it felt like,' I said. I felt like my heart was bursting. 'To know what it feels like to lose everything.'

'Do you think I don't know that?' she said. 'You know nothing about me!'

She was such an idiot. 'Oh I do, Gemma. I know everything.'

'So you know that your husband – your own husband – has been blackmailing me?' she said. 'You know that?'

I shook my head. 'You had that coming to you,' I said. 'It's what you deserve.' I drew myself up then and pushed my shoulders back. 'And he hardly did anything anyway.' I moved away a little, my eyes still on hers. 'Unlike you.'

'Unlike me?' she shrieked, as though she were blameless. 'What have I done?'

I was cold now; the heat had left my face. Left my body. I could feel my hands shaking. 'You've no idea, have you?' I said.

'What?'

I took a deep breath. 'You've no idea who I am.'

'What?' she said again, and to be fair, she looked completely bewildered. 'Of course I know who you are!'

'No, you don't,' I said. 'I'd always wondered if you knew.' I drew my shoulders back and looked her straight in the eye. 'I'm Alex's sister.'

43

Gemma

Fifteen years ago

It's odd the dreams you have sometimes; they're so powerful, so vivid, and yet the second you wake up, they vanish, no matter how hard you try to cling on to them. How does that happen? And other times they morph into reality and you find you're no longer dreaming. You're living in a nightmare.

When I woke that night at the party, my body was heavy and exhausted. My face was buried deep in the pillows and the smell of laundry was so intense I had to lift my head up to breathe fresh air. As I opened my eyes all I could see was darkness, and for a drunken moment I didn't know where I was. Then I remembered. This was Alex's room. I'd fallen asleep here while the party was going on downstairs.

I thought I'd go and find Lauren and realized I couldn't. The heaviness on my body wasn't exhaustion. It wasn't that I was too tired to move.

I *couldn't* move.

Something was on top of me, weighing me down. Something heavy. I tried to take a breath and couldn't. Then my legs were suddenly wide apart and something was moving inside me in hard, vicious stabs. I tried to turn but I couldn't. I wanted to shout but something was pressing down on my chest. I felt like I was being buried into the mattress, as though all the air in my lungs had been pushed out of me.

My arms were dead by my sides. I tried to move them, but couldn't.

And then I heard the breathing. A rasping breath, hot on the back of my neck, just beside my ear. I wrenched my head away and the weight lifted slightly.

This time when I tried to turn, the pressure lifted completely and I gasped in air. I struggled to sit up and a blanket was thrown over me, over my face. In the pitch black I heard someone moving around, then the sound of a zip. I tried to push the blanket off me but then another one was thrown on top of me and I was tangled up in them.

I was still drunk, still unable to think straight. Panicking, I tore at the blankets, but everything was dark and I couldn't find a way out. And then I heard the bedroom door open and the landing light shone briefly in the room. I turned towards the light, ripping the blankets away from my head. In the second it took for the door to quietly shut again, I saw someone tall and dark-haired, wearing a T-shirt with *The Coral* on the back, hurrying from the room.

I fell back onto the bed.

Alex?

After he closed the door, the room was back in darkness. Panicking, I tried to get off the bed, to work out what to do. I couldn't think clearly; couldn't see anything. What had happened? Why was Alex in here? I floundered around in the dark, then remembered there'd been a lamp on in the room when I first lay down; it was on the bedside table. I scrambled over the bed towards it and fumbled for the switch.

In the lamplight I looked at myself in disbelief. My dress was up around my waist and my knickers were on the floor beside the bed. My head was fuzzy from sleep and alcohol and I couldn't think straight.

And then I heard Tom calling from downstairs.

'Gemma? Gemma! The taxi's here!'

I scrambled off the bed and pulled on my knickers. My new sandals were on the floor by the window and quickly I slid them on. I looked around frantically. I hadn't left anything behind.

I ran to the door, wrenched it open, and ran downstairs as fast as I could, my blistered feet rubbing against my sandals.

Tom was waiting for me. 'Lauren's in the taxi,' he said. 'Where were you?'

I shook my head and said nothing. I just wanted to get out of there. Outside I got into the front passenger seat. Lauren was behind me, with Tom next to her. They talked about the party, about how strange it would be to not see people again until they got back from university at Christmas, about how it wasn't long now and how they'd visit each other every weekend. Everything they said was interspersed with kisses.

I leaned my head against the window, feeling it cold against my burning skin. I couldn't think about what had happened to me. I couldn't talk about it. What would I say? So when Lauren spoke to me, I closed my eyes and I heard Tom say, 'She's asleep.' Lauren laughed and said, 'Lightweight.'

The journey seemed to take hours. My face was pressed against the glass the whole time, each bump in the road punishing me. I didn't cry. I didn't think about what had happened. I couldn't. I didn't feel safe enough to let myself do that.

When we arrived at Lauren's house, Tom took the money her mum had left us in the hall and paid the taxi driver. I went straight into the spare room, where I'd slept so many times before. I couldn't take off my clothes. I didn't want to look at myself. The curtains were drawn and the room was almost dark, with only the faint glimmer of the light from the lamp-post outside shining through. I sat on the floor by the wall, rested my head on my knees and hugged my legs tightly.

Someone went into the bathroom across the landing from my room, and just the sound of them shutting the door was enough to make me leap up. I stood panting in the dark, ready to scream. And then I heard Lauren say, 'Sorry!' and realized she must have woken her mum. As my breathing slowed I realized that of course it was only Lauren. It wasn't anything to worry about.

I sat down by the wall again and stayed there until six, when the sun was rising. Then I picked up my bag, holding my house key tightly in my hand, and tiptoed downstairs. Once outside in the cool morning air, I ran the half-mile to my own house on the same estate, focusing only on my feet as the blisters rubbed and burst with each step I took.

Safely home, I ripped off all my clothes, put them into a plastic bag and buried them at the bottom of the bin outside. I wouldn't wear them again. Then I stood in the shower, scrubbing my body until it was raw, not daring to look down at the blood that coloured the water pink as it swirled down the drain.

I still didn't cry. Perhaps if I had, things would have been different.

44

Gemma

Present day

Monday, August 14

I took a step backwards, unable to believe what I'd heard.

'Alex's sister?'

'Yes, Alex Clarke's sister. You remember him, don't you?'

I nodded. 'Yes, of course I remember him.' How could I not? 'But you don't look anything like him. And your surname's Thomas. Is that your married name?'

'It's my mother's name. Her maiden name. When my parents divorced, she and I changed our names. We didn't want anything to do with my dad.'

'Why didn't you tell me you were his sister?'

She laughed. 'Like you would have given me the job!'

I thought back to the application she'd written. She'd seemed so enthusiastic and her qualifications were great. She hadn't used Alex's address, I knew that. I would never forget that address, even now, fifteen years later. 'Did you know who I was when you applied for the job?'

'Of course I did.' She gave me a scornful look. 'I'm not stupid.'

'But why? Why would you want to come and work for me?'

She said nothing, just stood staring at me, her knuckles white as she gripped the clipboard.

And then I realized just what was going on. 'Are you in on this with David Sanderson?' Her sneer only reminded me that I didn't know his name. 'Or whatever he's really called.'

'You needed to be taught a lesson,' she said.

'I did? Why? What have I done?'

'Did you really think,' she said, then stopped. I could see tears in her eyes. She began again. 'Did you really think that you could ruin my brother's life and get away with it?'

'But Rachel,' I said, 'I was raped. Alex raped me.'

Even though it happened years ago, I still struggled to say those words.

'Don't you dare say that! He wouldn't do that.' Her voice broke. 'You know what he was like – how could you think he'd rape someone?'

'I was there,' I said. 'I was the one it happened to.'

'Nothing happened!' she shrieked. 'You lied to the police and Alex was arrested. And then you said you wouldn't testify. After doing all that damage! You're the reason Alex died. You're the reason my dad left. And it's because of you that my mum died. Everything bad that's happened to my family has happened because of you.'

She stood in front of me, red-faced and triumphant, but all I could think about were those years after the party where I'd had no self-respect and had put myself in dodgy situations with men I didn't even know, stupidly thinking that initiating things with them would mean I was in control. It had taken a therapist to show me that I was no more in control with them than I'd been that night at the party. If I hadn't had that help, I don't know what would have happened to me. And even now, I knew that my problems with Joe were because I couldn't assert myself. I couldn't do it that night at the party and I hadn't been able to do it since.

My mother was on my side – she had been every day of my life – but she'd worried that I wouldn't be believed. I refused to testify because of that, and now, fifteen years on, I could see that she was right.

45

Rachel

Last year

It was on the night of my mother's funeral that I decided to take revenge on Gemma.

After he kissed me, David said, 'Come on, Coco,' and we drank our cocktails in a hurry and left the bar. We were at the Albert Dock in Liverpool and there was a hotel facing us. I said, 'Serendipity,' and he laughed and kissed me again. Within minutes we were in bed. When he discovered it was my first time, he was so tender. So gentle. I hadn't dreamed it would be like that.

Much later, he rang room service for drinks and we sat out on the balcony overlooking the river, watching as the lights popped on along the dockside. The sky was growing dark, the breeze was fresh, and though it was chilly and there was the threat of rain in the air, there was nowhere I'd rather have been. Being with David felt like I'd been given the chance of a new life, as though I was reborn, not as something new, but as the girl I'd been before it all went wrong. Before I lost my family. Now it was like my family had returned to me. When he put his arms around me, I felt sheltered. Protected. Something I hadn't experienced in such a long time. Like family, it didn't take long to catch up with what we'd done in the years since we'd last met.

I knew at the time that he'd gone to Bristol University when Alex went to Oxford, and my mum had heard from someone that he'd gone abroad to work after his degree. Philadelphia, she'd said. He'd married someone there. I hadn't known the marriage had ended until he told me that afternoon. He told me a bit about it then, though he seldom mentioned it later. He told me he hadn't known her well on their wedding day, that he was in love with her until they'd been married a few months, when he really got to know her. He said that was when he knew it was over.

Of course I didn't have much to contribute when it came to my past. I was so much younger than he was, but I'd hardly done anything anyway.

'So you had to be with your mum the whole time?' he asked in disbelief. 'But aren't you working?'

'I haven't worked for over a year,' I said. 'I'll be looking for jobs now, of course. When she became ill – well, when she admitted to being ill – I had to stay at home with her. At least she couldn't drink as much then.'

'She had a drink problem?' He frowned. 'I don't remember that. Alex never told me.'

You can't believe how good it was to have a conversation where Alex's name was dropped in as though he were still here. Ever since he'd died I'd wanted to share my memories of him with someone who knew him too. My mother talked about him incessantly. If I spoke, she just spoke louder. She wanted me to be there, but only as an audience for her monologue. If I talked about him, I could predict the time it would take for her to find a bottle to comfort her. It was her loss, that was made clear, not mine. She said I was too young to remember him properly and that only a mother knows true love. Friends avoided talking about him, in case I got upset, and of course my dad went after a year or so, so there was nobody, until I met up with David again, to whom I could talk about Alex. Not about what happened, so much, not about his death, but just passing remarks about him, about what he liked to do, things he'd said.

'It started after Alex died. She hadn't really drunk that much before. I'd never noticed it, anyway, but then I was only young. But afterwards . . . She became a full-on alcoholic. Within a couple of years I couldn't ask anyone home. I couldn't go to sleepovers; I was too worried that she'd fall down the stairs or choke on her own vomit.'

He hugged me. 'That sounds really tough.'

'I think she'd known for years that she was ill. She kept it from me.' Tears sprang to my eyes. 'I think she just wanted to die. She didn't tell me anything was wrong until that last year. I'd noticed she'd lost weight, but then she'd been thin for years. She wasn't interested in eating.'

'I had so many meals at your house when I was a kid,' said David. 'She was a great cook.'

'All that went straight away,' I said. 'I can hardly remember it now.'

But I could. If I let myself, I could remember walking home with my friends that last year of junior school, the summer before Alex died. I'd say goodbye to them at the end of my road and run up to my house. I'd come panting into the kitchen, my face red, excited to see my mum, and I'd find her listening to the radio, our dinner in the oven. She'd look up when she heard me at the door and I'd run over to hug her. I can still remember my face against hers, feel the softness of her cheeks, smell her perfume. I'd sit with her and have a biscuit and some milk while we waited for my dad and Alex to come home. We wouldn't eat dinner until they were there. And when Alex came in, she'd leap up to greet him. I noticed that even as a child: I ran to her and she ran to him.

He grimaced. 'And your dad couldn't help?'

'He'd gone by then.' I think I made it clear I didn't want to talk about him again.

'That's terrible, Rachel. Really terrible.'

'I still miss Alex,' I said. 'Every day.'

'I know, babe. I do too.'

'And do you know what?' I said. 'There's one person to blame for this.' I jabbed my finger at his chest. 'Just. One. Person.'

'Your mum?'

'No,' I scoffed. 'She couldn't help it. She just had one long fourteen-year breakdown.'

'You don't mean Alex, do you?'

'No.' I drank some more wine. I'd had too much to drink but it was one of those days when it seemed I couldn't have enough. 'I mean Gemma Brogan.'

'Who? Not *that* Gemma?'

I saw his hand grip his glass and I knew he was thinking of her, the woman who'd ruined my brother's life.

'Yes, the one who accused Alex.'

'Don't worry,' he said. 'I haven't forgotten her. How could I? But I thought she was Gemma Taylor.'

'She was. Brogan is her married name. I've been keeping tabs on her. She's married now, with a little boy. She's got a business in Chester and she's doing very well for herself.' I poured myself another drink. 'Very well indeed. But not for much longer.'

He gave me a questioning look.

'I intend to do something about it,' I said.

He laughed. 'What? What are you planning?'

Full of bravado, I blurted out, 'I want to stop her happy little life in its tracks, just as she stopped Alex's.' I saw him looking at me and stopped, embarrassed. 'Sorry, you must think I'm mad.'

'Are you kidding?' he said. 'Alex died because of her lies. That bitch needs bringing down.' He raised his glass and clinked it against mine. 'Count me in, Coco.'

46

Gemma

Present day

For a moment neither of us said anything; her accusations rang in the air. I could hear our breathing, high and fast in the empty room. We were both panting, both furious.

Rachel's face was so pale. She was staring at me as though she couldn't believe what she'd said. I'd never really thought about the impact this had had on other people. Just one action, one accusation, and wham, everyone's life changes.

'You'll have to forgive me if I see things differently,' I said. 'I'm sorry Alex died.' For the first time since it happened I realized it was true. I wondered whether his death had been an accident, or whether he'd felt guilty because of what he'd done. Whether he was too ashamed to live. 'Whatever happened, for him to be in such a bad way that he took his own life is really awful.'

Her mouth twisted and I knew she couldn't speak. I wouldn't have been able to either. I took a new bottle of water from my bag and passed it to her. She hesitated and I thought she'd refuse, but she took it from me and drank some of it.

'I'm not sure he meant to do it,' she said heavily, 'but what do I know? I was only eleven at the time. It was as though I didn't know anything any more. But my mum . . . well, she thinks . . . she *thought* he'd done it on purpose.' She glared at me. 'You have no idea what it was like for me after he died. It was all she could talk about. All she could think about.'

'You can't blame her,' I said quietly. 'He was her child.'

'And so was I! And I was alive and needed her. And she begrudged that. Hated me for it. Every single day I was made aware of the fact that I wasn't him.'

'Don't think that, Rachel,' I said. 'Of course she didn't hate you.'

'What do you know? You weren't there. I was, day after day, with all her memories.' She grimaced and I could tell she was trying not to cry. 'What about *my* memories? I learned to say nothing, though. There was no point.'

She took some tissues from her bag and scrubbed at her face. Rachel's make-up was usually perfect, her hair glossy and smooth. Now mascara was smeared over her face, her hair tangled where she'd knotted it with her hands. She clutched the tissues now and crouched down by the wall. Suddenly she looked exhausted.

'Why don't you just go? Leave the keys and I'll lock up,' she said. 'I need a few minutes.'

I shook my head, too scared to leave her like this. 'I'll wait with you.'

She started to speak but gave up. Her head on her knees, she started to cry in earnest. I sat down beside her. For a long time we said nothing. When her tears had stopped and her breathing was back to normal, I said, 'So all these things, these things that David's been doing . . . they were to punish me for Alex's death?'

'If you hadn't lied,' she said, 'if you hadn't said it was Alex, then he'd still be alive. He'd be in his thirties now, like you. He'd probably have a family. A good job. Like you.' She looked at me, anger and guilt on her face. 'Why should you have those things when he doesn't?'

'And David? What kind of man would do those things to a woman he doesn't know?'

'A man who lost his friend. His best friend. He's Alex's best friend. Was. We became close last year, when my mum died. We married not long after that. He's the only one who understands.'

I frowned. 'Was he at school with us? I don't remember him.'

'No, he didn't go to the same school as Alex. He lived a few miles away; they'd always gone to different schools. They played sport together. Hockey. That's how they met.'

'Whose idea was it that he did those things?'

She gave me a proud, truculent look. 'Mine. I wanted to pay you back.'

I sighed. She clearly wasn't going to listen to me tell her how my life had changed because of Alex. How overnight I'd gone from a quiet, confident girl to someone who I couldn't recognize at times. I couldn't tell her how I still longed to be the girl I used to be, the girl who wasn't scared of shadows, who could sleep in the dark.

'You don't deserve the life you have,' she said.

That much was true. I didn't deserve any of the things that she and David had done to me.

'You realize you've both committed criminal offences?' I asked. 'I've spoken to the police. They've told me which laws you've broken.'

She looked at me, astonished. 'We haven't broken any laws!'

'Are you joking? You think threatening to post photos on a voyeur site is legal?'

She looked at me as though I'd gone mad. 'What are you talking about? A voyeur site? I don't even know what that is!'

'Neither did I until your husband sent me a link to it. It's a site where men post photos and videos of women without the women knowing. Photos of them naked or asleep. Doing intimate things.' I swallowed. 'You wouldn't believe some of the things on that site. I don't know how it's not closed down.'

'Photos?' she said. 'You mean the photo of him kissing you outside your hotel room?'

So she knew about that. And then it dawned on me. I had a dim memory of turning when I reached my room and seeing someone standing at the far end of the corridor. 'You were there? At the hotel?'

She was pale but nodded. 'That's not against the law.'

'And was it you that photographed me outside my room?'

I could see shame in her face. 'I wanted your husband to think you were having an affair.'

'But you sent it to me.'

She said nothing, just stared out in front of her, and I knew she'd been prepared to send it to Joe.

'And so was it you, Rachel, who took the photos of me naked?'

Her head swung round. 'What? What are you talking about?'

You know sometimes you hear someone speak and you recognize the ring of truth. That was what happened then. I didn't want to believe her, but I had to.

'The naked photos,' I said again.

'Naked? You had your green dress on. Don't be stupid, you were in the corridor! How could you be naked?'

'I don't know,' I said. 'I don't remember.'

'I don't believe you! Where are they? Show me them!'

'They were on Instagram and he withdrew them. I don't have a copy of them and I've deleted my account now anyway.'

'That's convenient!' I could hear the cogs whirring in her head. 'Where were you when these photos were taken?'

'In my hotel room. On my bed.'

She was silent for a long time then. When she looked up at me, her face was pale and strained. 'Why did you let him do that?'

'Do what?'

'Go into your hotel room with you.' She was shaking. 'Take the photos.'

I stared at her. 'I didn't let him do anything! I didn't know anything about them until they were sent to me. I don't remember anything of that night after I got back to my room.'

'He wasn't meant to go into your room,' she said at last. 'I took the photo of you both outside your door and went back to our hotel and waited for him. He wasn't long after me, perhaps half an hour. He said he'd stopped to have a drink at the bar.'

'So you didn't know he'd changed my underwear?'

Her head shot up. 'What?'

'Or that he took my knickers home with him?'

She looked horrified.

'I woke up in different underwear from the ones I wore to bed,' I said. 'The underwear I was wearing that night had gone.'

'Gone?'

'He sent it to my home address a few days ago.'

I could see her mind racing, trying to make sense of it all.

'I don't remember anything after I got back to my hotel room,' I repeated. And then it dawned on me. Finally. What an idiot I'd been. 'He drugged me, didn't he?'

47

Gemma

'No,' said Rachel. 'No. You were drunk. Really, really drunk. I saw you, don't forget. You nearly fell over when you got out of the lift at the hotel.'

It was as though she wasn't there. 'He must have drugged me,' I said. 'I wondered why I couldn't remember anything.'

'Gemma, you walked up to your hotel room all right. You weren't drugged.' Her voice was desperate. 'You drank two bottles of wine!'

'No, I didn't! We ordered two bottles, but I didn't drink all that. I wouldn't be able to. I don't drink much, Rachel. I haven't drunk that much for years.' I couldn't look at her. 'The next morning I felt awful. And yes, I know I would have felt bad just from the alcohol. I would have expected a hangover. But I've never drunk so much that I couldn't remember what I'd done the night before. Never.'

'Except when you were eighteen,' she said spitefully. 'You did that night.'

'Do you really think I can't remember what happened that night?'

She flushed.

'But the night I was in London ... I can't remember

anything after I left the restaurant. I paid the bill, I remember that. David said his room was on the tenth floor. We went up in the lift and I nearly fell over getting out. And I remember when I got to my door he kissed me and I turned away and I saw someone there.' I paused, remembering. 'How did I not know that was you?' I knew the answer, though. I was completely out of it.

'You were drunk,' she said.

'I've told you; I don't drink like that. Or I haven't since my early twenties, anyway. I had a few years after . . . after I left school when I hated myself. I drank then, just to forget. But now, now I don't see the point. And I can't remember any of it. It's not as though I remember going into my room, brushing my teeth or anything like that. I can't remember a single thing until I woke up the next morning.'

We sat quietly. I was trying to recall what had happened that night; a glance at Rachel told me that she was wondering the same thing.

'So when did you get the photos?' she asked. 'The other ones.' She grimaced. 'Not the one through the post.'

I stood up and went to the door to fetch my bag. Inside was my mobile, and I sat back down next to Rachel and opened my e-mails.

'Last Saturday. Here's the e-mail with the voyeur address. I'll open the link.'

She quickly shook her head. 'No.'

I ignored her. 'You need to know what you're dealing with.'

I opened the link and showed it to her. She scrolled down past video stills of women in the shower, on the tube, at work. She paused at a photo of a woman who could be seen through the opaque glass of her bathroom window and closed the screen, a look of disgust on her face.

'I hope you don't think I had anything to do with that.'

I didn't know anything any more.

She looked down at the e-mail address that had been used to send the link. 'I don't recognize this.'

'I wrote back,' I said. 'It bounced. It must have been set up just to send that. And there's another, too, from a different address.' I opened the e-mail containing the timer gif and showed her. The counter had stopped at 00:00:00.

'I don't get it,' she said. 'What is it?'

'It was a timer.'

She looked startled. 'What do you mean?'

'It was ticking when I opened the e-mail. It was counting down to midnight.'

Realization dawned on her. 'What happened at midnight?' she whispered.

'I didn't stay to find out,' I said. 'It was the night before Joe and Rory came back and I was on my own in the house. I thought someone was going to break in. I went to a hotel.'

She winced. 'I didn't know anything about this.'

'Was he with you that night?'

'He's usually with me. Which night?'

'Last Tuesday.'

She nodded. 'He was at home with me.'

'Were you awake at midnight? Did he do anything? Was he using his phone or iPad or something?'

She looked away. 'No. He wasn't doing anything.'

One glance at her was all it took to know exactly what he was doing at midnight. I shuddered at the thought of him having sex with her while he knew I was terrified something was about to happen to me. He was getting a kick out of this.

'So you met David again after your mum died?'

She kept her eyes averted, but nodded. 'My mum never recovered from Alex's death,' she said. 'She'd always had a problem with depression, but this really tipped her over the edge.'

I thought of Rory and how it would feel to lose him. 'I'd be the same.'

'And nothing seemed to work. She had antidepressants, she had sleeping pills, the lot. None of it made a difference. The house was a shrine to Alex. Photos everywhere, videos running, candles burning. It brought her no comfort. Basically she spent all those years wanting to die, wanting to be with him. And in the end she had breast cancer. By the time she saw the doctor, it had spread to her liver. Apparently she'd found a lump years before and didn't say a word. By the time I realized something was wrong, it was too late.' Her eyes were wet with tears. 'Don't tell me that would have happened if Alex hadn't died.'

'Rachel, I'm really sorry Alex died. I'm sorry you lost your mum, too. But that doesn't change the fact that he raped me.'

'But you withdrew the charge,' she said. 'Why would you do that if you thought he'd done it?'

'I know,' I said. 'I did withdraw it. You know what it was like back then. Well, maybe you don't; you're younger than I am. I'd been to a party; I was drunk. My family were going on holiday the day after the party; we'd been looking forward to it all year. It was supposed to be a celebration. I'd got into university and my parents were so proud of me. I cried the whole holiday and my mum thought I just didn't want to leave home.' I sat for a few minutes, thinking of that holiday, how I'd stayed indoors in the baking heat, scrubbing and scrubbing myself in the shower. 'And then when I got back I told my friend Lauren and she took me to the police station. When my mum and dad found out I'd told the police, they begged me not to take it any further. My dad had been on a jury in a rape trial a few years before. There was a not guilty verdict; he was the only juror who disagreed with it. He was horrified at the way the woman was cross-examined, and he was frightened that would happen to me. He said Alex's defence lawyers would pull me to pieces.' I met her eyes. 'They would have, too. I would have been destroyed.'

She was quiet, then she said, 'I was eleven when Alex went to Oxford. I remember that New Year, just a few months later. He came home for Christmas but he wouldn't leave the house. And then when he did, a couple of days before New Year, he came home crying. He never told us what happened.'

I turned away. I knew my friend, Lauren, had seen him while she and Tom were out in a pub in town. I hadn't asked what she'd said to him, but I guessed it was pretty brutal.

'The next day he went back to Oxford. The term hadn't started, of course, so I guess there weren't many people around.' She put her head on her knees and wrapped her arms around herself. I could barely hear her. 'On New Year's Eve he phoned my mum and said he was going down to the river. There would be fireworks there, he said. And the next day we got a visit from the police. His body was discovered in the river early the next morning.'

She was crying now and there was nothing I could do to comfort her. I wanted to tell her it wasn't my fault, but there was a dead brother between us. Whatever had happened to me, I hadn't died, though I'd wanted to at times. I made a move to hug her, but she wrenched herself away.

'Don't,' she said. 'Don't touch me.'

A shift in the light in the room made me look at my watch. I stood up. 'I'm sorry, Rachel,' I said. 'I'm going to have to go. Joe's got something on at the running club tonight.' I sent him a quick text telling him I'd be five minutes.

She scrambled up and picked up her bag off the breakfast bar, then hesitated. 'Gemma, what are you going to do?' I said nothing, and once again she broke the silence. 'Are you going to tell the police?'

'I have to. You know that.'

'Can you just give me some time? He wasn't meant to go

The Girl I Used to Be

that far. It's just . . . if you do tell the police, will you let me know in advance, so I can be prepared?'

I laughed. 'What, you want me to give you both time to get your story straight?'

'No! I don't want to be with him when he's arrested. I know I need to speak to them. I know I shouldn't have done those things. It's just . . . I think he could be trouble if he's confronted. I don't want to be there.'

Something about the way she said that made me ask, 'Has he hurt you, Rachel?'

She shook her head, but I wasn't convinced.

'Don't say anything to him about this, will you?' I said. 'Keep yourself safe.'

She stared at me then, her eyes brimming with tears, then she turned, her shoulders hunched, and hurried to the lift.

48

Rachel

I checked my phone as soon as I left the building and saw that David had sent a text saying he'd be late coming home. He was waiting for a call from a client and couldn't leave the office until he'd spoken to them. I looked at the time of his message; he'd sent it three minutes before. Quickly I sent a reply, Will miss you, sweetheart xx, and breathed a sigh of relief. He hated it if I didn't reply quickly. I'd had a warning from Gemma about using my mobile in the office when I'd been working for her a few weeks, and after that I had to tell him I couldn't just answer the phone whenever he wanted. Actually it was a relief she'd warned me; I was finding it stressful having to respond when I was meant to be working.

'I'm always worried something's happened to you, Coco!' he'd say. 'I can't help it; I love you so much, and if you don't reply I think the worst.'

It was romantic, really, I knew that, but I wanted to be seen as a professional, and more than once in that first month at work I'd looked up from replying to see clients exchanging glances. I'd make up an excuse, but I knew it sounded pathetic. Once I'd been warned, though, he backed off. The last thing either of us wanted was for me to lose my job.

I was so glad he was going to be home late. When I glanced in the rearview mirror I realized how shocked he'd be to see me like that. My eyes were pink and all my make-up had gone. My skin was shiny and my hair looked damp and bedraggled. I winced. I'd have to get back quickly and get into the shower before David got home.

It was rush hour now and the traffic was congested on the route home. My mind was full of the things Gemma had told me. Voyeur sites. Her underwear. Naked photographs.

I wanted to disbelieve her. I wanted to be able to laugh at her and tell her she was mad. That if those things had actually happened to her – and after all, where was the proof? – David had nothing to do with it.

I couldn't.

None of this really surprised me. Not really. There was a dark side to David; I knew that. I hadn't been married to him for a year yet, but I knew what he was like. He liked control. He liked secrets.

He liked to mess with people's minds.

Once I was home, I got straight into the shower and washed my hair and face, to cover up the fact that I'd cried away my make-up. I'd just stepped out of the shower when I heard David come into the flat and call my name.

My body went into full alert then. I could tell, just from the way he'd spoken, that he wasn't happy about something.

'Hi, David,' I called.

He came into the bathroom and stood in the doorway, watching me.

'How come you're having a shower?' he asked.

'I was so hot today,' I said. 'I just couldn't cool down at work. And I've been stuck in traffic for ages.'

He said nothing and I knew he wasn't convinced.

'And Sophie had styled her hair in a different way,' I said. 'I thought I'd have a go at doing it myself.'

Sophie was always safe ground with David. He found her absolutely no threat at all.

'I would have thought you'd be cooking dinner,' he said. 'It's nearly seven o'clock.' He smiled at me, but it didn't reach his eyes. 'How long does a guy have to wait round here for something to eat?'

'We've got chicken and salad in the fridge,' I said. 'You said last night that that's what you wanted today. I went out to Tesco, remember?'

He stood watching while I put on my robe, then walked behind me into the kitchen.

'Are you okay?' he asked. 'Your eyes look pink. Has someone upset you?'

Yes, you have, I wanted to say, but instead I said, 'No, I squirted shampoo in them when I was washing my hair.' I smiled up at him. 'I'll put some make-up on after dinner, sweetheart. You won't notice it then.'

David was the sort of man who liked women to look immaculate. I think he thought it reflected on him somehow. When Gemma had taken him out to view the properties that day, he'd bitched about her all evening, talking about the state of her car – apparently Rory had left his mark on the back seat – and the fact that she looked tired and didn't have much make-up on. He kept saying how unprofessional she appeared, though really she just looked like any other working woman. Her flaws needled him; I never knew why.

Tonight he seemed on edge. I wondered whether there was a problem at work, but I didn't dare ask. He'd already fallen out with a female colleague who'd picked him up on a mistake he'd made. Apparently she'd been promoted beyond her capacity and would soon be found out for the charlatan she was.

I'd heard quite a bit about her for the last few weeks; I used to want to write to her and ask her to quit, just for my sake.

We sat and watched television – there was a film he'd been wanting to watch on Netflix – and I brought him a bottle of beer and then another. He asked me to get him some whisky while I was in the kitchen and refused to pause the film, so I missed a crucial scene. I knew that appeased him in some way and I wondered what I was meant to have done to him. When someone is like this, you spend all your time trying to second-guess them and it is really, really tiring. Yet I massaged the back of his neck when he complained it was sore from driving, and I laughed as he told me about a guy at work who'd made a fool of himself. All the while I knew something was wrong. I would probably never know what it was; I was used to that.

At ten o'clock I was ready for bed. David said he was going to stay up for a while; he was looking at something on his iPad, and he put it face down when I kissed him good night. I was used to this and normally never let myself think about what he was looking at, but that night as I pressed my lips against his cheek I thought of the website that Gemma had told me about. And though I smiled and said good night, all I felt was disgust. Disgust with him and disgust with myself for putting up with it.

49

Gemma

Once again I got home to find Joe fuming because he thought he was going to be late for his running group.

'You won't be late if you go now,' I said, tired of taking the blame for this all the time. There was an early-morning group he could run with, but in his mind the evening one was more convenient. It wasn't, and I was tired of explaining that every week.

'What's for dinner, Mummy?' asked Rory once Joe had left.

'Haven't you eaten yet, sweetheart? It's getting late.'

'I wasn't hungry before,' he said, sitting at the kitchen island with a hopeful look on his face. 'Can I have a buffet for my dinner?'

I laughed and hugged him. We'd been to a wedding a while ago and Rory couldn't believe his luck when he saw the buffet. He spent most of the afternoon going up there with his plate and choosing what he wanted to eat. I opened the fridge and was so glad I'd remembered to order an online shop to be delivered that morning.

Quickly I prepared a few snacks for Rory, and after he'd eaten I let him beat me in a dozen games of Snap, but all the while my mind was racing with what Rachel had told me.

I had believed her when she'd said she didn't know that David had been in my hotel room that night. She was married to him, so why would she want him to do that? And if she knew I was drugged, she would have been there, just to be sure of what he'd done.

I shuddered. Had she been there? Was she lying to me about that? But then I thought of the look on her face when she saw the voyeur website. She wasn't that good an actress; that was true disgust.

While Rory splashed around in the bath, in his own imaginary world, I sat on the bathroom floor and wondered whether she'd be able to act normal tonight, to pretend nothing had happened. I knew I wouldn't be able to do that.

I thought about what she'd done. She'd started work for me without explaining who she was. That wasn't a crime. She might have passed my home address to David, but it was available online anyway. I wondered about the phone calls I'd received at home, where all I could hear was silence. Was that him? Or even her? I'd given him my mobile number and my e-mail address myself, but everyone at work had my home landline number just in case. And then in London she'd taken my photo, but she hadn't done anything with it, though sending it to me might indicate blackmail was intended. I had a feeling Joe would have received a copy of it one day, but he hadn't so far. What had she done, exactly?

I wanted to talk to Joe, but I worried that instead of thinking about what Rachel had done, he'd think about what I'd done. I'd lied repeatedly to him. Did it matter that I was being set up? All he would think about were my lies. I thought of Caitlin and yearned to talk to her too, the way we used to back in the day. When I met and married Joe, I was so happy. It was as though my family was complete. I knew, though, that no matter how hard she tried, her allegiance would always be to him. In marrying Joe, I'd lost my best friend, in a way.

Of course it wasn't like that really. She'd come round and it would be just like the old days, and we could sprawl on the sofas and chat and everything would be fine. Great, even. She was happy for me to criticize Joe as long as it made her laugh, as long as it was gentle and said with love. But how could I talk to her about a man in my hotel room and the lies I'd told Joe over and over again? Just that day I'd had a text from her saying, Ugh, you saw a mouse? I can't believe you didn't call me! and I thought, *Well, that's because there was no mouse*, but what I actually wrote was It was awful. Don't make me talk about it. Lies upon lies.

After Rory was out of the bath and had been read to, I went downstairs for something to eat. I couldn't face cooking anything then, but I knew Joe would be starving when he came back from his run. I made up a plate of sandwiches and put together a fruit salad, then sat in the living room, thinking about Rachel and how she'd got on that night. Had she spoken to David about it? Lost her temper over him taking things too far? Or maybe he'd noticed a difference in her and wouldn't rest until he found out what was bothering her. And was she really innocent? Perhaps I'd been wrong to believe her when she'd said she knew nothing about the photos and the website.

I grabbed my laptop, went into Incognito mode, and checked the voyeur site, scrolling through it, trying to both see whether I was on it and not look at the other women. My phone beeped, startling me. It was Joe.

Hey Gem, mind if I go for a drink with the boys? xx

Immediately I replied, Of course not. If he stayed out, I could stay on the voyeur site without worrying about him noticing and thinking I was a pervert. I added, Have a great night xxx

After another ten minutes on that site, though, I felt disgusting, and on impulse I reactivated my Facebook account. For old times' sake, I looked up Lauren's page. She and I had been Facebook friends for a long time, but I'd hidden her notifications after a while. She had twins a few years ago and would post on there hourly, updating the world on their achievements. But that night I was thinking about the past, thinking about Alex and the party, so I looked at her page to see what she was up to nowadays.

She must have noticed that I was online, because within ten minutes a message came up.

Hi Gemma! How are you? It's ages since we spoke x

Hi Lauren, I replied. Great to hear from you. I was just thinking about the old days.

Oh me too, she wrote. Especially after seeing Jack's photos. Can't believe how young we look!

Jack?

Jack Howard. Remember him? That geeky boy who took Business Studies in school. He's quite good-looking now – I should've gone out with him when I had the chance! He's put photos up of that trip to London we went on, remember?

I thought back. Jack Howard. That was a name from the past. He'd had a crush on Lauren, but she hadn't had time for anyone except Tom.

I hadn't kept in touch with anybody from school. Even my friendship with Lauren had faded pretty quickly. I'd wanted to put that part of my life behind me, to start again, and in those days, before social media was so popular, it was easy to lose touch. When I met Caitlin, she easily replaced the friendship I'd had with Lauren, and although I knew that was unfair, I think Lauren was relieved by it too. By the time she married Tom and they moved to Australia, our friendship was reduced to Christmas and birthday cards.

I searched for Jack on Facebook. His profile was locked down, so I sent a friend request and went back to chat to Lauren.

We talked for a while, but it was difficult, really. I hardly knew her now. I didn't know her friends, had never met her children. In a way, though, she was living the life I'd thought I'd lead when I went to university. I'd thought I'd emigrate; go as far away from home as I could. The thought of bumping into people from school for the rest of my life had horrified me. Even though my name hadn't been in the press, everyone had known. I knew there had been reunions over the years and normally I would have loved that, loved to have gone back and reminisced with old friends, reliving our youth and celebrating new achievements. I doubted I could have done that even if Alex had lived, but once he'd died, he was deified.

50

Gemma

I'd gone to bed by the time Jack accepted my friend request on Facebook. Joe was still out, clearly making the most of his late pass.

As soon as I found he'd accepted me, I went to search his photos. He was surprisingly organized and his albums were clearly labelled. I opened *Term 1, School* and there we all were. I found Lauren with her long blonde hair standing next to me. That morning we'd both straightened our hair; it had taken us ages and we'd both burned ourselves. We were laughing at Tom. My heart thumped at the sight of myself then, aged sixteen. Contrary to everything I'd thought about myself, my skin looked smooth, my hair shone, and I was much, much thinner than I remembered.

Alex was in that first album. Unlike Lauren and me, he wasn't taking any notice of the camera at all. There were photos of him standing for class rep, of him playing football, and of him lying asleep along three chairs in the canteen, surrounded by hundreds of students. One photo was a close-up. He was doing an experiment in a science lab and the photo showed him looking at the results of a test tube, his expression thoughtful and clever. The photo was used later for the school's prospectus and he was overheard saying he was actually thinking about what he'd have for lunch rather than the results of the experiment.

I lay back in bed and looked at the photos of him. He looked so young. There was nothing predatory about him in those images, yet he'd come into a room where I was sleeping and he'd shut the door and turned off the lamps and he'd raped me, before leaving like a thief in the night. He stole something that night. I was never the same again.

There must have been twenty or thirty albums there. I was just looking through the photos to see whether I recognized anyone when I heard the key turn in the front door. Joe was home.

It took him about half an hour to shower and get into bed and tell me all the exciting things that the running club were up to. Given that I didn't know many of the people he was talking about, I struggled at times to keep track of what he was on about, but I let him talk and talk until eventually his breathing slowed down and finally I knew he was asleep. I got out of bed to go to the bathroom and he didn't stir. He was lying on his side, facing away from me, so I was able to prop myself up on my pillows and open my iPad again.

I could see on Facebook that Jack was online. I looked at the time – it was after midnight. Quickly I typed a message:

Hi, sorry it's late, just wanted to say hello. I was at Wirral School with you – I was Gemma Taylor then. I was Lauren's friend, remember?

I was nervous about his response. He'd been a friend of Alex's – how would he react to me now, after everything that had happened? Just a couple of minutes later a response popped up.

Hi Gemma! Nice to hear from you.

How're things? I asked. Just looking through some of

the photos you've posted - brought back so many memories.

While I waited for him to reply, I flicked through more of them. There were so many people I hadn't thought about in years.

It must be tough for you to look back, he replied.

I stared at the screen. Did that mean he believed me? I'd always thought everyone would have been on Alex's side. Facebook hadn't been around then, thank God, but I knew there would have been a lot of speculation and guessed I wouldn't have come out of it well. He was far more popular than I was at school. That was why I'd rarely gone home in the years following the party; I felt protected from the gossip when I was hundreds of miles from home.

Jack hadn't waited for a reply. He sent another message: Time's gone so fast. You and Lauren look great in your photos. I was badly in need of a makeover!

I laughed, relieved. It seemed he didn't want to discuss it any more than I did. If you knew the effort we went to every single day. I sent that message, then steeled myself and asked: Jack, do you have photos from the party? The party when we got our results?

I held my breath.

Are you sure you want to look at them? I thought it was better I didn't put them up here.

I hesitated. I knew what he meant and didn't want to explain myself. It's OK. I do want to look at them. That was a great night until it all went wrong. I wanted to see what I could remember about it.

There was a five-minute wait then, and I thought maybe he'd gone to bed without logging off, but then he replied:

Yeah, I have loads from that night. I don't have time to go through them and sort out which you might want. I'll stick them on Dropbox if you like.

That would be great, I replied quickly, relieved that I wouldn't have to face comments from old friends who were there. Thanks so much.

I sent him my e-mail address and he replied, Thanks, doing it now.

True to his word, in just a short time I received an e-mail telling me I could view the photos. I had to steel myself to open the album once they were ready to view. I'd never seen any photos from the party. Photos from other events were always posted on the noticeboard in the common room at school, but of course we'd finished school by the time of the party. Besides, I didn't speak to anyone apart from Lauren in those weeks before we went to university. After a while I saw a therapist every week for a few months, but by the time I'd been with Joe for a while I'd dealt with that period of my life. I thought I'd been successful, but now when I opened the album it all came back to me.

The first photos showed everyone arriving at the party at about seven o'clock, when the sun was low. There was a driveway up to the house, with tall trees either side; the road beyond was hidden from the house. It had been a long, hot summer and we were all tanned from the break. I scrolled through the photos and once again realized how young we looked, and how happy and relaxed we were. We'd all been together for those last two years, though some people had come from other schools, and others, like Lauren and me, had been friends since we were very young. Most of us arrived at the party at the same time; when I got there with Lauren and Tom, there were dozens of cars and taxis dropping students off. Everyone carried bottles of wine or crates of beer. There were shouted warnings from parents as they left, but nobody thought the night would be anything other than a fantastic end to our school days.

The photos then moved into the house, where huge bowls

of punch and bottles of beer filled the kitchen table and countertops. There were photos of people I hadn't thought of for years, happy and animated, talking to friends and drinking. Everyone was drinking.

And then I scrolled down and saw a photo of myself, holding a huge glass that was half empty. I knew it would have been full just minutes earlier. That was the thing we all did, then. There was no finesse, no tasting what we were drinking. The goal was to get drunk.

Lauren was there, too, wearing her little white dress with pink flowers. Mine was identical, though the colours were reversed, with white flowers on a dark pink background. We looked like mirror images and were so pleased with ourselves. We'd been shopping that day for our clothes and had hit the shops early so that we had time to get ready all afternoon.

Scrolling through again, I saw my first photo of Alex at the party. He was in the kitchen and the clock was behind him. It was just after eight P.M. and through the window I could see it was dusk. His face was flushed, his eyes bright. He looked just as he had when I'd seen him play football or when we'd bump into him in a pub in town. We didn't know him, didn't know him to talk to, that is. We couldn't have said he was a friend, except that on that night, of course, everyone was our friend. It was the last time we'd see most of the people from school, and besides, we were drunk. But even on the night of the party we didn't talk to him, though we were happy to stand and listen if he was talking to his friends. We'd seen him as in a different league from us. Looking at the photos again, I could see how hard we were on ourselves.

The next photos were outside, where the fairy lights lit up the trees and the barbecue could be seen smoking in the distance. I don't remember eating anything that night, but every time I smelled a barbecue for years afterwards I'd feel ill. I'd been able to smell it in the bedroom. As the night grew darker, you could see from our flushed cheeks and stupid grins that we were getting more and more drunk.

I paused and closed my eyes. There were only a few more albums to go. Soon I would see what was happening while I was upstairs. Asleep.

I heard Joe stir behind me and pushed my iPad under the quilt. He moved further into the middle of the bed, nudging me towards the edge. I tried to move him back, but he grunted and turned over. I held the iPad over the edge of the bed, hoping he wouldn't wake and see it, but the drink had seen to it he wouldn't. He flung his arm over mine, trapping me under it.

I clicked the Off button on the iPad and dropped it gently onto the floor. I was about to settle down to sleep, but a glance at the clock told me it was after one A.M. I groaned. I'd have to be up at seven. I snuggled down in bed, pressing my back against Joe. *Or maybe half past.* I reached for my phone to reset the alarm and changed my mind when I saw a text from Rachel.

I need to talk to you. Can you get to work at 8 tomorrow?

51

Gemma

Tuesday, August 15

I wasn't popular with Joe the next morning as I was up and ready to go to work at seven thirty A.M. I shook him awake just before I left.

'Rory will be up soon,' I said. 'I've put a carton of juice and a banana on my side of the bed so he can get in with you and have that, but don't go back to sleep, will you?'

He groaned. 'It's still early! Why are you going in now? The office doesn't open until nine.'

'I've got things I need to do,' I said. 'I couldn't get back to the office last night, so I have to get things ready for the meeting.'

He'd lost interest already.

Rory shot into our bedroom just before I left and I gave him a huge hug. 'Your drink's here, sweetheart, and you can have that banana if you can't wait for breakfast. Dad's still dozing. Don't let him sleep too long, will you?' I winked at him. 'But don't torture him!'

He laughed and I could see he was trying to think up punishments for a sleepy dad. 'Can I go on your iPad?'

'Just for half an hour,' I warned, and set the alarm on it. 'When the alarm goes off, it's time for breakfast.'

I closed down Facebook and deleted my history. The last thing I needed was Rory looking at voyeur sites or photos of me when I was young and drunk. He found the game he wanted to play, then opened his carton and accidentally spilled some of his juice down Joe's back.

When I reached the office at eight A.M., Rachel was waiting for me at her desk. Her face was pale and I wondered if she'd had as little sleep as I'd had that night. Her eyes were red-rimmed and her hands shook on her mug of coffee.

She saw me looking at her and flushed. 'I know, I look awful.'

'You're fine,' I said. 'Tell people you have a cold.'

'In August?'

'Hay fever, then.'

I picked up the coffee she'd made for me and sat down next to her.

'I have something to tell you,' she said. 'Last night.' She swallowed hard. 'Last night I didn't say anything to David, obviously.'

So his name *was* David.

I waited.

'We watched a film on Netflix and he had a few beers.' She grimaced. 'With whisky chasers.'

'Does he drink too much?'

She nodded. 'He does sometimes. There's always an excuse, you know? He's celebrating something or someone's annoyed him . . .'

I wondered what excuse he had for drinking the nights he was terrorizing me. Was that a time for celebration?

'Anyway, last night he was annoyed because I wouldn't have a drink. I was frightened of telling him I knew what had happened, so I wouldn't even have one.'

'Good idea.'

'Anyway, I went to bed before him. I had a shower, said I was tired. He was on his iPad and stayed up for a while. I don't know what he was doing.'

My heart sank. *We'll probably find out in the next day or two.*

'Anyway, I went to bed and fell asleep quite quickly.' She looked away from me and started to fiddle with a pen on my desk. 'Have you ever woken up suddenly when you hear something that you wouldn't pay any attention to when you were awake?' I sat quietly, waiting for her to go on. 'I used to have an alarm clock that made a tiny sound – a little click – a second before the alarm went off. I would always wake up when I heard it.'

I nodded. 'Yes, I know what you mean.'

'Last night I woke up like that. I jumped awake but I didn't know why. It was really hot when I went to bed, and when I woke up, David was getting into bed. He pulled the quilt up over us; I must have kicked it off.' Her face was red now. 'I wear a T-shirt to bed – one of David's. It comes down to here.' She gestured to her thighs. 'When I woke up, it was pulled up around my waist. I didn't think anything of it; I never sleep well when it's really hot, so I thought I must have been kicking around.'

I sat very still, suddenly terrified of what she'd say.

'The thing is, Gemma . . .' She stopped, then looked at the clock and started again, speaking faster this time. 'I began to think about why I'd woken up. I couldn't go back to sleep afterwards; I never can if I wake up really quickly like that. And as I was lying there I was trying to think what had woken me. I hadn't heard David in the bathroom; I can sleep through anything, normally, so even if he'd had a shower it wouldn't disturb me.'

'Maybe you heard your bedroom door open?'

'It wasn't closed. We never close it. No, it wasn't that.'

'The bathroom door?'

She shook her head. 'It wasn't that, either. It doesn't click shut. And we leave the hall light on overnight, so it wasn't as though I heard him switch that off, either.'

Outside the window a bus stopped and I saw Sophie get off and cross the road to go into the corner shop. She'd be here any minute. I could hardly complain about her being early, but I knew we needed more time.

'Sophie will be here in a minute,' I said urgently. 'What do you think it was?'

Her eyes filled with tears. 'I think he was taking photos of me,' she said. 'While I was asleep. I heard the click and that's what woke me. Then he got into bed. He's got one of those lamps that charges up a phone. He plugged his phone into that, then kissed me good night and went to sleep.' She looked really miserable. 'I couldn't sleep.'

'Has he ever taken photos of you before?'

She shook her head. 'No, nothing like that.' There was a pause, and she said, 'Or at least not as far as I'm aware. How would I know, though?'

52

Rachel

Sophie came up to us then and I had to busy myself with the voicemail messages and e-mails, and get ready for the morning meeting. It was hard to concentrate and I could tell from the expression on Gemma's face that she was finding it equally difficult. Brian was back at work and I noticed she passed on the keys from the flats we'd viewed the day before, asking him to take them back to Bill later that day. My face smarted at the memory of that conversation.

I could tell that Gemma wanted to speak to me. She kept looking over and checking where Sophie was, as though she was going to come and talk to me if she got the chance. I kept my eyes averted. I couldn't focus on work and think of everything we'd talked about. I needed to keep my mind off David's activities last night, but now that I'd seen the voyeur site I was terrified that photos of me would end up there. I desperately wanted to check it, and I think that was when I realized what it had been like for Gemma. She'd said that she'd been obsessive about viewing it every day, looking at the new pictures that appeared there hourly, trying to work out if she was on there. I felt sick at the thought of David doing that to either of us, and I had to force myself to be friendly to him when he sent his regular texts.

Eventually Gemma sent me an e-mail.

Are you feeling OK? Do you need to go home?

I gave a quick look around the office. A young couple were looking at the details of some first-time-buyer properties; otherwise only Sophie was there and she was preoccupied with the coffee machine.

No, I don't want to go home. He's working from home today and I'll end up saying something to him.

Sophie clattered in, bringing drinks for all of us and the biscuit tin.

'What were those flats like yesterday?' she asked me.

I didn't dare meet Gemma's eye. 'They were great, yeah.'

'Ask Brian to take you next time he goes,' Gemma told her. 'Have a good look around before we get tenants in.'

As soon as Sophie was back at her desk, Gemma sent me another message.

You need to say something. Those photos could be anywhere.

Instantly my face became hot. I know.

The clients came over to speak to Gemma then, and I heard them ask whether they could view a house that evening. She called the vendors to arrange it, and then when they'd left the office she took her purse from her bag. 'Sophie, would you do me a huge favour? It's Lucy's daughter's birthday next week. Would you pop out and get her a card and a present? Oh, and some wrapping paper, too.'

Sophie looked delighted. Time out of the office and shopping with someone else's money! She took the money and was gone before Gemma could change her mind.

As soon as the office was empty, Gemma pulled up a chair next to my desk.

'We need to go to the police.' She spoke in a low voice,

even though nobody was around. 'He took those photos of me and now he's taken photos of you. He could be sending them anywhere. It's illegal; you know it is. We need to do something. We need to stop him.'

'I know,' I said. 'But you know it'll get into the press, don't you? It's the sort of thing they love. Especially with him doing it to both of us. I read about a court case a while ago where a man was filming his wife at home and it was all over the newspapers. Aren't you worried about that?'

'Of course I am. Legally they can't print our names, but it doesn't stop people talking. They kept my name out of the paper before, but it didn't make much difference. Everyone knew about it before too long. It was awful.'

I couldn't help it. I snapped, 'What do you think it was like for us? At least you're still alive.'

She stood up, her face pale and strained. She leaned over and whispered, 'You think there wasn't a cost to me, too? I was raped!' Her voice shook. 'And now your husband is abusing me.'

I watched as she went back to her desk and put the files and stationery into her drawer. She locked the drawer and logged out of her computer. I couldn't take my eyes off her; she didn't give me a second glance.

Without another word to me she walked out of the office.

53

Gemma

Tuesday, August 15

I drove round aimlessly for a while, too shaken to go home. I parked the car in the car park overlooking the River Dee and paid for an hour so that I could sit and think.

I felt the bite of Rachel's words more than she probably expected. She loved her brother, clearly, and when he died she was only young. No matter what I thought of him, the idea of her seeing the police arrive at their house at New Year with such terrible news was truly awful. I didn't hear about it until a few weeks later. My parents had read about it in the local newspapers, but they didn't tell me, and by then, just months after leaving school, I wasn't really in touch with anyone any more. We were all away at different universities and it was too easy to slip away from the group. I'd refused to go home that Christmas and so we all went to my grandparents' in Staffordshire instead. I went back to London from there.

I do remember the shock of hearing about Alex's death, though. I'd been invited to Lauren's nineteenth birthday party at her place in Nottingham, where she was studying

English. Her birthday was at the end of January and I hadn't seen her since we'd started university the previous September, so I got the train from London and went to stay with her for the weekend.

As soon as I saw her, I knew something had happened. Her eyes were red and swollen and at first I thought she and Tom had broken up. She linked her arm through mine, just as she used to on the way to school, and we walked out of the station and into the cold night and she told me then that Alex had died.

I was really shocked at my reaction. I couldn't stop sobbing and she was trying to tell me it wasn't my fault and I knew it wasn't, of course it wasn't, but it felt like one big burden on top of the rest of it. I think what got to me was that I'd suddenly remembered him as the boy who dressed up as a girl for the school play. There was a moment where he was so clearly enjoying himself and everyone had laughed. I remember leaning forward to watch him, loving his confidence and the way his smile lit up his face when the audience laughed with him.

Rachel was probably at the school that night. It was odd to think we'd shared that experience, so many years before we met. I pictured her as an eleven-year-old girl, and in that instant I didn't know how I hadn't seen the resemblance between her and Alex. They had different colouring and he was six feet tall and built for the rugby pitch, which had made his acting debut even funnier. Now when I thought about it, I remember seeing him in the middle of our summer exams, looking as though he was really trying hard to think of the right way to say something in an essay, and I knew I'd seen that look on Rachel's face at work.

I winced. I wished I hadn't thought of that resemblance now. It would make it so hard to see her again.

Suddenly I felt overwhelmed. I couldn't go on like this, working with someone who hated me. Being destroyed by her husband. I picked up my phone.

'Mum? Can we come up and stay with you for a few days?'

54

Gemma

I went back to the office then and luckily Sophie was there, so I focused on work and avoided speaking to Rachel on my own. I knew I'd have to talk to her again about David, to persuade her to go to the police, but I couldn't summon up the courage to do it just then. I sent them both home ten minutes before closing time and phoned Lucy to tell her that I wasn't feeling well and that I would be taking some time off. She was great, offering to work every day for the next week.

'I'll ask my mum to take Maisie to school and back,' she said. 'She won't mind. I can be there nine to five.'

'I'll drop the keys off at your house on my way home,' I said. 'All my appointments are in the diary. But Lucy, you're in charge, okay?'

'Not Rachel? You said you were promoting her.'

'You're in charge,' I said again. 'I'll let the others know.'

She was quiet, then said, 'Is something the matter?'

My eyes filled with tears and I started to speak, but I couldn't go on.

'It's okay,' she said. 'Talk to me about it when you get back. And don't worry. I'll keep an eye on everything. I'm really glad of the work and if you need to stay off a bit longer, then that's fine.'

Within a couple of hours I was driving to my parents' house with Rory. Joe hadn't been keen on coming up and offered to do some work on the living room and kitchen while we were away.

'There's no point us all going,' he said. 'It's not like I'd have much to do there. I might as well stay behind and get some jobs done in the house. It's impossible to do anything like that while Rory's around. I could paint the kitchen if you like? Freshen it up a bit.'

Part of me wanted him to come with me, but I knew I wouldn't be able to talk properly to my mum with him there. And I needed to. There was too much for me to deal with now.

It's only about thirty miles from my house to my mum's, but we tend to meet up in Chester to do some shopping and then she comes back to my house for dinner, rather than us going to visit them. It had been the same since I left home at eighteen. Every month my parents would come down to London for the day. My room there had been so small it was impossible for us to stay in it together, so we'd walk for miles, talking about my course and my new friends, and my mum and dad would talk about their jobs and the holidays they planned. We never spoke about what had happened.

That day, travelling up with Rory for company in the car, I found myself yearning to be back home, as I still saw it, despite everything.

Rory had been delighted to be visiting them with me.

'Just you and me, Mum?' he'd asked. 'No Dad?'

'Daddy will stay behind and do some painting.'

Rory had looked bemused, and I guessed he was thinking of Joe using his watercolours.

We'd packed our bags and set off on our little trip. He was

excited to be sleeping in my old bedroom and chatted constantly throughout the journey, telling me all the things he was going to do with his grandparents. I felt guilty then that he didn't see them more often; they'd been really excited to have us visit too, though I knew my mum had been concerned when I called her.

'Everything's okay with you and Joe?' she'd asked nervously. 'You'd tell me if there was a problem, wouldn't you?'

I pictured myself telling her everything that had happened. She would have had a heart attack before I'd finished.

'Everything's fine,' I'd said instead, but she didn't seem convinced.

We parked in their driveway and Rory jumped out, eager to ring their doorbell. This was the game they always had to play, to be amazed we were there.

As soon as my mum opened the door and shouted, 'Grandad, we've got surprise visitors!' Rory ran through the house to find him. I must have been looking a real state because my mum took one look at me and hugged me tightly.

We went into the house to find my dad. The game was that he would hide and Rory would have to find him. Although my dad was over six feet tall, this took longer than you might think.

Eventually, after finding him in the garden shed, where he was actually oblivious to our arrival, Rory and I sat at the patio table while my mum brought us some dinner and my dad made drinks.

It was so peaceful sitting there with them. The garden was enclosed and private, giving an aura of safety and security that I badly needed. Rory chattered away to them about all the things he and Joe had got up to in Ireland and I was able to sit back and relax.

'You've been working too hard,' said my mum. 'You'll stay for a few days?'

'I'm having a week off,' I said. 'I'm going to sort something out with Lucy, too.' I hadn't even thought of that until now. 'I'm going to ask her to work every weekday for a while, just for a few hours, so that I can have a break.'

'When did you last manage a day off work?'

'I took a day when Joe and Rory came back from Ireland.'

'And before that?'

'When Rory wasn't well.'

'It's not right, Gemma,' said my mum softly. 'And it's not fair, either, that you're taking on the whole burden. I thought Joe would go back to work soon, but you need to have a think about the way you want to live your life. It's not fair that you're the one working all the time.'

I was glad Joe wasn't there; she would have said the same thing even if he had been. It always caused problems when she complained about the way we lived.

'I know,' I said. 'I need to reconsider things. But Joe wants us to go and live in Ireland. His brother Brendan is moving there.'

'What will he do over there? Is there work?'

'He seems to think I could set up my business over there.'

'And he'll stay home with Rory?' Her mouth tightened. 'But surely you couldn't just start up in another country?'

Luckily Rory interrupted us to ask if he could have a bath. They'd had a Jacuzzi put in when they had their bathroom refitted the year before and it was always the highlight of his day. Mum's attention was on him then; she took him upstairs while my dad cleared the table and tidied up the kitchen.

'No, sit down,' he said, when I tried to help. 'Have a rest.'

I closed my eyes and tried to blank my mind but couldn't. I had so many thoughts racing around my head. Joe was the least of my problems right then, though of course my main concern was stopping him from finding out what had happened. I knew I should go to the police. I knew now where David lived, and as long as Rachel hadn't warned him, it would be easy for them to question him. I was furious that he thought he could get away with it, but I was terrified, too, at what he might do next. I knew I needed to act before he could do anything more.

At seven o'clock I heard my phone beep from my handbag in the living room. My dad passed me my bag. 'It might be Joe,' he said. I knew he thought I was there because we'd fallen out.

It was a text from Rachel.

I'm really sorry. I shouldn't have shouted at you.

Relief surged through me.

It's OK, I replied. He's your brother. I know you loved him.

I sat in the sun a minute longer, then sent another message: You know you have to delete these texts?

Immediately she replied: I will. I'm deleting them straight away.

I had to know. What are you going to do?

This answer took longer. I need to get away from him. I might go abroad and put all this behind me. I thought I'd better warn you because of work.

Don't worry about that, I replied. As long as you're safe.

She asked: What are you going to do? You should tell the police now. Please, just tell me before you do.

She was right on both counts. She needed to get away. I needed to tell the police.

A second later she sent another message: We should go to the police together.

But Rachel, I wrote, if I talk to the police then you are implicated.

I know, she replied. I'll admit everything. I can't

believe the way I've acted. I've told David I overheard you on the phone saying you were thinking of going to the police, so he shouldn't do anything for a while. I said you wouldn't tell me what was going on.

Then another message popped up: He's back.

55

Gemma

Upstairs, my mum was sitting on a chair in the bathroom, watching Rory in the bath. It was a huge corner whirlpool bath and he would happily spend hours in there with all his toy fish and dolphins. I stood in the doorway and watched my mum as she chatted to him. Her face was soft and happy, and she smiled when she saw me there.

'It's like looking at you all over again,' she said. 'It's just wonderful, like a glimpse into the past.'

I knelt down by the side of the bath and tipped some water over Rory's hair. He laughed and splashed me, drenching me.

'Will you tell me what's troubling you, sweetheart?' she whispered. 'What's on your mind?'

Rory's ears pricked up at this. 'What's on your mind, Mum?'

I gave my mum an exasperated look.

'She's trying to guess what's for supper.' She stood up and reached for a warm, soft towel. 'Can you guess what it is?'

Rory stood up so quickly he almost slipped over. He clambered out of the bath and let my mum wrap the towel around him. 'And put one round my head,' he said. 'Like in the spa.'

My mum raised her eyebrows at me.

'We play spas, sometimes,' I admitted. 'He has cucumber on his eyes and I have to paint his toenails.'

'And does Daddy do that, too?' she asked Rory.

'No, but we did it to him when he was asleep on the sofa.' He laughed. 'Show her the photos, Mum.' He hugged me and just for that moment I forgot all my worries.

Later, while Rory was in bed and my dad was at a quiz night at their local pub, my mum and I sat on the patio. They have a fire pit, which my dad had lit before he went, to take the chill off the evening. She'd poured me a gin and tonic and I guessed she was trying to get me to open up to her.

'Is there something wrong at home? Have you and Joe been arguing?'

'No. Well, in a way. He's got himself all excited, thinking we could move to Ireland. But I couldn't do that. I've got the office and I wouldn't be able to operate over there. As you said, I don't know the area and I'm not qualified to work in a different country. It's just a pipe dream for him, really.'

'Does he accept that?'

I sighed. 'He and Brendan seem to think it could work.'

'Well, why doesn't he find work over there and let you take a few years off with Rory and get qualified then? You could keep the office open here and take on a manager. It's doable, isn't it? You could even come back every month or so. Flights are very cheap from Liverpool to Ireland.'

I kept quiet. I couldn't say to her that Joe had no intention of getting work. I knew what my mum thought of that. She'd been wary ever since he gave up his job to look after Rory.

'That's not the problem, though,' I said. 'I can deal with him.' I wanted to tell her what the problem was, but how could I? And then I thought, if I couldn't speak to her, I couldn't speak to anyone, so I said, tentatively, 'You remember what happened to me when I was eighteen? At that party?'

She stiffened. 'Of course I do, pet.'

'I've been thinking about it. I should have let the police take it to court. It wasn't fair, what I did.'

'What *you* did wasn't fair?'

'No. Alex was arrested but then let go without being charged, and people thought he was guilty just because he was arrested.'

'But he *was* guilty, Gemma! You mustn't feel bad about that.'

'I know, but he didn't have the chance to put his case forward, did he? Going to court would have been horrible, but at least he would have had an opportunity to have his say.'

'What could he say?' she asked angrily. 'He'd either say you agreed to it – and how could you prove you hadn't? – or that he hadn't done anything. There was no evidence by then. If you'd gone to the police at the time, it would have been different, but two weeks later? You think he would've just admitted it?'

'I had no choice,' I said, trying to keep my temper. 'We went on holiday the next day. By the time I was ready to tell the police, I was in another country.'

'I know, pet,' she said. 'I'm sorry. I wasn't blaming you. I just meant that after two weeks there was no evidence. His lawyers would have made things really difficult for you.'

'I know,' I said. 'I know. But . . . I don't know. I just think he should have had a voice. If he had, he might not have . . . Well, he might still be alive.'

'It was terrible what happened to him,' she said. 'It was. But that's not your fault, Gemma. And his death may well have been an accident anyway. There was nothing to show he'd done it on purpose.'

I knew he had, though. Even though we weren't friends, I'd seen him most days for two years and I'd got an idea of the sort of person he was. He was proud and ambitious; he lost his reputation and his dreams when he was arrested. It couldn't be a coincidence that he drowned at New Year, just four months later.

'He'd always wanted to go to Oxford, you know,' I said after a pause. 'I remember on our induction day when we were sixteen, we had to say what we wanted to achieve by the end of the course. I could tell from the way he talked about it that he'd succeed.'

My mum said nothing, her lips tight.

'And I don't think the arrest would have stopped him practising law,' I said. 'I rang the Law Society a few years ago to ask them.'

She looked sharply at me. 'What did you do that for?'

'I needed to know. I phoned a long time after I heard that he'd died. Years. Of course I thought he'd killed himself and then Caitlin said maybe he'd done it because he couldn't have the future he'd wanted.'

My mother made a sound, then, a kind of *Well, he should have thought of that* kind of noise.

'But when I spoke to them, they said that as the charge had been dropped, it would be possible for him to practise. He'd have to declare the charge, but they thought it would be okay.'

'And you're thinking you would have done better taking it to court, to let him have his say? Gemma, sweetheart, you did the right thing. The only thing,' said my mum. 'What would that have done to you? And they could have paid for the best lawyers; you know that.' Her voice wobbled and I could see she was holding back tears. 'Think how you would have felt if they'd found him not guilty.'

I knew that would have crushed me, and I knew, too, that that was exactly how I would feel if I were accused and couldn't have my say, too.

And I thought of the ripples from that one night in August, when everything changed forever for Alex and for me, and for our families, too. We'd all suffered the after-effects of that night. The pain didn't just belong to me.

I spoke without thinking. 'I met his sister the other day.'

'Alex's sister? I didn't know you knew her.'

'I didn't even know he had a sister until recently,' I said. 'I didn't know anything about him.'

'I only knew because Lauren's mum told me,' said my mum. 'She came round to see me after you and Lauren had moved away.' She grimaced. 'I think she wanted to gossip about it. I had to avoid her for a while.'

I knew how she felt. After I'd reported the rape, a few girls from school wanted to talk to me, and I'd felt there was something almost indecent about their interest. After a while I wouldn't answer the door to them and would get my brother to say I was out when they phoned.

'Their mother died last year,' I said.

My mum was quiet, and then said, 'She must have been young. What was the matter with her?'

'She had cancer.'

'Oh, the poor woman. That on top of everything else.'

I wanted to tell her what Rachel had told me, about their mother's dependency on her, the fact that she'd wanted to die. I couldn't. Though I wasn't to blame, I was involved. I would have given anything for that not to be the case. My mum, though, didn't need to be. She didn't deserve to hear those things.

'How did you meet her?'

Just then my dad came back and spared me from having to answer that. We chatted then about the quiz and the team that had won, and we didn't go back to talking about Rachel and her family, though my mum kept looking at me all evening, and I knew the question was preying on her mind.

56

Gemma

Wednesday, August 16

The next morning I waited until the office was open, then sent Rachel an e-mail through the work system. It was the only safe means of communicating as there was no way David could intercept the messages.

```
Everything OK last night?
```

She must have been on her own at her desk, because she replied quite quickly:

```
I think so. I'm not sure. Who can tell, though?
```

I winced. Surely she should be able to go to sleep without worrying about someone taking explicit photos of her. And then I thought of myself, in my hotel room in London, and became fired up. I started to type an e-mail, saying:

```
I'm going to talk to the police when I come back to
Chester. You can come with me if you want to but I'm
going anyway.
```

Before I clicked Send, I stopped. David was her husband. Was she really going to wait for the police to come round? Surely she would tell him – or he would guess. That would be worse. Much worse. I shuddered. What would he do if he discovered she knew and hadn't told him?

I deleted my message. Instead, I wrote: You shouldn't have to live like that, and she replied, I know.

There the conversation ended. I went out with my mum and dad to take Rory on the ferry over to Liverpool and spent the day at the museums. Later we went for afternoon tea at a hotel, before going back to our car on the underground train. That was the thing that impressed Rory the most; he hadn't been on an underground train before and was beside himself. The fact that he was carrying a box of cakes from the hotel only added to his happiness.

Later in the afternoon, back at my parents' home, we borrowed the paddling pool from the next-door neighbour and she kindly sent her little girl, Evie, in to play, too. I don't know what it is about Rory, but if you want to keep him amused, just give him some water and he'll be happy for hours. So I sat outside to make sure the children were safe while my mum and dad napped on their garden chairs. Clearly the day had taken it out of them.

I pulled out my iPad and went back to look at the photos that Jack had put on Facebook, the photos of us throughout the two years we'd all spent together. I'd meant to tell Rachel to send Jack a friend request so that she could look at them, but I wasn't sure whether they would upset her too much. From the comments under the photos it was clear Jack had only recently put them up, and name after name of friends I'd had in school popped up to make fun of us all. I wondered if any of them remembered how that summer term had ended, though they would have known at the time, of course.

'Who was that girl . . .' I imagined them saying. 'That scruffy little redhead . . . Didn't something happen to her?

I can't remember now what it was . . . Did she die or something?'

I blinked hard to stop the tears falling.

And then I gathered my courage and looked at the photos from the party that Jack had put on Dropbox.

I turned the iPad away from the sun. I could see which albums I'd viewed, and clicked on the next one. It was clear that Jack had run out of steam, or maybe even just run out of film, because of course it wasn't a digital camera that he was using then. The last fifty or so photos were random ones rather than several at a scene. So there was a group of girls doing karaoke, then a photo of the fire pit with all the smokers sitting around with bottles of beer. Then there was Lauren, sitting in the hammock with Tom. I stopped at that one, remembering that I'd wanted to go home at that point, but Lauren had avoided my eyes. I could just about see the love bite on her neck; it looked at first like one of the pink flowers on her dress.

I steeled myself. Now I was about to see what happened while I was upstairs. There were people dancing on the patio, though I think they were just doing it for a laugh. Or at least I hoped so. The next scene was the kitchen. Jack must have been making his way back into the house. Lauren was there now.

I remembered her telling me in the taxi going home that night that someone had tipped them out of the hammock and she'd got mud on her dress. I didn't reply, didn't say a word. I'd pretended to be asleep.

In the first shot she was at the kitchen sink, splashing her face with water. Tom was holding her hair up and for a second I saw how much Jack had liked her, as the droplets of water splashed her face, her hair held aloft giving her an air of grace that the love bite completely destroyed.

In the next shot she was sitting on Tom's knee, her arm casually around his neck. How much had it hurt Jack to take that photo? And behind her, just about to walk out of the kitchen door into the hallway beyond was a young man. Not a boy. You could never have called him a boy.

This man was dressed in jeans and a Coral T-shirt. It was a T-shirt that was on sale at Glastonbury that summer. The same T-shirt that Alex had been wearing all evening.

It wasn't Alex, though, who was leaving the room unnoticed by the crowd.

It was David.

57

Gemma

My reaction was so physical it was as though someone had thumped me in the chest. For a second or two, no matter how wide I opened my mouth, I couldn't breathe. I put my head between my legs and tried to breathe, just as I had in the days and months, even, after that party. My parents were napping on their chairs on the deck and I could hear the distant sounds of Rory and his little friend as they splashed around.

And then it was as though the air burst out of me and with one huge gasp I started to hyperventilate.

'Mum!' Rory ran over to me and shook my arm. 'Mum! What's wrong?' He screamed. 'Granny! Granny!'

I heard my mother gasp, then shout my dad's name. She came running over to me, but all I could see was a blur.

'What is it, Gemma? What's the matter?'

I was struggling to breathe again. My chest was tight and felt like a balloon was about to explode, but I just couldn't get the air out.

I heard my dad in the kitchen, pulling open drawers, swearing under his breath, and then he was uncurling my fists and I could feel the rough rasp of a paper bag in my hands. He knelt in front of me, his eyes fixed on mine.

'Breathe into it, pet,' he said, and then I remembered him saying that all those years before and tears streamed down my cheeks. 'Breathe in and let's count. One, two, three, four. That's right. Now breathe out. Come on, blow hard. As hard as you can. And look at me. Look at me!' He counted again and I watched his face intently. 'You can do it. Come on, let's count again.'

My mum was hovering in the background, trying to reassure Rory and Evie that I was okay. She made Rory pull out the plug of the paddling pool with the promise of a spa night later if he was good now, then sent him off to find the biscuit tin for both of them.

'I knew we shouldn't have talked about it,' she kept saying. 'It's my fault. You never get over that sort of thing. I shouldn't have asked her questions.'

I could see my dad didn't know what she was talking about, but then something in him recalled doing this in the past, when he'd had to help me to breathe to cope with what happened. There was anger in his eyes, not at my mum or me, but fury that something that had happened to me, his only daughter, was still hurting me even fifteen years later.

Slowly, my eyes fixed on my dad's, my breathing returned to normal. My mum was inside now with Rory, having packed Evie off home. When the panic attack was finally over, my dad got up and pulled a chair over next to mine.

'We'll talk about it, Gem,' he said, 'but not now. Have a rest and we'll get Rory to bed. And if you're not up to it tonight, don't worry. You're here for a few days. There's plenty of time.'

My iPad had turned itself off while I was away from it. I couldn't bear the thought of seeing that picture again, but at the same time I panicked in case I might lose it. I asked my dad to go and check that Rory was okay, and in the couple of minutes he was gone, I sent it to myself on my private e-mail.

When my e-mail alert sounded, I knew it was safe.

* * *

That night I went to bed early, exhausted from the day. The tiredness I felt then seemed like the result of having to hold myself in for fifteen years.

I couldn't risk looking at the photo again. There was no one I could speak to except Rachel, and she was running her own gauntlet at the moment. I heard my mum downstairs, talking to Joe on the phone. She'd told him I was having an early night, but I'd made her promise not to tell him about my panic attack.

Why was David at the party? This thought raced around my mind for hours. What was he doing there? Rachel had said he and Alex were best friends, but that party had only been for people from school. I remember him saying that when a girl asked him if she could bring a friend.

'It's just for us,' he'd said. 'I don't want anyone else there, just us lot. It's the last time we'll all get together.'

I'd been there from the beginning and I hadn't seen David. I would have noticed him simply because he wasn't someone I'd met before. Everywhere I'd looked that night there were people I'd known for two years. Even if someone took completely different subjects, I had still seen them in the canteen or in the library or on the school bus. And he was a good-looking man, too, but that was the thing – all of the other students, well, they were more like boys to me. We called them boys, not men. David looked older than us and would have stuck out a mile.

I picked up my phone and sent a Facebook message to Jack Howard, the guy who'd taken the photos, asking him to call me whenever he was free for a quick chat. Within a few minutes, my phone rang.

'Hi,' I said. 'Sorry it's late.'

'Don't worry,' he said. 'What is it?' His voice was deeper than I remembered, but I knew I would have recognized it. He sounded friendly and I realized again how cut off I'd been from my old school friends.

'Thanks for sending the photos,' I said. 'There's one that I wanted to ask you about. It's a photo of Lauren.'

'Which one?' he said drily. 'I took tons of her.'

I laughed. 'You liked her, didn't you?'

'I was crazy about her. Took me a while to get over her. Still, that's a long time ago.'

I remembered his Facebook status. 'You're married now?'

'Yes; we're having a baby in a few months.'

'Oh that's lovely,' I said. 'Congratulations.'

'Thanks. So the photo – which one was it?'

'It's the one where Lauren's in the kitchen, sitting on Tom's knee.'

'Just a second, I'll have a look at it on my laptop.' I waited a few seconds, then he said, 'Oh that one. Yeah, I was a bit of a masochist, wasn't I?'

'You see that guy in the background? Do you know him?'

'That's weird. I never noticed him standing there. He wasn't at our school, was he?'

'No, he wasn't.'

'What was he doing there?' he said. 'It was just meant to be us, wasn't it? I remember I had to tell some guys they couldn't bring their girlfriends because they weren't from Wirral. Alex's mum and dad were really strict about that.'

'I heard Alex tell someone that too,' I said.

'I have seen him before, though. He looks older than the rest of us, doesn't he?' He was quiet for a while, and then he said, 'Oh yeah, I know who he is.'

I held my breath.

'I met him once or twice when he played hockey for All Saints School. We'd play against him sometimes. Alex went to All Saints until he was sixteen, before he came to Wirral.' There was a pause. 'I remember now. He went to Glastonbury with Alex.'

'Are you sure?'

'Yes, just the two of them went. The rest of us couldn't afford it. I heard all about it when Alex got back. He'd had a great time.'

'Do you know his name?' I asked.

'I don't know. I would have known it then. I'll get back to you if I remember.'

'Thanks. You've been a great help.'

'Gemma, is this something to do with what happened that night?' he asked.

'I don't know,' I said. 'I really don't know.'

'I just couldn't believe Alex had done that. I thought I knew him pretty well.' I said nothing and he went on. 'I'm not saying you were lying. Honestly I'm not. It's just . . . well, he was one of the last people I would've thought was capable of rape.'

I ended the call without another word and found that my face was drenched with tears. I wanted Joe. I wanted him to hug me and tell me everything would be all right. I knew he'd be out with Mike but sent him a message:

I love you, Joe. I miss you. I'll be home soon xx

Immediately my phone beeped.

I miss you too, sweetheart. It's not the same without you here. I love you. I'll call tomorrow xx

I smiled and sent him a photo that my mum had taken in the garden. I had my arms around Rory, my face next to his.

When I heard my phone beep a second later I expected it to be a quick reply from Joe, but it was a message from Jack.

I'm sorry if I upset you, he wrote. I feel awful about that. It's just that Alex was one of my best friends. About that guy - I've just found my old hockey fixtures. His name is David Henderson.

I felt a flash of victory at discovering David's real name. I replied immediately: Did you see him at the party? I know he's in the photo, but did you notice him there?

No, he replied. I didn't notice him at all. I would have wondered why he was there and said something to Alex.

If he had, none of this might have happened.

Desperate to speak to Rachel, but knowing she couldn't receive a call from me at home, I sent her an e-mail she'd get at work the next day.

Rachel, I need to talk to you. Can you call me as soon as you get this? Make sure nobody can overhear you.

58

Gemma

Thursday, August 17

I didn't sleep that night. How could I? I had a long bath to try to calm myself down, but hours later, my heart was still pounding.

I didn't get out of bed until nine A.M. the following morning. I was expecting Rachel to call me, but my phone was quiet. I had a quick shower, taking my phone into the bathroom with me, but she still didn't call. I tried to rationalize it: She'd call when things were quiet. They'd be having the morning meeting, and then she'd say she was going out to view a property and she'd call me from her car, I knew it.

I looked terrible that morning and my mum wanted me to stay in bed, but I was too agitated for that. Instead she said she and my dad would take Rory out for the day.

'Unless you want us to stay with you?' she asked. 'I think one of us should. What do you think?'

I needed to have that conversation with Rachel in private, so I refused.

'It's okay. I'll be fine. I'll catch up on a box set or something and just stay on the sofa all day.'

Eventually they left, with worried glances at me as they drove off. I breathed a sigh of relief. As soon as their car had disappeared, I was on the phone to the office.

'Hey, Gemma,' said Lucy. 'How're you feeling?'

'Okay, thanks. It's nice to be with my mum and dad.'

'I bet. It's good for you to have a rest. But you're missing out on something here,' she said. 'That postman – you know, the surfer guy – has only gone and asked Sophie on a date.'

Despite myself, I laughed. 'Oh, I wish I'd been there. I bet she's bouncing off the ceiling, isn't she?'

'She hasn't shut up about it,' she said. 'He only asked her half an hour ago and I've already got a headache.' She lowered her voice. 'Are you all right? You sounded upset the other day.'

'I'm fine, thanks. I just got so tired and I thought if I went to my mum's she'd look after me.'

She laughed. 'I bet she's thrilled you're there.'

'Yes, she is. Lucy, I need to talk to Rachel. Is she there?'

'She's chasing a mortgage offer for Mrs Davies at the moment, but I'll get her to call you as soon as she's free.'

It was half an hour later before Rachel called back. She sounded subdued. I could hear traffic in the background and guessed she was in the car park, out of sight of the office.

'It's me,' she said. 'Is everything okay?'

'I need to talk to you. Do you have time now?'

'Not really,' she said. 'I've got Mrs Johnson coming by in ten minutes and I need to make a phone call before then.'

I couldn't tell her then. I just couldn't. I dithered, not knowing what to do. She needed to know David was at the party, but how was I going to tell her when she was either at work or at home with him?

'Is everything all right?' I asked.

'I've decided to sell my mum's house. I can't use our office to sell it, though. I hope you understand.'

'Of course. Of *course* you can't do that. Don't even think about it. I didn't realize you hadn't sold it.' I hesitated. 'How long has it been empty?'

'About ten months. My mum died last October. I've not been there since. I went away to France with David for a month after she died – it was our honeymoon – and then I moved to Chester.'

'It'll be a lot of work, won't it, sorting everything out? We can help you, Rachel,' I said. 'Me and the girls in the office. You don't have to deal with it on your own.'

She gave a strangled 'Thanks,' then said, 'I have to go,' and the call ended.

Later that morning I got an e-mail from Rachel.

Sorry. Mrs Johnson was walking towards me so I had to go.

Instantly I replied:

I need to talk to you. Something's come up. It's really important.

Within ten minutes my mobile rang.

'It's me, Rachel. I'm having an early lunch break. What's happened?'

'You might be better going outside to talk about this,' I said. 'Can you do that?'

'It's okay,' she said. 'I'm in the car and I've parked somewhere quiet. What is it?'

'I should be telling you this face to face, Rachel. I'm sorry.'

'What?' she said. 'What's up? You're frightening me.'

'David was at the party.'

There was silence, and then she said, 'What did you say?'

'The party. Where . . .'

'Yes, I know which party. But he wasn't there. It was just for people from Alex's school. David was at All Saints.'

'I know that's what it was meant to be, but he *was* there. I have a photo of him. Hold on a second.' I pulled my iPad to me and sent her the photo. 'Check your messages.'

There was silence as she opened my message, and then she gasped.

'But how do you know this was the party?'

'See that girl in front of him? She was my best friend.' I didn't say Lauren's name, not wanting Rachel to realize she was the one who'd yelled at Alex in the pub, the one who made him go back to Oxford a couple of days before he died. 'We went to the party together. She bought that dress the same day. I was with her when she bought it.'

'Yes, but . . .' She was flailing around now. 'But it might have been another night.'

'There was another party in your house after that one?'

There was silence.

'He never told me he was there. And his name wasn't on the guest list. Alex had to write it up for the police. He had to ask the school for a list of all the students in his year and use that as a guide.' Her voice faltered. 'I've seen it. It's still at my mum's house. David's name isn't on it.'

'Maybe he just heard about the party and thought he'd turn up. Who knows? But Rachel, he was there.'

'Alex didn't know he was there,' she said, sounding puzzled. 'He couldn't have known.'

'Maybe he was in the garden when David arrived. A lot of people were outside. It was a really hot night.' I paused; I had something to tell her and I was scared to say it. 'You know I identified Alex because of his T-shirt.'

'Yes, the Glastonbury T-shirt. The Coral.'

I said nothing. I closed my eyes and waited for it to dawn on her.

When it did, her voice was unsteady. 'David's wearing a Coral T-shirt in the photo.'

And I waited again for her to make that connection.

'Does . . . Oh God. Does this mean it might have been David who . . .' I could hear the tears and the fury in her voice. 'Are you telling me now that it was David who raped you?'

59

Gemma

I couldn't speak. What could I say? I'd accused her brother of rape. He'd died as a result of my accusation, and her mother had died because she'd lost her son. Now I was saying it was her husband who'd done it.

'So you were lying?' she screamed. 'If you weren't sure, why didn't you say so?'

I couldn't answer. I sat with my head bowed, my phone clamped to my ear, listening to her outrage.

'Say something!' she yelled. 'All this has happened because of you!'

And suddenly I was sick of it. Sick of taking the blame for something that had been done to me so many years before. 'It hasn't happened because of me,' I shouted back. 'I was asleep on Alex's bed and someone raped me. I looked up and saw someone of Alex's height, Alex's build, with Alex's T-shirt on leaving the room. What was I meant to think?'

'I don't know. I don't know.'

We sat in silence for a while, both too upset to speak. I could hear her crying, then blowing her nose. She said, 'Where did you get the photo from?'

'Jack Howard. He was a boy from school who was there that night.'

'I used to know him. He was one of Alex's friends,' she said. 'He played hockey with him. We gave him a lift to matches sometimes.'

'He's the one who took the photo,' I said. 'He took hundreds of photos that night and David was only in this one. He knew David. Well, he'd met him a few times. He was taking a photo of my friend – he was crazy about her – and he didn't notice anyone in the background. But I talked to him last night. I asked him if he recognized the person behind Lauren and he said it was David.' I hesitated. 'David Henderson. That's his name?'

'Yes, it is.' She was quiet for a few moments, then said, 'I remember Alex and David going to Glastonbury. They loved The Coral. Even now . . . even now David plays their songs. I don't like it; it reminds me of that summer when Alex would play them and he'd dance with me.' She started to laugh but I could hear the tears there. 'And you're sure this is the night of the party? Absolutely certain?'

'Yes. There's no doubt, Rachel.'

'So Alex *didn't* do it,' she said. 'I knew he didn't.'

We said nothing for a minute or two. I was looking at the photo on my iPad and I knew she was looking at it too.

'I think we should go to the police,' I said. 'We should both go to the police together.'

'I thought that too,' she said. 'But do you know what, Gemma?'

'What?'

'I'd rather tackle him ourselves.'

I started to say, 'We can't do that,' but the line was dead.

60

Gemma

I was exhausted after that conversation with Rachel. I wanted to just go to the police and tell them everything, but I knew I had to get her to agree to that for her own sake. She'd been so powerless for so long; she needed to have some control now.

While I waited for Rory and my parents to come home, I went back to look at the rest of the photos from the party. David wasn't in any of them, and after a flurry of early photos, neither was Alex. There was one photo of Lauren on her own; Jack must have wanted to take a last shot of her before she left. She was standing in the hallway at the foot of the stairs looking impatient, and I realized she must have been calling my name. I felt sick at the thought of what had just happened to me. The front door was wide open and I wondered whether David had run out just a minute before Lauren got there or whether he'd waited upstairs until he'd heard me leave.

I made myself go through the albums again. I saved each photo in sequence to a new album I set up on my iPad. There were hundreds and I knew I wouldn't need them all, but I kept them anyway. I couldn't take the risk of Jack taking them down again or, worse, deleting them. Quite why he'd do that, I had no idea, but the thought of it made me panic.

By the time my parents arrived back with Rory I was desperate for him. I didn't want them to go off with him again; I wanted to spend time with him. But I knew, too, that I had to get this sorted and that would involve time away from him. I vowed things would change after that.

While I played with Rory and cooked him some dinner and listened to his stories of what he'd done that day, all I could think was: what did Rachel mean that she wanted us to tackle David ourselves? When I knew things would be quiet at work, I sent her an e-mail.

What did you mean?

Quick as a flash, she replied:

I think we should talk to him first. See what he has to say. Catch him off guard.

He'd just deny it, I replied.

A minute later she sent another e-mail with a link to a website. I clicked on it, and when the site opened I stared in disbelief. It was a site that sold covert recording devices and on the screen was a button that operated as a camera. A button that you could sew onto a shirt or jacket. It looked just like any button you'd have on a shirt and the set came with extra ones so that all your buttons would match. I looked at it closely. I couldn't tell the camera was there! And then the description stated it was a video recorder, too.

I replied: What is this?

He had it on his shirt when you had dinner.

How do you know? I asked. Did he tell you?

It was several minutes later that she replied, and when I saw her answer, I guessed she hadn't wanted to reply at all.

I sewed them on. I'm so sorry, Gemma.

I felt fury then, that they'd done that to me. And she'd known about it. I'd talked and talked that night and all the time he was recording me. And of course he was in my room, too, and all that would be recorded, as well.

Was there anything else? I asked.

I don't know. I don't think so.

I need to go, I replied, and switched off my phone. I couldn't stand to talk to her right then.

61

Gemma

That evening, after Rory had gone to bed, I sat with my parents and watched a film on television. I could see them eyeing me cautiously. They knew that I had something on my mind, I could tell. When the film ended, there was an awkward pause where my dad opened his mouth to speak and my mum shook her head. I pretended not to notice, but stood up and yawned, saying I was ready for bed.

I called Joe from my bed that night, but when he answered the phone all I could hear was background noise.

'Sorry, sweetheart,' he said when he called me back a few minutes later. 'I was watching football at The Crown. I've missed you, Gem. It's lonely here without you and Rory.'

'Lonely in the pub?' I teased. 'Sounds like you're having a good time.'

'I was the first night,' he admitted. 'It was great. I'm never in the house on my own usually.'

I hadn't thought of that. He had plenty of chances to go out, what with running and football and seeing his friends, but of course if he was in the house, Rory was there with him.

'Did you like it?'

He laughed. 'Last night was really weird. The daytime was

fine. I finished the kitchen and it was so much easier without Rory there. But . . . it made me think of how different my life is now compared to how it was. And it was nice going out when I wanted and staying out late. But then when I got home the house seemed so quiet. I didn't like it!'

'I know. I didn't like it when you were away, either.' He was quiet and immediately I felt guilty. 'I'm sorry,' I said. 'I don't want to get into point-scoring.'

'Me neither. I thought you'd enjoy it, though.'

'I like the idea of it more than the reality.'

'Me too,' he said. 'When will you be back?'

'Not long,' I said. 'A couple of days.' And then suddenly I found the courage to be open with him. 'But Joe, we need to talk. I'm not happy with the way things are.'

There was a strained silence. 'You're not happy with us?'

'Of course I am. It's just work. It's not working out, the way it is. Not for me. I can't do it much longer.'

'What? You can't work?'

'I can. Of course I can. But it's not how I want to live.' I struggled to stay calm. 'I miss Rory. I'm . . . I'm jealous of you.' I could hear that he was about to speak and hurried on. 'I feel outside the family. As though I'm just there to bring in the money.'

'Oh, now . . .'

'Don't. Let me say this. Sometimes I feel it's like you and he are the family. That's what I see. He turns to you first. You always know what's best for him. I hardly see him some weeks. I'm up before him a lot of the time and I have to work most nights after he's gone to bed. I'm so tired.' I couldn't stop the tears. 'And I love the way you are with him. It's great. But I love being with him too. I want to do things for him.'

'But you do! He looks forward to you coming home all day.'

'But when he cries now, he goes to you. I'm his mum! He should be coming to me!'

'Gemma, sweetheart, don't be daft. We're both his parents.'

'I know. I'm just saying I want things to change. I don't want to work nonstop. I want to be part of his life. I'm happy to work, but . . .' He said nothing. I had no idea what I was even thinking, but then I blurted out, 'Why should it always be you at home and me at work? Why shouldn't I be at home some of the time? Why can't you go out to work as well?' I knew this would hurt him. I knew he'd think that I was criticizing him. But once the floodgates were open I couldn't stop. 'Sometimes you make out like I don't know my own child! I feel like a spare part in the family.'

And then I couldn't stop crying. I heard a knock on my bedroom door and my mum looked in.

I grabbed some tissues from the box on the bedside table. 'I'm on the phone to Joe,' I said.

She gave a quick sympathetic nod and quietly closed the door. And then I realized that she thought I was talking to him about the night of the party and that made me cry even harder, that I couldn't talk to him about that. Not now. That would have to be done face to face.

'Just a second, I need to go to the bathroom,' I said to Joe.

'I'll wait.'

In the bathroom I tried to calm down. I rinsed a flannel in cold water and pressed it against my burning eyes. I was glad I'd told him. He needed to know.

Back in my room, Joe said, 'Gem, we need to talk about this. Talk about it properly. I knew you were tired. I'm really sorry. I hadn't thought about it.' He was quiet, and then he said, 'You must hate me.'

'Of course I don't. I love you. I've always loved you.' I lay down and it was as though he were next to me. 'Right from the moment I saw you. You saved me.'

'I love you too.' I could almost hear his mind racing. I knew he'd be going over what I'd said. I should have said it before. 'And I'm sorry. I'm really sorry. I should have noticed you weren't happy. We'll sort something out.'

I felt then that we would, but of course there was a whole other story that he knew nothing about. That I'd have to admit to. I couldn't do it that night. I just couldn't. I knew the time was coming when I'd tell him everything. I just hoped he'd be able to forgive me.

62

Gemma

Friday, August 18

I woke late the next morning and found Rory and my dad having breakfast in the garden.

'This is my second breakfast!' said Rory. 'I had one with Granny when she got up, then one with Grandad when he got up.'

He came over to me and sat on my lap, leaning back until his body was aligned with mine. He stroked my arm with his hand while he told my mum and dad in great detail what he had planned for the day, and then he wriggled round until he was facing me and whispered in my ear, 'Are you coming with us, Mum?'

I whispered back, 'Do you want me to?'

He nodded vigorously.

'Of course I will.'

As we got ready for the day ahead, packing up a picnic and spare clothes for Rory, I thought of Rachel in her flat with David last night. Had she challenged him? Was she safe? Despite everything, I wanted to contact her but I didn't know whether David would be with her. I couldn't risk that, for her or for me.

And while we sat in the car and sang songs with Rory, and as we walked on the beach and built a sandcastle with him and raced down to the waves and ate ice cream and chased the gulls, I thought of her again. She'd married David thinking she'd have a new family, but yet again, she was alone. I didn't know whether she had any cousins or other relatives who could help her get through this, but it seemed as though her role as caregiver to her mum had meant she was pretty isolated.

When my parents offered to take Rory for a long walk along the beach, I agreed quickly. I sat on the sand and thought about what had happened. If David was the one who'd raped me that night, then Alex had died because of him. But he'd died because of me, too.

Why had I thought it was Alex? But try as I might, when I thought of that figure as he hurried from the room that night, I could see why I'd thought it was him. He was the same height, a similar build. It was the T-shirt, though, that had convinced me.

The Glastonbury festival had been on after our exams had ended. I'd known he was going. I don't even know who had told me, but it was probably Lauren.

And then on the day of the party, we'd picked up our exam results in the morning and he was wearing that T-shirt then. I'd stood behind him in the queue and I'd heard him talking about it, about The Coral, and how brilliant they were. For those ten minutes or so I was in that queue I was standing just inches from his back and I knew the image well by the time I saw it on the back of the man leaving Alex's bedroom.

I didn't see David at the party. I certainly would have

noticed someone wearing the same T-shirt. The photos that Jack had taken were pretty thorough. I couldn't think of anyone he'd missed out. And David was only in one of them, one that was taken just before I went upstairs. I'd looked through them again and again, and he wasn't there.

Rachel had told me about the list that Alex had written: a list of those at the party. He hadn't written David's name down. He mustn't have seen him there.

And Jack knew him and hadn't noticed he was there. I wondered then whether that had been deliberate on David's part. I remembered what the therapist I'd seen when I was living in London had said about rape, about how it wasn't caused by the desire for sex but for domination. Control. It was driven by anger, she'd said. Anger and hatred. It had confused me so much. I could never link those emotions to the Alex I'd known in school.

My phone beeped, startling me. It was a text from Rachel.

I'm so sorry I did those things to you.

63

Gemma

As soon as I saw Rachel's message, my anger towards her vanished. We both needed to focus on the person who'd done this to us, not on each other. I was about to call the office to see whether she was there when she called me.

'Rachel,' I said quickly, 'I'm sorry too.'

'It's not your fault,' she said. 'Neither of us is to blame.'

'I know,' I said. 'But are you all right? What about last night?'

'It was okay,' she said. 'Nothing happened. We just watched a couple of films and went to bed early. He had to be in Newcastle today for a meeting, so he set off at about five this morning.'

'Where does he work?'

'Andrews and Fitch,' she said. 'They're in Warrington, a big engineering company.'

'He's in sales there?'

'No, he works in their legal department.'

So everything he'd told me was a lie. Of course it was. And then I thought about it. 'He studied law at university?'

'Yes,' she said. 'At Bristol. Why?'

She started to say something else, but I interrupted her. 'Did he apply to Oxford?'

She stopped in her tracks. 'Yes, he did. He didn't get in, though. He missed out on an A grade in one subject.' She paused. 'Why? Why does it matter where he went to university?'

I shrugged. 'He told me he'd studied in London. Maths.' She was quiet and I guessed she already knew he'd told me that. I shook my head. I had to get over her involvement in this. So he lied about studying in London. Presumably he was trying to give us something in common. 'He must have been angry that Alex got into Oxford and he didn't.'

'I've never thought of that,' she said slowly. 'He would have been angry with himself, too. He sets really high standards for himself. Actually I don't think he would have been able to keep up the friendship with Alex long-term. It would always be a reminder of his own failure.'

I thought of David turning up at the party, furious and jealous. There must have been six or seven students from my year that had got into Oxford, and I wondered how he'd felt as he hovered on the edge of groups that were excited about a future he was denied. I wondered whether that was what led him upstairs to me, the desire to punish. To take revenge.

How had he felt when Alex was arrested? Was that when he really started to celebrate his own success?

'I know I said I wanted to confront him,' said Rachel, 'but I'm terrified.'

'So am I.' Just the thought of being in the same room as him made my heart pound. 'I can't do it. I'm too frightened of him.'

In the distance I saw my parents walking with Rory. Each of them was holding one of his hands and he was swinging between them. When he saw me looking at him, he started to run towards me. I felt awful for Rachel but I really couldn't talk to her. All I had time to say was 'Sorry, I have to go. Call me later,' before Rory bounded on top of me, pinning me to the ground with hugs and kisses. I wrapped my arms around him and breathed in the summer smells of suntan lotion and ice cream, but my pulse was still racing at the thought of what we had to do.

Rachel called again later that day. We were all out in the garden when my phone rang.

'Is that Joe?' asked my mum. I could tell from her face that she was worried about my marriage, that it would all end in tears.

'It's work.'

'You're meant to be having a break from work!'

I could hear my dad hushing her as I took the phone upstairs to my bedroom.

'I think we're right not to confront him ourselves,' Rachel said as soon as I was able to talk. 'Shall we go to the police in the morning, while he's away? I'm not expecting him back until tomorrow evening.'

'Yes. Let's do it.' I felt a huge sense of relief that this would soon be over. 'I'll drive down early. I can be at the police station near the office at eight o'clock.'

'I'll be there,' she said. 'I'm going up to my mum's house after work tonight. There are some things I don't want David to get hold of. Papers, financial stuff. Will you be able to keep them for me, until it's all over?'

'Yes, of course. You can put them in the safe at work if you like.'

She hesitated. 'Gemma, you wouldn't come with me, would you?'

'What, to your mum's house?'

'Just for a few minutes.' Her voice was strained. 'I don't want to be there on my own.'

'No!' I said, horrified at the thought of being back in that house. 'I'm sorry, Rachel. I can't do that.'

'It's okay.' She sounded resigned. 'I didn't think you would.'

'Why do you need to go there now and not after you've told the police?'

'I need to make sure everything's safe,' she said. 'Just in case I have to get away quickly.'

'How come you didn't take all your mum's documents to your flat when you moved in?'

'I don't know,' she said slowly. 'I think I knew early on that I shouldn't let him know about all my mum's finances. She had a lot more money than I realized, and once we were married there was something about the way he thought he was entitled to it that I didn't like. I didn't tell him about her stocks and shares, though he asked several times whether she had any. If I don't get them now and he has the chance, he'll be all over that house.' Her voice broke. 'I just don't want to go in there on my own.'

I thought about her going back into her mother's house after everything that had happened there. She'd had to deal with so much. I summoned up all my courage. 'And you'll only be a few minutes?'

She breathed a huge sigh of relief. 'I know where the papers are. That's all I want, to just run in and get them, then get out again.'

I looked out of the window at Rory. He glanced up and waved at me. 'I promised Rory I'd spend all day with him,' I said. 'I could be there for seven o'clock, if you like.'

'Thanks so much. I know I don't deserve it, after everything I've done.'

'Forget it,' I said. 'Let's just get this over with.'

'I'll text you the address.'

'There's no need.' Even fifteen years later, I could still remember her family home.

* * *

My parents agreed to put Rory to bed that night. I took a while getting ready, and when I came downstairs my mum was waiting for me.

'You look nice,' she said. 'New top?' She gestured towards my blue cotton shirt.

'I bought it yesterday. It was in the package that arrived in the post this afternoon.'

'Oh, I saw you had a couple of parcels. What else did you buy?'

I held my wrist out to her and she smelled my perfume.

'Oh that's lovely. Isn't it similar to the one you had at Christmas, though?'

I ignored her and looked at my watch. 'I'd better run. I won't be late back.' I fastened her house key onto my car key fob. 'Don't wait up.'

But still she hung around the hallway. 'So you're just meeting a friend? Anyone I know?'

I was prepared for this. 'She's called Helen,' I said. 'I went to university with her. She's in Liverpool with work and asked if I wanted to meet up for a drink.'

'Helen,' she mused. 'Did I know her?'

'No, I don't think so. She studied languages. French and Spanish, I think.'

'Oh, okay.' My mum didn't sound convinced. 'I don't remember you mentioning her.'

I didn't reply, but just opened my shoulder bag and checked that I had my phone and purse. Once out of the house I breathed a sigh of relief. I loved my mother but she really had missed out on her true vocation; she would have been a fantastic detective. If she'd had any idea where I was going tonight, though, I knew she wouldn't have gone back into the house with a wave and a smile.

It took thirty minutes to drive from my parents' home to Rachel's. On the way I passed Lauren's old house. A different family lived there now; they'd been there for years. There were lights on in the bedroom windows at the front of the house and my mind flashed back to the last night I was there: the night of the party.

Tonight I took the same route that the taxi driver had taken then. Unlike that night, there was no music playing, no excitement, and no breeze rushing through my hair. I wasn't with my friend, looking forward to the night ahead. Where last time I felt free, as though my life was beginning, tonight I was dreading going into the house again.

I slowed down as I approached Rachel's house. It was so much easier to think of it as her house, rather than Alex's. The front garden was surrounded by high hedges and I started to shake as I drove past them. I'd intended to park on her driveway but my palms were sweating and at the last moment I overshot the entrance and parked further down the road, just after the bend. There was a little shop there with a car park for customers and I pulled into an empty space. I was feeling dizzy with tension just at the thought of going into their house.

My phone beeped on the dashboard. It was Rachel.

`Just saw you drive past. I'm here now.`

I thought of her there in her mother's house, a house that had seen nothing but sadness in all those years. She seemed friendless, lonely, and it was only the pity I had for her that made me go there that night.

I climbed out of the car, then took my phone from my bag and left the bag in the locked boot. It would just be in the way if I had to carry boxes of papers. I slid my phone into the pocket of my jeans and put my key fob into the other pocket, pushing it right down.

I had to gather all my courage to walk towards the house. Rachel's car was parked on the gravel driveway and she was waiting for me by the front door. As I approached her she waved then turned and pushed the door wide open.

'Hi, come on in,' she said, and all I could think was that was exactly what Alex had said when we arrived at the party that night.

64

Gemma

In the hallway I tried to keep a lid on the panic that rose in me. I hadn't been here since that night, fifteen years ago, but I remembered it well. Then, though, it looked well tended and loved. The oak floor had been polished and glossy; the Persian rug in the centre of the large hallway had been thick and expensive, its colours rich and vivid. I remember when Lauren and I had first arrived we'd looked around and she'd whispered, 'This is exactly what I thought Alex's house would be like.'

Now, though it was exactly the same inside, everything was dull, untended. There were marks on the rug, scratches on the floor. It was clear nobody had redecorated since I was last here. The curtains lay heavy and dusty and lifeless and I saw cobwebs draped over the chandelier that hung unlit from the ceiling. Everything was drab and I knew then that when Alex had died, the light had gone out of their lives.

I shuddered.

I saw Rachel watching me and my face flamed. This was her house, after all.

'It must be hard for you, being here,' she said. 'Thanks for coming.'

'It's okay.' I felt far from okay, though. My stomach was tight with nerves and I couldn't stop thinking how stupid I was to come here. Rachel looked so expectant, though, so trusting and so young that I smiled at her to reassure her. 'Where are the documents?'

'They're in my mum's room,' she said. 'Can you give me a hand?'

I hesitated.

'What?' she asked.

'I don't want to go upstairs.'

'I won't be able to carry them on my own,' she said. 'It'll just be one trip if we both do it.'

I took a deep breath. 'Okay.'

She took my arm and we walked upstairs. I clung onto the banister, wishing I hadn't come, wishing I were at home with Joe. Why hadn't I told him? He could have come with me, helped us do this.

My heart thumped as we reached the top of the stairs. The bathroom was ahead, just as I remembered. Its door stood open and I recognized the black-and-white tiles in a diamond pattern on the floor. Though I hadn't thought of it in all those years, in that one glance I remembered kicking a towel that was on the floor that night, knowing I was so drunk that if I bent to pick it up I would have fallen and hurt myself. I wished now I had picked it up. Wished I'd hurt myself and called for help and gone home. None of this would have happened.

We paused at the top of the stairs. I glanced to the right. The door to Alex's room stood ajar. Immediately I averted my eyes.

'Mum's room is here,' said Rachel. She led me past Alex's door and to a room at the front of the house. There were windows overlooking the front garden and the room was lined with photos of Alex. You wouldn't know she had another child. At the foot of her bed she had a large flat-screen television on a stand, with a DVD player underneath it. It seemed to jar with the rest of the room, which was old-fashioned and dreary.

'She had all our old family videos put onto DVD,' explained Rachel. She wouldn't meet my eyes and I wondered whether she was embarrassed or ashamed. 'She would play them all the time.' She winced. 'Constantly. Wherever I was in the house, I'd hear them. And she'd fast-forward through the bits I was in, or my dad. She'd replay the parts with Alex in again and again. All his old rugby matches. Every time he won a prize. Every party and every holiday.'

I thought of Rachel living there with that running commentary of her dead brother's life playing on and on while she gave up the chance of her own life to care for their mother. She must have experienced such mixed emotions when her mother died.

She put her shoulder bag on the floor and crouched down to look under the bed. 'Oh thank God, they're still here.' She reached under it and dragged out several box files. They had stickers on them: *Maths*, *English*, *French*, *Psychology*.

'They look like your old school files.'

'That's what I wanted them to look like,' she said, 'in case he saw them.'

I was desperate to get out of there. 'Do you want us to pack all this up while we're here?' I picked up a pile of her family DVDs and looked around for something to put them in. 'Have you got a box? A suitcase?'

'Until the other day,' she said, 'I didn't want to see any of it again. And now . . . now I don't know what to do.' She turned away, but not before I saw that her cheeks were flushed. After a few seconds she said, 'Gemma, you have no idea what it was like.'

A photo of Alex with his arm around his mum caught my eye. It looked like they were on holiday; a bright blue pool was behind them and a white towel lay on the edge of a sun lounger. He was about sixteen, tanned, his dark hair wavy and wet. His mother stood beside him, looking so proud. She was inches shorter than her son; even at that age he towered above her.

I turned away. I couldn't look at him. I felt such a complicated mix of shame and pity and anger.

'Rachel, there are no photos of you here.'

She tried to laugh but didn't quite make it. 'Well, no. He was the one, wasn't he? He always was.'

My heart ached for her. 'What, always? Even before he died?'

She shrugged. 'Look at her room, Gemma. You decide.'

'And yet you and he got on so well.'

'Oh I loved him,' she said. 'Absolutely loved him. My mum used to say, "He was the light of my life," and I'd agree. He was the light of mine, too. But he'd gone and she and I were the only ones left.'

I closed my eyes as I thought of them both losing that one person who meant more to them than anyone else. How could either of them go on?

Then the tension in the room changed. I noticed it even with my eyes closed. I turned to Rachel. She was at the window, looking out at the driveway.

'Oh no,' she said. 'He's here.'

'What?' For a wild moment I thought she meant Alex. 'Who?'

'It's David. He's here!'

I dropped the DVDs onto her mother's bed and flattened myself against the bedroom wall. My heart banged in my chest. 'David?' I felt dizzy at the thought of seeing him. 'What's he doing here?'

Rachel's face was white with shock. 'I don't know! What should I do?'

'Don't let him in. Pretend you're not here.'

'But my car's in the drive. I'll have to go down.'

'Put him off. If you have to go with him, don't worry about me. Try to get him away from here.'

'Okay, okay,' she whispered. 'But you'll have to hide.' She backed away from the window and quickly shoved the box files back under her mother's bed. 'Have you got your phone? Mute it, just in case.'

Quickly I did as she said, and then his car door slammed and we both jumped. Rachel grabbed my arm and pushed me out of the room. I was willing to go; I wanted to run out of the house. 'Don't stay in here!' she hissed. 'He might come in.' She hurried me along the corridor and pushed open the door to Alex's room. 'Wait in there. Quick!'

I found myself flung into the room, and then she pulled the door so that it was open just a few inches. 'Don't make a sound,' she whispered.

I stood behind the door, staring at a room I'd last seen fifteen years before.

Everything was as it was then. His bed was made, the quilt cover and pillows just the same. Two blankets lay folded on a chair by the window; I remembered blankets had been thrown over my head as he left the room. I'd had nightmares about that for years, where I'd relived the struggle to break free of them. In the corner were his drums and guitar, beside me the large chest of drawers. His desk overlooked the rear garden, and books and cardboard files were piled up high. I swallowed. He'd died after a term at Oxford. I thought of his mum – and Rachel, probably, too – going there to his rooms to collect his things and knew how broken-hearted they would have been.

And then I heard the doorbell ring and David call Rachel's name. My heart pounded. He was here, within reach of me.

65

Rachel

I've never been as frightened in my life as I was then, going downstairs to let David into the house.

'Hey,' he said, when I opened the door. He came into the house and put his arms around me. I reached around and squeezed him tightly and kissed his cheek. The last thing I wanted was for him to notice any difference in me.

'What are you doing here?' I said. 'I thought you were staying over in Newcastle?'

'Yeah, the last meeting was cancelled and I couldn't be bothered hanging around for the guys to finish work,' he said. 'I'll see them next time I'm up there.'

'How did you know I'd be here?'

'Oh, I was coming through Liverpool and thought I'd see what you were up to. Find My Phone showed you were here, so I thought I'd turn up and surprise you.' He spoke as though this were completely normal behaviour. I didn't know anyone else whose partner tracked them like that, but he always said he liked to know where I was. It was hard to believe I'd thought it was romantic when he first did it.

'I had nothing to do so I thought I'd come up and check that everything was okay here,' I said.

He walked around the hallway, pushing the doors to the kitchen and living room open and looking inside. 'Everything seems all right, doesn't it?'

'Yes, it's fine. I was just about to leave, actually,' I said. 'I'm starving. Fancy a takeaway? Chinese?'

I was really struggling to sound normal. David could pick up anything different about me from a mile away; my heart raced at the thought of him noticing anything now.

'Are you okay, darling?' he asked. 'Are you tired?'

'I'm fine,' I said. 'I just hate being here. It makes me feel really weird.' I put my hand in his and he kissed my knuckles. 'I want to be back home.'

'Come on, then,' he said. 'Pity we're in separate cars. Fancy going for a meal somewhere near here instead?'

'If you like.' It was always important that I gave him the choice, let him make the decisions. 'Though I'd like to get into a hot bath and have a glass of wine.'

He gave a soft laugh and said, 'I'll join you.' My skin prickled with disgust. 'Got your keys?'

In a flash I remembered that my handbag was in my mother's room. I cursed the fact that I hadn't just let him take me home in his car.

'My bag's upstairs,' I said. 'I won't be a second. You go and get the car started.'

'Don't worry,' he said. 'I'll fetch it.'

He took the stairs two at a time and I hurried after him.

'It's in my mum's room,' I said.

'Is there anything you want me to bring back now? Have you decided what you'll keep?'

I thought of the boxes of papers under the bed and hoped he wouldn't notice them. He would never believe that I knew nothing about them. 'Honestly?' I said. 'I never want to see any of it again.'

'Oh, sweetheart.'

We went into my mum's room. I wanted to shut the door, to give Gemma the chance to escape, but I didn't have the nerve. He'd know something was up immediately if I did that. And then he'd see her from the window. I nearly collapsed at the thought of him chasing her.

I picked up my handbag. 'Come on,' I said. 'Let's go. I'll call around some charities tomorrow and ask them to take the whole lot. They can sell whatever they want and chuck the rest.'

'But there'll be things you want, surely?' He stood in the doorway. 'What about the television? It's fairly new, isn't it? We could have it in our bedroom.'

'No,' I said. 'I don't want it. They can take it all.'

I was just about to say that I could afford a new television if I wanted one. I could afford a new house to put the new television in, if it came to that, and then I realized that in his mind, the money belonged to him. Not that it belonged to both of us, even, but that it was his. I knew if I wanted to buy something, whether it was a television or a house, he'd have to approve, and if he said no, it wouldn't happen. The rage I'd felt since I realized what he'd done nearly overwhelmed me: he'd caused my brother to commit suicide and my mother to die young and yet he thought her money was his.

And it was then that the courage to say something struck me. I knew Gemma was in Alex's room and she'd hear everything I said. I hoped she had her phone out, ready to call the police if he turned nasty. So quick as anything, before I could think about the sheer lunacy of what I was doing, I stopped dead in the hallway, just outside Alex's room.

'I'm glad you're here,' I said. 'I wanted to have a chat with you about Alex's party.'

66

Rachel

I felt as though my lungs were only half full of air; my voice sounded completely different. Higher-pitched. Breathless.

He stared at me for a couple of seconds. I could feel my chest heaving. He glanced down, then at my face. He sounded bewildered. 'What? What about it?'

'I didn't realize you were there,' I said. I tried to sound matter-of-fact, but my heart was racing. 'You weren't on Alex's guest list. I saw it, after he died. My mum used to go through everything. She phoned everyone on it several times, checking again and again. Well, you know that. I've told you often enough. But she didn't phone you, did she?'

'Why would she?' he said, slowly. 'I wasn't there. I wasn't invited. It was just for his friends from school.'

Now that I had started I had to go on, even though I felt like a lemming running towards a cliff. 'Well, yes, that was the idea. My mum and dad made him promise that. But you were there anyway. And Alex didn't know.' I stepped back a couple of feet. 'Why was that?'

'I wasn't *at* the party,' he said again, his voice louder now. He sounded confident; I would have believed him if I hadn't known otherwise. 'I don't know what you're talking about.' There was a silence, and then he went on, 'Look, this must be upsetting for you, coming back here. I wish you'd let me sort it out with you at the weekend. We could have got the house emptied.'

'It's not upsetting at all,' I said. It was as though I could hear my voice from elsewhere. I thought of Gemma behind that door and hoped to God she was texting someone who'd help us. 'Hearing that my brother had committed suicide was upsetting. Sitting next to my mother in the ambulance as she *died* was upsetting. This is nothing in comparison.'

Irritation flitted across his face. 'I know, babe,' he said. 'You've been through such a lot. Come on, let's get you back home.' He reached out to hug me. 'You need a good sleep.'

And then I couldn't help it. I laughed, though nothing about it was funny. 'I don't think so.' I didn't dare look at him. He was standing between me and the staircase and I realized too late there was no other way out. The silence was thick and frightening, and I couldn't stop myself from breaking it. 'Do you really think I sleep well in my bed? With you beside me?'

'What?'

The memory of that night flashed before me and I shouted, 'You with your phone, taking photos in the dark? You must think I'm stupid.'

'I don't know what you're talking about,' he said again. 'Come on, sweetie, let's get back home.' The floorboard creaked as he took a step towards me. I took a step back and banged into the wall next to Alex's door. 'You're just upset because you're back here.'

'I'm not. I hate being here, but this is nothing to do with that.' He reached out and put his arms around me. 'David, you were at the party and . . .' His hands were all over my body now, stroking me as though he owned me. As though he could do whatever he wanted with me. 'Get off me! Keep away from me!'

Now his voice changed. He sounded hesitant. Confused. 'You're not wearing perfume, are you?'

My stomach tilted. 'What?'

'When you opened the door, you kissed me,' he said. 'When I hugged you, I noticed that you weren't wearing perfume. You know I love it when you do.' He stared at me as though he couldn't recognize me and he sounded perplexed, as though he was trying to figure something out. 'But when I walked upstairs with you I thought I could smell it. I can smell it now.' He took a step back. 'And I think I recognize it.'

67

Gemma

There was such a long, tense silence that I thought I would collapse. When Rachel spoke, her voice was further away, back towards her mother's room.

'My mum had some perfume in her room. I sprayed it. It reminds me of her.' She was a good liar. Very convincing. But then she'd convinced me for months that she hadn't known who I was.

David had stayed in the same place, just beside the bathroom, outside Alex's room. Inches from me. 'I don't think so.' I didn't dare breathe. 'I think you're lying to me, Rachel,' he said. 'Why would you do that?'

Terrified, I leaned back against the wall. My hip touched something. Something hard. I slid my hand behind my back and felt around.

It was a hockey stick. Alex's hockey stick.

And I thought of the only time I'd spoken to Alex in school, right at the start of our course, when we were sixteen. He was getting onto a coach to go on a sports trip and he was carrying too much kit and dropped his hockey stick. I'd handed it to him and he'd smiled and said, 'Thanks, Gemma.' I hadn't realized he'd known my name.

Now, with my hands around that stick, I felt he'd passed it to me, just when I needed it.

And then the door to Alex's room opened wider and David walked in. His back was to me. He walked over to the window, past the lamp he'd switched off that night so many years before, past the bed where he'd raped me and the blankets he'd thrown over my head so that I wouldn't see him. I could hear him breathing in the stale air. My body was coiled like a spring.

Then he turned and my legs buckled.

'Well, well, well,' he said. 'Look who's here.'

He stood in the darkening room, looking straight at me. He was shocked, I could tell, but confident in his strength. Now, as then, I was no threat to him.

I stood motionless, my hands behind my back, gripping Alex's hockey stick so hard that my skin felt raw. I stared at David, not wanting to show any fear. My stomach had plummeted, though. I was scared, and in the instant I looked at his face, I knew that he knew that too. From a movement near me, I realized Rachel was standing in the doorway; the open door stood between us.

'What's going on?' he said. He glanced over at Rachel. 'What's she doing here?'

'Gemma and I have been talking,' said Rachel. She was trying to sound strong, but I could hear a slight tremor in her voice and I knew that of course he would have heard that too. He'd recognize it as a weakness. I knew he'd be good at spotting those. 'Talking about the party.'

'What about it?' he said. 'You've talked about it a million times. I've told you I wasn't there.'

I took a deep breath. 'But you *were* there.' My voice was shaky. 'You *were* at the party.'

'Oh, and how would you know about that?' he said.

'There's a photo of you there in the kitchen that night.' From the tightening of his jaw I guessed he hadn't expected that. 'You were wearing the Coral T-shirt.'

'The Coral? I don't have a T-shirt like that. You're mistaking me for someone else. For Alex.'

'You do,' said Rachel from the doorway. 'Or you did. Alex had photos of you both at Glastonbury that summer, wearing the same T-shirt. I've seen them.'

'Yeah, I had one then. It got ripped there, the night they played, and I left it behind.'

He was a good liar. His voice was steady. Reasonable. If I hadn't seen that photo, if I hadn't seen him wearing that T-shirt, I probably would have believed him.

'I don't think so.' Rachel was agitated now. 'You were at the party and you were wearing the T-shirt. There's proof of it.' She gave a mocking laugh, designed to make anyone angry. 'You're just making a fool of yourself if you deny it.'

He stared at her for ages then, the realization that she was on my side, not his, dawning on him. Then he looked back at me.

My legs began to shake. He was still the same man I'd taken to view properties in Chester, the man who'd charmed me at dinner in the hotel in London. He was still as tall, as dark and as handsome as he had been, but something had changed. He was now under threat. His body was tense, ready for battle, and in that moment I knew he'd do anything to win.

'So,' he said. 'You two are in this together? That's interesting.' There was a pause and I knew neither Rachel nor I dared to break it. 'After all the things you said about her, Rachel. I'm surprised.'

Her face was crimson.

'So all those nights you told me about how you wanted to

pay her back for ruining your life, for your brother dying . . . you were lying then? Were you lying when you told me how much you hate her?'

'That was before I knew what really happened.'

'You *know* what happened, babe. I've told you. I wasn't there. You were mistaken.' His voice went soft. 'I've always been honest with you, Coco.'

Coco? I thought. I saw Rachel hesitate and guessed it was an affectionate name he used for her. My stomach tightened. Was she going to be taken in by that? Where would that leave me, if she was?

'Remember what you said about her husband and son?' He mimicked her again. 'Why should she have a happy marriage? Why should she have a good job? Alex didn't have any of that.'

'He didn't,' she said. 'And I'm wondering why, now.'

He carried on, speaking as though he were her, in a high, breathless voice. 'And that poor son. He's being brought up by his father. I bet he wouldn't even recognize his mother!'

'Shut up!' she yelled. 'Ignore him, Gemma! I didn't say that.'

But she had. I knew she had. I thought of Rory in his pyjamas that evening, fresh and damp from his bath. He'd hugged me before I left, holding his toy rabbit to his face, rubbing it across his cheek as he always did when he was tired. My eyes prickled. He was my reason for working so hard, and I just wasn't spending enough time with him. The thought of someone criticizing my relationship with my son made the fear inside me turn to strength.

'Why are you focusing on what she said rather than what you've done?' I said softly. 'The night of the party, you came in here and you raped me.'

'I did what?' He sounded so shocked I almost believed him.

'You raped me.'

68

Gemma

His eyes flickered towards Rachel. 'What's she talking about?'

When she spoke, I knew she was crying. 'You did it, David. And you let Alex take the blame.'

He flinched, then. 'What? I didn't! I wouldn't do that!'

I wanted to get out of there. He was going to keep on denying it and I couldn't stand to hear him. But Rachel was blocking the doorway and she was shouting.

'You did do it! I *knew* Alex hadn't done it! And you let him . . .' She almost choked on her tears. 'You let Alex take the blame and then he killed himself. And you came round night after night and sympathized with my mum when it was you that had done it all along!'

'I wasn't here,' he insisted. 'I've told you!'

And then Rachel turned to me and said, 'Gemma, were you wearing a hair bobble, the night of the party?'

I stared at her, confused at the change of subject. 'What?'

Her voice was strange. It was as though she was thinking something over and couldn't quite believe it. 'Can you remember?'

'I can remember everything,' I said. 'And no, I wasn't wearing a hair bobble.'

I heard David take a step or two back. I glanced at him; his eyes were fixed on Rachel and he held himself very still.

'What about lip gloss?' she said. 'When you were at the party, when you were eighteen, did you wear lip gloss?'

'What the hell are you talking about?' said David.

'Yes, I wore lip gloss,' I said. 'Why?'

'Did you take it with you to the party?'

I nodded.

'Did you take it home with you?'

I stared at her. 'No. I didn't. I must have lost it.'

Her face was pale and her hair was spiked with sweat. 'Was it raspberry ripple? Or blackberry? Or maybe vanilla fudge?'

At her words, I felt a kaleidoscope of memories form into shape. I remembered dipping my finger into the little pot of raspberry ripple lip gloss as our taxi approached Alex's house. Lauren had dipped her finger into it too, and we'd smeared it over our lips and giggled, before going into the party. I'd slipped it into my pocket and hadn't thought of it from that day to this.

'It was raspberry ripple,' I whispered. 'How did you know?'

'I found it, didn't I?' she said to David in a conversational tone. 'There was a pile of stuff in an old bag of yours. It looked like a load of junk. That's what you told me it was, didn't you? You said an ex-girlfriend had borrowed your bag and left it all behind. You said you'd throw it away, but you didn't, did you? Didn't you think I'd check?' Her face was pink with strain, but she looked him straight in the eye.

David was breathing hard and fast and staring at her so fiercely I took a step back. I knew something was going to happen.

'You've done this before, haven't you?' she said. 'Those things . . . what are they, something from each girl?'

A muscle moved in his jaw. I was on high alert now.

'They looked like trash, but they were precious to you,

weren't they? They were significant. Did you keep them to remember your victims by?'

'You're insane,' he said. 'I don't know what you're talking about.'

'Funny,' she said. 'Because you made enough effort to hide them the second time.' He stared at her and she said, 'You really need to think twice before you let your wife borrow your car. You lent it to me last night without even thinking. You were so keen that I should go out and buy you some whisky that you completely fell for it when I said my car was out of petrol.'

His jaw was tight, his eyes on her.

'Did you really think I wouldn't look in the boot?' There was a tense silence and she said, 'Underneath the spare tyre? Odd place to put things that mean nothing to you.' She glanced at me. 'Gemma, there were *loads* of them.'

And then he broke. He reared back and suddenly he was taller. Broader. I steeled myself and faced him head-on.

Here it comes. Here it comes.

'You stupid bitch,' he said to Rachel. 'She wasn't even awake. All that fuss, calling the police, when she was asleep the whole time.'

I nodded, once, and moved into his view. 'And how do you know that?'

'You,' he sneered. I steeled myself. 'You were so drunk. Lying there with your skirt up round your waist. Anyone could have had you. You pathetic bitch. If you didn't want it, you shouldn't have flaunted it.'

And there it was. The last fifteen years of my life had been a lie.

69

Rachel

For a moment I don't think either Gemma or I could speak. The sound of him admitting what he'd done resonated in the air, and for that moment all was still. And then my body responded.

I pushed the door wide open.

David stood, poised for action, in the middle of the room. He was staring at Gemma – I think he thought she was his main threat.

He was wrong.

I leaped into the air and slapped him hard across the face. He swore and swung away from me. He'd taken his eyes off Gemma and I could see her standing still, staring at him.

He turned back towards her.

Big mistake.

I hit him again. A loud slap resonated in the room. At the same time, Gemma shouted, 'You bastard!'

My eyes met hers and in that moment we were united. His reign over us was about to end; I didn't know how and neither did she, I think, but that look between us decided it.

We had had enough.

'It was so long ago, Rachel,' he said, attempting a beseeching look. He put his hand out to me. I think he intended to caress me. 'It meant nothing.'

I relaxed and he saw it and smiled. Then I leaped onto Alex's bed, using the wooden frame as a lever to push myself off again, just as I used to when Alex and I played Pirates when we were kids, that game where we weren't allowed to touch the ground. My body must have kept the memory of that move he taught me all those years ago just for this moment, as I kicked and spun around and threw myself as hard as I could against David.

He staggered, and just as he started to right himself, I kicked out again, catching his shoulder. He crashed to the ground and I leaped on top of him, hitting him over and over again.

All I could think of was Alex and my mother and the way my dad had left, without even saying goodbye. I thought of the house, full of memories of them all. And now this memory would override it: my own husband had raped Gemma and made everyone think his friend, my brother, had done it.

And I thought, just for a second, of the girl I used to be, the girl who played chase around the house with Alex, who taught him to dance. The girl who lay on the floor next to his bed night after night after he was accused of rape, listening to him cry.

I was thinking all those things, and more, when I saw, out of the corner of my eye, David's fist coming towards my face.

70

Gemma

Rachel crashed to the ground like someone in a cartoon. I blinked, thinking she'd bounce back up, but she lay still, her head against the wooden leg of the bed. Almost immediately there was a swelling the size of an egg on her temple and for one mad moment I thought she was dead.

'So,' said David. He was breathing hard and took no notice of his wife's body lying on the floor. He stepped over her: one step nearer to me. 'It's just you and me now, Gemma.'

I stumbled back until I banged into the door. I could feel my phone in my jeans pocket and I was desperate to take it out and call for help. I needed to get out of the room, to run away from him.

He clearly knew what I wanted to do. He reached out, his hand almost brushing my face, and I flinched. He touched my hair then and it felt like an assault. My eyes met his; I saw excitement there. He let go of my hair and reached out beyond me to slam the door shut.

I jumped.

He smiled at me. 'Not quite what you were expecting?'

I couldn't say a word. It was like being in a room with an

animal, one you can't take your eyes off. One that you're terrified of.

'So, who thought we'd meet up again here?' he said. 'This is where it all started between us, isn't it?'

I froze.

'Remember that bed?' he asked, his voice soft, almost a caress. 'How much do you recall? I'd love to know that. When did you become aware of me, Gemma? What woke you? Do you remember the first touch? I've always wondered.' His tongue flicked out to wet his lips. 'I liked to think of that, afterwards.'

Acid rose at the back of my throat. I tried to make myself not listen, to plan instead what I should do. I could feel Alex's hockey stick behind me and I tried desperately to gather strength from it.

'You were always my special one,' he said. His eyes were bright and I saw beads of spittle foaming at the corners of his mouth. I couldn't take my eyes off him. 'You were the first, you see.' For a moment he looked proud. 'I did pretty well, didn't I? It took you fifteen years to figure out it was me. In a way I would have liked more of a challenge, but you know, if you'd been a bit brighter, I wouldn't have had the chance to do the others. And not all of them were quite as acquiescent as you, Gemma. I wouldn't have missed out on that for anything. So in a way I should thank you.' His eyes glittered. 'You gave me the idea, the opportunity. You gave me everything.' He smiled at me. 'You made me what I am.'

I shuddered. His eyes were fixed on me, and while my mind raced as it thought of escape routes, I knew I had to distract him.

'America didn't work out for you, then?' I said.

'Let's just say my time was up there,' he said, and smiled at me.

I knew that Rachel had been right about the other women.

My body shook at the thought of what he'd done, and I had to gather all my strength to talk to him when what I wanted was to run as fast as I could.

'Funny you turned up at the funeral,' I said. 'Paying your respects, were you?'

He shrugged. 'Well, yeah, in one way you could say that. She was always good to me.'

And look how he'd repaid her.

'Then you fell in love with Rachel. Bit convenient, wasn't it?'

He laughed. 'She called it serendipity. To be honest, I'd forgotten all about her until I saw her standing there, crying by the coffin. It's amazing how a bit of money can make someone so much more attractive.'

'So when she said she wanted to get revenge,' I said, conversationally, 'you just thought you'd go along with it? Bit of excitement for you, was it?' Out of the corner of my eye I saw something move behind him. Rachel's hand lifted, just an inch. My stomach tightened. I had to keep his attention away from her. 'Or was it your idea all along?'

'Nah,' he said. 'That was her idea.' He laughed again. 'One of her better ones. And of course I didn't exactly object. It was fun getting to know you better the second time around.'

Anger burned inside my stomach. 'Shame you had to drug me to do that.'

He shrugged. 'Sometimes I like to take the easy way. I couldn't risk you turning me down at the last minute, could I? Well, I could . . .' He smiled at me and I knew that he would have loved that challenge. 'But Rachel was waiting for me back at our hotel, and I didn't give you that much anyway.' His eyes gleamed. 'I saved the rest for her.'

I tried so hard not to express disgust at this. 'What, so that you could take photos of her without her knowing? Just as you did with me?'

'Well, I do like my souvenirs.'

I know it was stupid, but I had to ask. 'What have you done with those photos?'

He grinned. He knew this was my weak spot, the thing I'd worry about for years. 'You'll never know, sweetheart.' He glanced over at Rachel. 'And neither will she.' He moved a step closer. I stepped back and the hockey stick rubbed against me. I couldn't swing it from that angle, I knew, and I didn't want it to fall to the ground. I knew he hadn't noticed it was there. I needed him to move away. My mind was working frantically when he added, 'Speaking of which, that photo from the night we met . . .'

I frowned, unable to understand for a minute. 'What, in London?'

'No.' He laughed. 'The night of the party.'

'We didn't meet! You raped me when I was asleep.'

He shrugged. 'Same difference. Where is that photo? I'd like to see it.'

'Jack Howard has it,' I said.

'Who?'

'One of Alex's friends.'

'So how did you see it?'

'He showed it to me.'

'And you showed Rachel?'

I hesitated.

'One of you has a copy of it. Come on, Gemma. I just want to see it.' He winked at me. 'Add it to my collection. Where is it?'

'My phone's in my handbag,' I lied. 'Downstairs in the kitchen. The photo's in an e-mail to Rachel.' I needed to get him out of the room, to call the police.

I could see him trying to work out what to do. He couldn't let me go downstairs alone. He looked at Rachel. She was still on the floor, her eyes shut. Purple bruises were blooming on the side of her face.

He glanced around the room. There was a wooden chair next to Alex's desk, over by the window. 'Sit there,' he said.

I tried to buy some time. 'What?'

He grabbed my arm and pushed me over to the chair. There were files on it and I recognized them from school. It was the work Alex had done there; the work that had got him into Oxford. David tipped the chair and the files scattered across the floor. He kicked a couple out of the way, then opened the wardrobe. Inside the door were Alex's school ties. With such ease I knew he'd done this before, he grabbed one and tied me to the chair. I could see Rachel on the floor; his back was to her as he wrenched my arms behind my back. I saw her eyelids flicker, just once. I had to alert her and I had to cover up any noise she'd make.

So I started to yell. It took him by surprise, I could tell. He slapped my face hard, so that my head whipped to one side, but I carried on screaming. He reached over to the wardrobe for another tie and stood in front of me, trying to tie it around my mouth. I was wriggling and shrieking and in all the commotion he just didn't hear her.

But I did.

71

Rachel

I'd never thought for a minute that Gemma could yell like that. She was really going for it, screaming and shouting and swearing. It was the best thing she could have done.

David was frantic, trying to tie her up and shut her up at the same time. He was used to more passive victims. He was used to me.

He'd never seen me as a threat, more of an opportunity. He'd walked into that chapel at the crematorium last year and he'd winked at me – who winks at a bereaved daughter at a funeral? And when I winked back, he knew I'd be putty in his hands.

Well, you know what they say: pride comes before a fall.

There was no need for me to be quiet because Gemma was making enough noise to cover me, but still I slid my feet up slowly and waited a second. He hit her again – a punch in the jaw this time – and I knew she'd be as bruised as me soon. She screamed as though she were being murdered and I felt a surge of admiration for her.

And then I knew I was going to do this for her, as well as for Alex.

Within a second I was standing. David didn't notice a

thing, but I knew Gemma had. She'd leaned forward and grabbed his hair in her mouth and was pulling it so hard he couldn't turn to look in my direction. Now he was shouting too, calling her names that made me feel sick. In two steps I reached the door and grabbed Alex's hockey stick. I'd sat with him before he went to Oxford and we'd wound new binding tape around the handle so that he could grip it better, and written his initials, *A.C.*, on the tape. He hadn't played hockey in Oxford; the tape was pristine.

Now with both hands on the stick, I stood behind David. Gemma looked up at me and I mouthed, *Let go*.

She gave one more vicious tug that made him scream, then spat hair onto the floor.

I said, 'David?' in the sweetest voice I could muster.

In the split second between him hearing me and turning around, he let go of Gemma and I brought the stick down on his head, as hard as I could.

He fell to the ground, stunned. I hit him again and again and in the silence between blows I heard the sound of bone cracking.

Gemma shouted, 'Rachel!'

I turned, thinking she was telling me to stop, but she said, 'Quick, untie me!'

I twisted her chair away from David. 'You watch him,' I whispered, and she turned to look at him while I struggled with the knots. I gave up and pulled open the drawer to Alex's desk and grabbed the scissors that had always been there. I cut the ties and put the scissors in my back pocket in case I needed them later. Gemma stood, rubbing her legs.

Then David stirred.

She and I stood frozen to the spot as we watched him kneel, preparing to stand. He turned to look at us and I panicked.

Gemma didn't panic, though. She picked up that hockey

stick and she raised it high in the air. With a grim look on her face, she brought it crashing down on David's back.

He swore and fell back, landing heavily on his shoulder. I held my breath, but he started to push himself up again.

Gemma was panting and her knuckles were white where she gripped the stick. She looked terrified. I was, too, but more than that, I was exhilarated.

'Here,' I said. I stood behind her and put my arms around her, her back to my chest. I could feel her body shaking, and mine was, too. I grabbed hold of the stick so we were both holding it. Alex had stood like this with me when he was teaching me to play hockey in our garden the summer before he died.

David was about to rise when I felt Gemma lift her arms. I pressed against her, my body touching hers, my hands right next to hers on the hockey stick, and it was as though Alex were with us too, as though he were behind me, guiding me. Protecting me. As though the three of us were one.

David's eyes flicked from me to her and back again. I don't think he could believe we were sticking up for ourselves.

'This one's for you, *babe*,' I said to him.

We lifted our arms higher still and Gemma shouted, 'It's from all of us, you bastard.'

And then with our bodies together, united, we brought Alex's hockey stick down with full force on David's head.

This time he lay still.

72

Gemma

Saturday, August 19

Joe was waiting for me in the reception area of the police station when I was finally allowed to leave. It was after two A.M. by then. He looked as exhausted as I felt, and he held me to him for so long that I thought I'd go to sleep in his arms.

'Where's Rachel?' he asked. 'Is she coming with us?'

'They've taken her to hospital,' I said. 'They want her to stay in overnight, because she lost consciousness.'

He winced. 'And are you all right, sweetheart?' He put his arms around me again and held me to him. 'I've been so worried.'

'I'm fine,' I said. 'Let's just get out of here.' Poor Joe, he'd been sitting there for hours waiting for me, not knowing what was going on. The police had told him I was being questioned about an incident that had occurred in Rachel's house; that was all he knew up till then. 'It was to do with Rachel's husband. Long, long story.'

He raised his eyebrows at that, because of course he hadn't known she was married. I hadn't even known myself until recently. It was good now to have him sitting beside me, one hand on my leg as he drove. I said I'd tell him everything when we got back to my parents' house, and though I closed my eyes and pretended to sleep, I knew he wasn't fooled.

'My mum's going to be worried,' I said as Joe parked the car.

'I called her. I told her I was with you and we'd be back late.'

'You didn't tell her anything?'

'I didn't *know* anything,' he said. 'I said we'd talk to them in the morning.'

I could only imagine the self-restraint my mother had had to show then. My dad must have had his work cut out calming her down, but as we entered the house, all was quiet from their bedroom.

As soon as we were in the living room, Joe opened his mouth to speak, but I said, 'I need to shower,' and ran upstairs to the bathroom and closed the door.

I kept my eyes shut while I showered. All I could think of was David saying, *You made me what I am*. I scoured my skin, and the heat of the shower and the tears on my face and that scrubbing motion reminded me of the shower I'd taken after the party where I'd tried to wash away my shame.

Fifteen years later, it had finally ended.

Back downstairs in my dressing gown, I sat in the living room while Joe made a pot of tea and some toast. Although I hadn't thought I could eat a thing, I found I was ravenous and sat at the kitchen table while he toasted more bread. He sat quietly with me while I ate; I knew he was bursting with questions but he didn't say a word.

When I'd finished eating, he tidied away the plates and mugs, and we sat on the sofa, his arms around me, a blanket covering us.

'I want you to tell me everything,' he said. 'Don't miss anything out. Don't try to spare my feelings, or think you're doing me a favour by leaving things out.' He stroked my face and kissed me. 'I love you, Gemma. I'll love you no matter what you say. But please don't lie to me.'

And so I told him.

It was an hour before I finished. He kept quiet throughout, though he did prompt me occasionally.

'And then we ran out of the room and Rachel remembered there was a key to the bedroom. They hadn't used it since Alex died; it was by the front door on a hook. I held the door shut and she ran downstairs to find it. Once she'd locked him in, I called the police and we waited outside, in the driveway. They were there within minutes.'

Joe's face was pale and drawn by the time I'd finished. 'The same man,' he said at last. 'I've hated him for so long, Gem. You know that. When I think of what he did to you all those years ago, I want to kill him. But now. The things he's done since.' He put his arms around me and buried his head in my neck. 'You must have been terrified.'

'You wouldn't believe it. When Rachel was downstairs and I was holding the door shut . . . It was an old door handle and if he'd been fit he would have been able to get out of there easily.' I shuddered. 'I knew he wouldn't be able to get up. I knew we had a few minutes, at least. But that thought, that he'd pull open the door . . . I was so frightened.'

'I wish you'd told me you were going there. I wish I could have helped you.'

'But we weren't expecting him to turn up,' I said. 'I was just going to be with her to pick up some documents. She didn't want him to find them.'

'Even so,' he said. 'I hate to think of you going through that.' We were quiet for a while, then he said, 'So what's happened to him now?'

'I'm not sure. Apparently he was coming to just as the

police arrived. They carted him off to hospital and he's under guard now.' I winced. 'We hit him pretty hard.'

Joe shrugged. 'Shame. But when the police got there and found him unconscious and locked in a room, did they just believe what you said? You both clearly had something to do with it.'

'We were taken to the police station.' We'd been glad to go. We *asked* to go. At least we were safe there. 'And I gave them my shirt.'

'What? Why did you do that?'

'That night at the hotel in London, David was recording me while we had our meal. He'd planned it all, known what he wanted to do.'

'Recorded you with his phone? Didn't you notice?'

'No, he had a video camera that was in a button that Rachel had sewn onto his shirt,' I said.

'A button?'

'I know. I couldn't believe it. Rachel told me about it; she sent me a link to it just the other day. I thought that two could play at that game, so I sent off for a shirt with buttons and I ordered the same recorder he'd bought, and I sewed the buttons on before I went out. Everything that happened in her house last night was recorded.'

He looked at me as if I'd grown another head. 'Sound as well?'

I nodded. 'It was clear as a bell. You could hear that we broke a bone when we hit him.' I swallowed hard, remembering also the clarity of the video he'd made of me criticizing Joe. That was the only thing I hadn't told him. I hoped he'd never hear about it.

He winced. 'But why were you wearing the shirt? You thought you were just going to help Rachel, didn't you?'

'I was testing it,' I said. 'I knew that Rachel would have seen the buttons before, on David's shirt; she'd sewn them on. I wanted to see if she noticed them. If she didn't, I figured he wouldn't either. Before I had a chance to tell her, he'd turned up. The police wouldn't touch the button as it was evidence, but I gave them the login to the website where the footage was stored and they could see everything.'

He sat quietly, holding me to him. I knew it was going to take a long time for him to grasp what had been happening over the last couple of months. 'I just don't understand why you didn't go to the police straight away, as soon as you saw him going into Rachel's flat.'

'I wanted to talk to her first,' I said. 'I was worried about her. I knew that if I told the police before speaking to her, I'd never get the chance to ask her why she was with him. And then when I spoke to her she asked me not to go just yet. At first she said she wanted us to confront him together, but we were too scared to do that. We were going to go to the police tomorrow – today, now – and make a statement. And then he pre-empted us.'

'What do you think she'll do now?'

'She'll probably go abroad. She needs to get away.' We were quiet for a while; Joe's hands gripped mine as if he'd never let me go.

When he spoke next, he sounded so sad and confused. 'I just wish you'd told me, right from the beginning. When you came back from London, if you'd told me then, none of this would have happened.'

'I think it would, just in a different way. She was still determined to get revenge, and of course he loved having the chance to do whatever he wanted. And how could I have said to you, weeks later, "Oh, you remember that conference I went to a month ago? Remember I said I'd had dinner in my room and went to sleep early? Well, I didn't. I lied about that. And remember I texted you to say I was in bed, about to go to sleep? I wasn't. I was in a restaurant having dinner with a client instead and we got drunk and then I think he kissed me, but I don't remember. Nothing else happened, though. I don't remember but I know nothing happened."'

He grimaced. 'I wouldn't have believed you. I know it. And it's my fault, too. You looked awful when I picked you up off the London train and I still went out. I knew you wanted me to stay home, but I didn't. I'm so sorry, Gem.' He gave me a tentative look. 'Do you think him being arrested will help bring some peace to you now?'

I thought for a while about all that had happened and how Rachel and I had united to overcome him. 'I think so,' I said. 'I hope so. Rachel will have a bigger problem, though. She's lost everything.'

'Not quite everything,' Joe said quietly. 'You've been a really good friend to her.'

'And she has to me, too.'

We sat in silence for a while, and then he said, 'About your job. How do you fancy taking on someone new?'

I closed my eyes, exhausted. 'I've already advertised. I told you.'

'No,' he said. 'How about if I come in with you? I could train up for Brian's job and take over the lettings when he retires. We could work it so that one of us was always at home with Rory.'

'You'd do that? You've never wanted to work with me before.'

'All this,' he said, 'not David, but all the rest . . . You're out at work all the time and I know you want to spend time with Rory. You've done so well, building up the business, and it's as though you're being punished for that now. I want your business to thrive. I want to be part of that, Gemma. I want both of us to do it.'

I hardly dared ask. 'What about Ireland?'

'Can we think about that as something for the future?' he asked. 'In a few years' time, maybe?'

'What, not by Christmas?'

He laughed. 'I'm sorry. I was an idiot.'

I was exhausted. 'Let's talk about it tomorrow,' I said. 'I need to go to bed.'

Outside the sky was still dark. We had a few hours until Rory would wake. He was sprawled in the centre of my bed; before I'd left the evening before, I'd promised him he could sleep with me that night. He lay on his back, legs and arms spread wide, Buffy buried in the crook of his neck. Carefully Joe and I got into bed either side of him and Joe reached over to hold me in his arms. Rory lay between us, his chest slowly rising and falling. In his sleep he seemed to know we were there, and snuggled between us.

It was all over.

I held Rory and Joe close to me. They were my future, but they weren't the only ones I had to consider now.

I thought of Rachel in her hospital bed and hoped she was sleeping and not thinking about the man she'd married who'd destroyed her family. I hoped she could move past the tragedy of her childhood, knowing she'd overcome the worst things life could throw at her. I knew she'd always be part of my life, the way she had been for so many years without my realizing it.

And Alex, too. I thought of the boy he used to be and how at last he was vindicated. There'd been a moment when I'd stood in his bedroom where I'd felt connected to him. I'd sensed his presence there, not just in the way his hockey stick stood behind me, as though it had waited fifteen years to be put into my hands again, but in the way his sister and I had moved as one to bring David down. Alex was there with us in that moment, rooting for us, giving us strength.

Rachel and I had to live our lives for him, now.

Acknowledgements

Thank you so much to Toby Jones at Headline and to Danielle Perez at Berkley for your invaluable editorial advice and support. It's been such a pleasure working with you both.

Thanks to my writer friends, Fiona Collins and Sam Gough, who made the experience of writing this novel such fun. I'm so grateful for your support and your tact when I went off piste!

Thanks to Anne-Marie Thomson for your advice about what an estate agent does all day. It was so kind of you to answer all my questions.

Thank you to Graham Bartlett, author and ex–Chief Superintendent of Brighton and Hove, for your advice and for talking me through what would happen to a woman in Gemma's position.

Finally, thanks so much to Daisy Ambrose for your social media advice.

Reading Group Questions

1. Do you think Gemma's parents were right to persuade her to drop the charge against Alex? Was it really in her best interest?

2. Given the seriousness of the accusation against him, do you think Alex should have had the right to defend himself in court?

3. If the case had gone to court at the time, do you think Alex would have been found guilty?

4. Gemma met Caitlin at university and they were best friends for years before Gemma met Joe. Gemma assumed that if she confided in Caitlin, her loyalties would be to her brother rather than her friend. Do you think she was right?

5. How much do you think David's rejection from Oxford – and Alex's acceptance – was the reason for his behaviour that night?

6. Gemma is terrified that, if her marriage ended, she would no longer live with Rory. Do you think this fear prevents some women from fulfilling their career potential and encouraging their partner to be a stay-at-home dad?

7. In the final scene, Joe says he wishes Gemma had talked to him, but there were occasions throughout the book where he clearly knew she was unhappy. Do you think the responsibility also lay with him to talk to her and to try to discover the cause of her unhappiness?

8. Alex's father responded to his son's death by running away and starting a new family, whereas his mother responded by breaking down and refusing to leave the family home. Why do you think Rachel blamed her mother rather than her father for her subsequent lack of a healthy childhood? Why do you think people can react so differently to a tragedy?

9. What difference do you think it would have made to Alex's mother's physical and mental health if she'd known what really happened at the party?

10. Rachel has grown up believing Gemma was responsible for the destruction of her family. After everything they've been through in this book, do you think they have the chance of becoming true friends?

GONE WITHOUT A TRACE

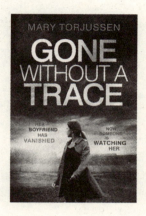

No one ever disappears completely . . .

You leave for work one morning.

Another day in your normal life.

Until you come home to discover that your boyfriend has gone.

Available now in Paperback and Ebook

THRILLINGLY GOOD BOOKS FROM CRIMINALLY GOOD WRITERS

CRIME FILES BRINGS YOU THE LATEST RELEASES FROM TOP CRIME AND THRILLER AUTHORS.

SIGN UP ONLINE FOR OUR MONTHLY NEWSLETTER AND BE THE FIRST TO KNOW ABOUT OUR COMPETITIONS, NEW BOOKS AND MORE.

VISIT OUR WEBSITE: WWW.CRIMEFILES.CO.UK
LIKE US ON FACEBOOK: FACEBOOK.COM/CRIMEFILES
FOLLOW US ON TWITTER: @CRIMEFILESBOOKS